*The honor of your presence is requested
at the Reel New York awards show gala....*

Everyone is talking about the single mother turned Cinderella who has been spied in very close company with a certain dashing action hero.

Sources say a sultry bartender/aspiring actress has been seen "rendezvousing" with a certain award-winning movie star.

Rumors abound that Cupid may strike again for two certain screenwriters, who are former flames.

*It's a star-studded evening, full of glamour and gossip.
A night of beautiful people and borrowed jewelry,
décolletage and designer gowns, where the "A" rules.*

D0468948

Dear Reader,

It's hard to believe that the Signature Select program is one year old—with seventy-two books already published by top Harlequin and Silhouette authors.

What an exciting and varied lineup we have in the year ahead! In the first quarter of the year, the Signature Spotlight program offers three very different reading experiences. Popular author Marie Ferrarella, well-known for her warm family-centered romances, has gone in quite a different direction to write a story that has been "haunting her" for years. Please check out *Sundays Are for Murder* in January. Hop aboard a Caribbean cruise with Joanne Rock in *The Pleasure Trip* for February, and don't miss a trademark romantic suspense from Debra Webb, *Vows of Silence* in March.

Our collections in the first quarter of the year explore a variety of contemporary themes. Our Valentine's collection—*Write It Up!*— homes in on the trend to online dating in three stories by Elizabeth Bevarly, Tracy Kelleher and Mary Leo. February is awards season, and Barbara Bretton, Isabel Sharpe and Emilie Rose join the fun and glamour in *And the Envelope, Please...*. And in March, Leslie Kelly, Heather MacAllister and Cindi Myers have penned novellas about women desperate enough to go to *Bootcamp* to learn how not to scare men away!

Three original sagas also come your way in the first quarter of this year. Silhouette author Gina Wilkins spins off her popular FAMILY FOUND miniseries in *Wealth Beyond Riches*. Janice Kay Johnson has written a powerful story of a tortured shared past in *Dead Wrong*, which is connected to her PATTON'S DAUGHTERS Superromance miniseries, and Kathleen O'Brien gives a haunting story of mysterious murder in *Quiet as the Grave*.

And don't miss reissues of some of your favorite authors, including Georgette Heyer, Joan Hohl, Jayne Ann Krentz and Fayrene Preston. We are also featuring a number of two-in-one connected stories in volumes by Janice Kay Johnson and Kathleen O'Brien, as well as Roz Denny Fox and Janelle Denison. And don't forget there is original bonus material in every single Signature Select book to give you the inside scoop on the creative process of your favorite authors!

Enjoy!

Marsha Zinberg

Marsha Zinberg
Executive Editor
The Signature Select Program

COLLECTION

USA TODAY bestselling author
BARBARA BRETTON
EMILIE ROSE
ISABEL SHARPE

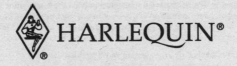

HARLEQUIN®

TORONTO • NEW YORK • LONDON
AMSTERDAM • PARIS • SYDNEY • HAMBURG
STOCKHOLM • ATHENS • TOKYO • MILAN • MADRID
PRAGUE • WARSAW • BUDAPEST • AUCKLAND

ISBN 0-373-83693-7

AND THE ENVELOPE, PLEASE...

Copyright © 2006 by Harlequin Books S.A.

The publisher acknowledges the copyright holder of the individual works as follows:

EVER AFTER
Copyright © 2006 by Barbara Bretton

AN AFFAIR TO REMEMBER
Copyright © 2006 by Emilie Rose Cunningham

IT HAPPEND ONE NIGHT
Copyright © 2006 by Muna Shehadi Sill

www.eHarlequin.com

Printed in U.S.A.

CONTENTS

Dear Reader,

My mother loved the movies. She loved everything about them. She loved the handsome actors and the beautiful actresses, the love stories, the mysteries, the Technicolor spectacles. I grew up reading *Photoplay* and *Modern Screen,* and for a while I figured Elizabeth Taylor had to be a distant relative because we spent more time talking about her many marriages than my own grandfather's multiple forays into wedded bliss.

But more than anything else, my mother loved the Oscars. Oscar night was a big deal in my house, right up there with birthdays and Christmas Eve. The lights in the living room were dimmed. Snacks were piled up on the end tables. The coffeepot was plugged in and ready. Even my father, who wasn't exactly a big movie fan, joined in the festivities.

We wrote down our guesses and gloated shamelessly when our pick took home the Oscar. We oohed and ahhed over the beautiful gowns and were merciless if one of the stars had a bad-hair day. We laughed at the jokes, winced when a winner got tongue-tied during an acceptance speech, then analyzed every last second of it for at least a week afterward.

My mother is gone now, but I still watch the awards shows. I love watching the celebrities strut their stuff on the red carpet. I love glitz and glamour and all of the silliness that comes along with it. I love the fact that the shows are live and the drama in unscripted. I love knowing that anything can happen and probably will. I even love those acceptance speeches that never end—the ones where the Best Whatever thanks everyone from his pet goldfish to his third-grade teacher.

When I was offered the chance to write a novella for this collection, I knew I was going to love every minute of writing Julia and Jack's story. Glitz, glamour and an awards ceremony of my very own. How could I refuse? I'd been preparing for this since I was a little girl.

And why not? I am, after all, my mother's daughter!

Warmly,

Barbara Bretton
Please visit me at my Web site www.barbarabretton.com.

EVER AFTER
Barbara Bretton

For Kali and Marie, good friends and Brooklyn goddesses
extraordinaire, with much love

CHAPTER ONE

Manhattan

JACK WYATT HAD ESCAPED twenty-three enemy ambushes, survived sixty-seven leaps from doomed fighter jets and dodged one hundred and seventy-three bullets with his name on them, but not even Hollywood's favorite action hero could find a taxi on Saturday night in midtown Manhattan.

"Sorry, Mr. W.," the doorman said as he scanned Park Avenue north and south. "No cabs anywhere. You want me to get you a dial-up?"

"How long would that take?"

"Ten, fifteen minutes," Horace said. "You'd be cutting it close but we'll get you there on time."

Jack was scheduled to appear at the Reel New York Film Festival awards ceremony, where he would be handing out the trophy for Lifetime Achievement in Directing.

Root canal without anesthesia would be more fun.

"It's only five blocks, Horace. I might as well walk it."

"Not that it's any of my business," Horace said, "but I wouldn't if I were you. Midtown's swarming with fans and you're one of the guys they're all waiting to see." According to Horace's grapevine, The Hotel, the trendy new establishment where the awards ceremony was taking place, didn't have its crowd-control chops yet and wouldn't know how to handle a celebrity who arrived on foot and without the requisite handlers and bodyguards.

Jack thanked Horace for his concern, then set off south on Park Avenue just the same. This was what he was looking for, wasn't it? No handlers. No bodyguards. A return to real life…or what passed for real life after twelve years in the public eye.

Tonight, after the show was over, he was going to get behind the wheel of his car and point it east toward Montauk, and he wasn't going to stop until he was up to his front tires in the Atlantic Ocean. What had started out as a plan to help an old friend had turned into something different. Jack needed this break more than he had realized. Years of living in a world of weekend grosses and six-pack abs had taken its toll on him and skewed his perception of what was normal and what wasn't.

Wearing a tux in broad daylight?

Definitely not normal.

Traffic on Park Avenue was at a standstill. The weather was unnaturally warm for early April, and frazzled drivers leaned out their open windows to see what was holding things up. It was tough enough to fly beneath the radar when you were six feet five and sporting a tux, but try keeping a low profile when your films were a regular feature at the local multiplex, where your face was projected higher than a two-story house. To his dismay the buzz of recognition was starting to build.

He deftly sidestepped a regal King Charles spaniel whose spaced-out owner daydreamed at the other end of the leash. It hadn't rained in New York for two weeks. The day had been sunny and dry. So could somebody explain to him why both the dog and its owner were wearing Burberry raincoats?

Money did weird things to people. The green stuff seemed to climb into the cerebral cortex and yank the wires that were linked to traits like common sense, perspective and a sense of humor. He saw it in Hollywood. He saw it here in Manhattan. Hell, he saw it in the mirror every morning and it was starting to scare him.

It started small, with Burberry raincoats for King Charles spaniels, and then before you knew it you actually believed you needed four houses, eight cars and a private jet. For the last year he had been teetering on the brink of craziness and he knew it. There was still time to make changes in his life before he found himself turned into a parody of a human being. When the opportunity to help his manager, Clive, and help himself at the same time arose, Jack had jumped on it.

"I understand your need for some downtime, but you cannot back out on the awards show," Clive had barked into the phone. "It's far too late to bring in a replacement."

"Call Tom or Harrison. I told you, Clive, my year off begins today." Jack had been careful not to let his manager suspect that his own welfare was in any way a part of the decision.

"Your year off begins at midnight as agreed. You dodged the rehearsal yesterday and I managed to explain that away. You bloody well better show up tonight for the show. You're presenting a lifetime achievement award and I'm too old to explain your absence to Clint."

"You're a year younger than Clint," Jack had said with a laugh. "The only award I'll be handing out tonight is for best bowl of Manhattan clam east of Riverhead."

Clive Bannister knew which buttons to push, which

was something that happened when your former father-in-law was also your friend and manager. Clive was family, and family had always been Jack's Achilles' heel.

"You need a new manager," a studio executive had told him over dinner a few months ago. "This is a young person's game."

It wasn't the first time someone in a position of power had told him Clive should retire, and each time, Jack had a vulgar two-word answer ready and waiting. They were a team, he and Clive. Clive and his late wife, Rosie, had seen something in a rough, unpolished dish-washer-busboy at the Union Square Café, and had handed him a life. They became his family. They helped him build a future. They didn't turn away when his marriage to their daughter, Linda, fell apart. They were family, all of them, and they always would be.

But lately he had begun to wonder if maybe Clive deserved more than the daily grind of keeping Jack's star burning bright. Clive had always seemed ageless, a force of nature who operated above the frailties of mere mortals, but over the last few months there had been enough for-gotten messages, tangled communications and downright screwups that even Jack had to admit his friend might be feeling the effects of his seventy-five years on the planet.

"Why don't I just tell him he needs to slow down?" he had said to Linda during one of their planning sessions.

"Because you know him as well as I do," his ex-wife had said. "The only way Dad will ever slow down is if we make sure he has no choice."

Which was how Jack finally decided to take a year off.

The idea had been floating around in his subconscious for a long time. The thought of climbing behind the wheel of his Jeep and taking off for parts unknown sounded pretty damn good to him. A year without contracts or commitments. A year where he could grow a beard, shave his head, forget cell phones and e-mail and box office grosses. A year where he didn't have to save the world from whatever ninety-four minute peril was threatening it this time.

"So are you seeing anyone these days?" Linda had asked after they had planned her father's future for him.

"A few people."

"But are you seeing anyone special?"

"You'll be the first to know when I do." Marriage had briefly interrupted a terrific friendship, which divorce had quickly restored.

"You have to put yourself out there, Jack, or it's never going to happen for you."

"I'm out there on 3,123 screens this week. You can't get more out there than that."

She gave him one of those disgusted looks that only family can deliver. "Fine," she said. "Swell. You don't want me to talk about it and I won't. But trust me on this—one day some woman is going to come along and knock you flat, and I hope I'm there to see it so I can say, 'I told you so.'"

Linda believed in the kind of love that knocked you off your feet and left you gasping for air while destiny stomped all over you. She had wanted the whole package: the can't-live-without-you romance, the fairy-tale wedding, the until-death-do-us-part marriage, with children and grandchildren and great-grandchildren all gathered around for the golden anniversary.

He hadn't been able to give her any of that, and when they parted he had been genuinely happy that she found everything she wanted and more in her husband, Mike. Maybe the second time really was the charm for some people.

Jack maneuvered around the Burberry spaniel and picked up speed. He had been knocked flat by love a hundred times in his movies. Love at first sight had rocked his world over and over again, to the delight of audiences in more countries than he knew existed. He had the dialogue filed away in his brain. He knew how it should feel, how he should act while it was happening, how it played out along the way to the happily ever after ending.

But he had never experienced it for real. The thunderbolt of legend, that pow! of recognition when the woman of your dreams walked into your life—it was all still Hollywood special effects to him, and he was beginning to think it always would be.

Brooklyn

FOR THE LAST THREE HOURS Julia McGraw Monahan had been primped, prodded, highlighted, colored, washed, blow dried, pinned up, brushed out, waxed, powdered, shadowed, mascaraed, perfumed, buffed and polished to a high-gloss gleam, all in the name of friendship.

By anyone's standards Julia was a low-maintenance woman. A single mother of preschool twins didn't have time to be anything else. Once upon a time she had had more than a passing acquaintance with elaborate beauty rituals designed to turn your average geeky computer nerd into a bombshell, but those days were long gone.

Or so she had thought before her best friend and part-time fairy godmother got her hands on her.

Julia's usual scruffy ponytail had been transformed into a sexy tumble of fiery red curls that skimmed her shoulders. Her everyday uniform of T-shirt and jeans had been replaced by a shimmering bronze Versace knockoff that fit her like a glove. Her skin was flawless alabaster. Her eyes were smoky jewels surrounded by thick curly lashes. And for the first time in years she smelled like perfume, instead of laundry detergent.

Miracle was the only word that covered it.

"Wow," she said, adjusting her glasses. "I think this qualifies as an extreme makeover."

"Take off those glasses," Bonnie, her best friend and fairy godmother, ordered. "You're ruining the effect."

"If I take them off, I won't be able to see."

"I don't care," Bonnie said. "You're not doing geek chic tonight. Off with 'em!"

Julia reluctantly slipped off her glasses and squinted in the general direction of the mirror. "This isn't going to work. I can't see a thing."

"Just for tonight," Bonnie said. "Think of it as one of those sacrifices women make for beauty. Besides, it will keep you from going crazy around all those movie stars."

The thought of Julia going crazy for a movie star made them both laugh out loud. She hadn't been to a movie since before the twins were born, and that was nearly five years ago. All you had to do was look at her to know she wasn't the type to gush and fawn over a celebrity. Julia was a self-described nerd who by day ran a computer repair business named Wired, and by night wrote how-to articles.

An extra 512MB of RAM would get a bigger response from her than a candlelight dinner with Brad Pitt.

Bonnie dashed from the room, and Julia took the opportunity to slip her glasses into her tiny sparkly purse. There were limits to what she would do in the name of beauty, even for her best friend.

Bonnie returned seconds later waving a pair of impossibly high, impossibly gorgeous strappy sandals overhead. "The pièce de résistance," she announced. "My lucky Manolo Blahniks!"

"The shoes you won at the Actors Equity raffle last year?"

Bonnie nodded, eyes gleaming with pride. "A moment of silence for perfection, please."

Even Julia, who wasn't a shoe person at all, knew a great pair when she saw them. A one-of-a-kind masterpiece created and signed by the master himself. The shoe lover's equivalent of the Holy Grail, and probably more famous than ninety percent of the actors who had purchased raffle tickets for a chance to win them.

"It's been a long time," she said. "I'm not sure I remember how to walk in heels."

"It's like riding a bike. No woman worth her estrogen could forget how to walk in heels." Bonnie gestured for her to sit down on the edge of the bed. "We don't have time to argue shoes, Jules, so you might as well just give in. Rachel's waiting outside in the limo and she's feeling mean as a snake." Bonnie had called in a favor, and apparently her cousin was finding it hard to be gracious.

Julia slid her feet into the obscenely expensive sandals and tried to ignore the ripple of pleasure she felt when she made contact. The straps felt like silky spiderwebs against her bare skin, fragile as a whisper. "What if I lose them? You know I'm always losing things."

Bonnie shot her a look. "They're shoes. They have straps. They won't come off unless you take them off, and I *know* you wouldn't do anything that foolish, would you."

"I don't know," Julia said. "Are they insured?"

"I'm lucky my car's insured."

"Forget it. I'm not wearing shoes that cost more than my entire wardrobe. There must be something more practical in my closet." Something that wouldn't give her an anxiety attack every time she took a step.

"I know what's in your closet, Jules—clogs and a pair of rubber flip-flops."

Julia's aversion to shoes was notorious. A trail of discarded footwear followed her wherever she went.

"They're gorgeous," she admitted, "but they're just not my style."

"Neither is that strapless Versace knockoff you're wearing, but this is a big-time Hollywood-style awards show you're going to, honey, not a potluck supper at St. Matthew's. Seat-fillers have to blend in with the crowd, and in this case that means glitz and glamour. If you're not going to enter into the spirit of the thing, tell me now and I'll find someone else to sub for me tonight."

Bonnie was a struggling theater actress who made extra money between gigs working as a seat-filler at undersold performances and the occasional Manhattan-based awards show. She had been booked for tonight's First Annual Reel New York ceremony, but a root canal gone bad had left her puffy-cheeked and in need of a last minute replacement.

"I thought there wasn't anyone else you could call," Julia reminded her.

"There are a million people I could call," Bonnie said, "but you're my best friend. Pardon me if I thought you might enjoy going to a celebrity event."

This was one of those times when Julia devoutly wished her friend hadn't attended drama school. Bonnie was giving an award-winning performance herself.

"If you want to stay home every night watching *Sesame Street* with your children and scribbling your stories, far be it from me to interfere."

"Oh, that reminds me," Julia said as she fiddled with

the narrow strap around her right ankle. "The Barney tapes are stacked on the coffee table, right next to the complete works of Mary-Kate and Ashley. I told the kids you'd love to have a little film festival with them tonight."

"Cruel and inhuman," Bonnie muttered darkly. "This is a side of you I don't like, Jules."

Julia laughed and stood up, swaying like a weeping willow in a hurricane. "The last time my center of gravity shifted like this I was pregnant with the twins." She glanced over at her best friend. "And you expect me to walk in these things?"

"Yes, and I also expect you to guard them with your life."

"I think a few hours with your godchildren will do you good tonight. You need a new perspective on life."

"So do you, Cinderella," Bonnie said. "It's about time you kicked off your clogs and put on your dancing shoes."

"Please tell me there won't be any dancing."

"I was speaking metaphorically."

And thank God for that. Standing upright would be tough enough.

She quickly ran through the usual domestic litany of emergency phone numbers, menu plans and bedtime rituals.

"Make sure they don't go near my office," Julia warned. "I have two Macs open and I'm building a work station. That room's definitely not childproofed."

"Gotcha." Bonnie pretended to scribble the instructions on an imaginary notepad.

"And stay away from my laptop."

"I resent that note of suspicion in your voice."

Julia laughed out loud. "Oh, stop looking so outraged, Bonnie. I know you like to snoop, but my laptop's off-limits."

"I wasn't snooping last week. I was looking for the aspirin, not poking around in your medicine cabinet."

"Just stay away from the laptop," Julia repeated. "I'll know if you so much as breathe on the keyboard."

"I'm not going to read your journal, if that's what you're worried about."

"Bingo," she said. "I know you too well, Bonnie Benitez. You were a snoop in kindergarten and you're a snoop now."

"I peeked into your lunch box. I was five, Jules! Gimme a—"

Bonnie's words were cut off as the brassy notes of "Here Comes the Bride" tumbled through the front window.

"I'm going to kill that cousin of mine," Bonnie said. "I begged Rachel not to bring that tacky white limo they use for weddings."

Julia was secretly delighted to see the outlandish car double-parked in front of the house. Bonnie might turn up her nose at the wedding limo, but Julia couldn't wait to settle herself into the back seat for the drive across the Bridge into Manhattan. She wanted to smell the rich leather upholstery and watch the other drivers as they tried to peer through the smoked glass windows for a glimpse of her.

She had written how-to articles on everything from safety ladders to banishing hiccups, and this experience was a gold mine of possibilities for her. With a little luck she could probably get three or four assignments out of the experience, and the extra money would be added to the twins' still-tiny college funds.

But there was more to her excitement than the thought of banking a few bucks for the future. She couldn't remember the last time she had felt pampered and feminine. She might not be beautiful, but this was the closest she was likely to come to that state in her lifetime, and she intended to enjoy every single minute of the experience.

Even if it meant wearing those ridiculous shoes.

"I think all of Bay Ridge showed up to see you off," Bonnie said as they stepped out onto the front porch of the three-family redbrick home.

"It's the limo," Julia said. "They probably think I'm about to elope."

She lived in a friendly, close-knit neighborhood of two- and three-family houses owned by recent immigrants and old-timers, and the arrival of a white stretch with bluebells and doves painted along the side panels drew everyone out to the street to see what was going on. Her wonderful landlady, Mrs. Wasserstein, Mrs. W.'s daughter-in-law and her three kids, old Mr. Domenico from across the street, his bocce cronies, the Lopezes from the corner house, Srini and Anu who owned the house next door, Ida and Bill Lukinovich from the video store, Pete the mail carrier, so many familiar faces.

Of course, without her glasses those familiar faces were all fuzzy, like a soft focus photograph, so she smiled into the middle distance and hoped for the best.

"You're gaw-jus!" Terri DiGregorio from St. Matthew's Day Care Center proclaimed. "Who knew?"

"Look at that hair, will you? It grew a foot overnight!" Mary O'Fallon nudged her sister, Brigid, in the ribs. "Maybe there's hope for us," she stage-whispered, and everybody laughed.

The men were mostly silent as they watched Julia with the kind of attention usually reserved for a Mets doubleheader.

She was the same woman who had popped out in her bathrobe and bare feet to bring in the mail that morning, to almost universal yawns, and now they were staring at her as if she were a goddess among mere mortals.

"You'll put the other Julia to shame," Mrs. Wasserstein said. "You look like the princess in a fairy tale."

"I'm starting to feel like one," Julia admitted. A flutter of excitement was building inside her chest, the kind she hadn't felt in longer than she could remember. "Thanks for watching the kids while Bonnie performed her magic on me."

Mrs. W. waved away her gratitude. "You're a beautiful girl. All you needed was a new dress and a place to go." She lowered her voice. "This would make Danny, may God bless his dear memory, very happy."

Julia knew she was right. Danny had loved life, and he had made her promise she wouldn't spend the rest of her life grieving for him. That had proved to be easier said than done. Julia had mourned her young husband's passing hard and long. She had been pregnant with the twins when Danny died, and there had been many days when they were the only reason she got up in the morning.

But just as they had all promised her, time really did heal even the most battered heart. There was something else filling the pages of her journal these days—a growing sense of anticipation, a renewal of joy. The feeling that her life was about to unfold before her like the first butter yellow daffodils of spring.

"Will you look at this?" Mrs. W. was saying as she pointed toward the Manolo Blahniks on Julia's feet. "Our girl didn't get those at Payless!"

"Mommy?" Kate's sweet soprano lifted above the clamor as the laughter and chatter stopped cold. "Is that you?"

Daniel, who was surveying the world from Mrs. Wasserstein's side, took one look at Julia and burst into tears. He was her sensitive child, the one who carried the weight of the world on his tiny shoulders. Change unnerved him. He liked life to be as predictable as a glass of milk.

"You smell funny," he said, wrinkling his nose.

"Just for tonight," Julia said. "Tomorrow I'll be plain old Mommy again." Goodbye Obsession; hello Irish Spring.

Daniel refused to be mollified, but Kate was absolutely enchanted with her new and improved mother. Kate cooed over the dress, slipped under the slim skirt to admire the borrowed Blahniks, played peekaboo beneath the billowing train, and begged to play stylist with her mother's hair extensions.

"You look just like Barbie," she said, which was high praise from the perspective of a four-year-old fashionista.

"Gimme a break," Rachel muttered loudly from inside the limo, and even Julia had to laugh.

Finally it was time to go. She kissed the kids again, asked Mrs. Wasserstein to look in on Bonnie later "just in case," then glided toward the limo. The fact that she was able to remain vertical in those glittery stilts that were strapped to her feet was amazing enough, but she was reasonably sure she had never glided before in her life.

"Wait!" Bonnie leaped into action. "Let me get your train!"

Words Julia would probably never hear again in her entire life unless she somehow found herself in succession to the British throne.

Bonnie was a wonder. She quickly gathered up the

yards of fabric into her arms and stage-managed Julia's entry into the limo.

"Where did you learn how to do this?" Julia asked as she carefully positioned herself in the back seat.

"Drama school," Bonnie said as she climbed in after her. "I played a lady's maid."

Rachel tapped on the steering wheel with her shiny crimson fingernails. "I have other places to go," she mumbled.

"No, you don't," Bonnie retorted. "You owe me six hours, Rachel Benitez, and not a second less."

"She's not going to leave me stranded in Manhattan, is she?" Julia asked. "This isn't exactly a subway kind of outfit."

"Rachel will drop you off at the employees' entrance to The Hotel and wait for you," Bonnie said sternly. "*Right,* Rach?"

Rachel shot a quick look at the rearview mirror. "Whatever."

"When you get there, make sure she parks so you're at curbside. You never exit into traffic in Manhattan. It's a good way to get killed." Bonnie raised her voice. "Are you listening, Rachel?"

"Curbside," Rachel muttered. "I'm hanging on every word."

"Sweep the train to your left, swing your legs out to the right, then ease your way from the car. There won't be a doorman at the employees' entrance and I don't think Miss Thing up there will be much help, so you'll have to manage on your own."

"I heard that, too," Rachel said. "Let me wear those shoes to the club next weekend and I'll *carry* her to the door."

Bonnie shot a deadly look in her cousin's direction,

then lowered her voice. "Those shoes are magic, Jules. The last time I wore them I scored a chewing gum commercial that paid my back rent. Who knows what might happen?"

Rachel's snicker could be heard three blocks away. "Somewhere in Brooklyn there's a house with a witch under it."

"I'm talking Cinderella," Bonnie snapped back, "not the *Wizard of Oz*." She glared over at Julia. "And stop laughing. You're just encouraging her."

"If the shoe fits," Julia muttered, and was rewarded with a soft punch on her forearm for the trouble.

"So sue me," Bonnie said. "If you ask me, a little extra good luck never hurt anyone. I'm an optimist and I think something wonderful's going to happen to you tonight."

Rachel turned the key and the engine leaped to life with a roar.

As far as Julia was concerned, she would settle for not having to take the subway home.

Traffic was light and they made it across the Bridge in record time. Julia flipped open her cell phone and snapped photos of the burled wood console, the flower bottle of Moet, and Bonnie's shoes.

Up front, Rachel muttered something they wouldn't even say on cable, and Julia realized they were no longer moving.

"Welcome to gridlock." Rachel tossed the remark over her shoulder. "Park is backed up from here to the east thirties. I might as well turn off the engine."

"What time is it?"

"Five minutes after six."

It didn't take Einstein to do the math.

"I think I'd better walk the rest of the way."

"In those shoes? You wouldn't make it to the corner."

"You're right." Julia leaned forward and started to unfasten the straps. "I'll take them off."

IN LESS THAN TEN MINUTES Jack was stopped three times for autographs, twice for pictures and once to father a woman's child.

With the exception of requests for sperm donations, he had never been good at saying no to fans. Put him face-to-face with people who had actually plunked down ten dollars to buy a movie ticket for one of his films, and he was putty in their hands.

He stepped up the pace and closed his ears to the greetings shouted from passing cars, the horns honking in salute.

"Ohmigod! Ohmigod!" A girl's high-pitched voice rang out from the other side of the avenue. "Jack Wyatt, I love you…!"

She sounded young. Little more than a kid. He told himself not to look in her direction—eye contact was always his undoing—but rudeness wasn't part of his nature, and he angled his head in the direction of the sound in time to see a small figure dart into traffic.

The adrenaline rush hit and next thing he knew, he was standing in the middle of Park Avenue holding back traffic while a skinny preteen clung to his arm and sobbed as if her heart was breaking.

"You're safe," he said, tightening his arm around her narrow shoulders, "but how about we get you back on the sidewalk."

They were met at the curb by a middle-aged woman with a high hairline and a bad attitude. "Gina, what the hell was that all about?"

The little girl barely registered her mother's words. She continued to clutch Jack's hand and sob.

He crouched down next to her. "Are you okay?"

She nodded, unable to look at him.

"Pretty dumb thing you did. You could've been hurt."

"I wasn't thinking." She met his eyes, then quickly glanced away.

"Duh," he said, and was rewarded with a smile. "You won't do that again, will you?"

"No."

He extended his right hand to her. "Shake on it?"

She had a good grip and a great smile. He turned to her angry mother. "She did something stupid, not something bad," he said pointedly to the woman. "I hope you'll keep that in mind."

"Talk to me after you've raised one of your own," she snapped and, linking her arm with her daughter's, stormed off.

A crowd was starting to gather. He knew enough about crowds to know he didn't want to be in the center of one. He signed a few quick autographs, posed for one cell phone snap, then quickly disengaged himself and plunged back into traffic.

And that, of course, was when his destiny finally found him.

CHAPTER TWO

"ARE YOU OKAY?" A woman's voice, pitched low, sounded from somewhere behind him.

"What happened?" Jack managed to wheeze between intakes of breath. "Was I hit by a truck?"

That was the only explanation he could come up with for why he was sprawled on his ass in the middle of Park Avenue gasping for air like a trout.

"I'm so sorry. I should have looked first." All he could see were her elegant feet, but that was enough for him to know a goddess had to be attached.

"What were you driving, a tank?" He struggled to a sitting position and tried to look macho.

"A limo."

He focused in on her. She was tall, curvy, and clad in a long shimmery column of bronze and copper that hugged her body like a second skin and made him think of sunsets in Maui.

"You drive a limo?"

"Actually, I was riding in one and I clipped you with the passenger door when I got out."

"Next time try looking first."

"You haven't been listening." She didn't raise her voice, but then, she didn't have to. She was a redhead. "Maybe you should have watched where you were going."

He stood up gingerly, aware of the blossoming pain

in his midsection. Where was the stunt double when he needed one?

"You look like you're about to pass out," she said, clearly unimpressed with his superior physical conditioning. "Go sit on the curb and put your head between your knees while I call 911."

Right after he started getting his hair highlighted and curled.

Come to think of it, this whole thing reeked of setup. The camera-ready redhead. The bridal limo with the hearts and flowers painted on the side panels. It had tabloid written all over it.

He glanced around. "Okay, so where are they?"

"Where are who?"

She answered a question with a question. She was either very clever or a native New Yorker.

"The paparazzi."

"You're not making sense." She gestured in the general vicinity of his forehead. "You're breaking into a sweat. Sit down before you fall down."

"Forget it. I'm fine." Of course he was breaking into a sweat. Redheads always had that effect on him.

She opened her sparkly purse and pulled out a beat-up cell phone. Scratch that. A camera phone.

He wasn't surprised. Welcome to the age of technology. You could snap a picture and sell it to the *Enquirer* just by pressing the speed dial.

Except she wasn't snapping pictures, she was actually talking into the phone.

"...yes," he heard her say, "male, around thirty-six—"

"Thirty-four."

She gave him a look that had probably sent more than one man running for cover. "Thirty-four," she said, and he could almost see the eye roll she withheld. "Male...

I hit him in the stomach with a car door…. No, it wasn't deliberate. I think he needs an—"

He grabbed for her cell. "I'm okay," he said into it. "No problem here…it's a misunderstanding…thanks."

"You shouldn't have hung up on them," she said as he handed back the phone. "I was calling for an ambulance."

"I don't need an ambulance," he said through gritted teeth. "I just need a minute to catch my breath."

"How do you know you don't have a concussion?"

"I didn't hit my head."

"Are you sure you didn't hit it on the sidewalk when you fell? Your eyes don't seem to be tracking too well."

Now that hurt more than a door to the gut. Most women liked his eyes just fine.

"I had the wind knocked out of me."

"So you're telling me that nothing hurts."

"That's what I'm telling you."

She had an unnervingly direct glance. "So if nothing hurts, why are you clutching your stomach?"

He stopped doing it immediately.

"You're a lousy actor," she said without even a hint of irony. "My four-year-old son gets the same look in his eyes when he skins his knee and doesn't want me to know how much it hurts."

"That's the first time anyone ever compared me to a four-year-old." Or called him a lousy actor.

Well, to his face at least.

"You should be flattered," she said. "He's an exceptional four-year-old."

Maybe she was right. Maybe Jack should sit down on the curb and put his head between his knees. But not for the reason she thought. The goddess had him completely off balance. He didn't know if she was flirting with him, mocking him or setting him up for a photo op.

Sure, she was young and beautiful, but not in the way the women he knew were young and beautiful. Soft shadows hovered beneath her wide hazel eyes. Faint worry lines on her brow hadn't been airbrushed or Botoxed into oblivion. Her life showed on her face. Maybe that was why he couldn't look away, why he really couldn't seem to catch his breath.

The entire city had vanished. Traffic, buildings, the people hurrying by—they had all disappeared. There was only the two of them…only her…and it wasn't a red carpet she was gliding down, it was a white one strewn with roses, and he was waiting for her at the altar, where—

"I think that Hummer's heading straight for us."

He blinked at the sound of her voice as the city came back into focus around him. He felt like a space traveler returning to earth after a long absence. Instinctively, he reached for her hand, and the unexpected softness of her skin sent his brain cells tumbling once again into a free fall.

What the hell was wrong with him?

He was the guy who didn't flinch in the face of danger. The guy who had made the Coolest Man on the Planet list so many times he'd been inducted into the Hall of Fame.

Right now the Coolest Man on the Planet felt like a fifteen-year-old kid whose voice hadn't quite finished changing, a kid whose main goal in life was finding the nerve to ask the prettiest girl in school to the prom.

If his touch did anything at all to her equilibrium, it was the best kept secret in the city. He'd read about this kind of chemical attraction, and it was usually reciprocal. No way could he be feeling this way without some feedback in return. Add two parts of hydrogen to one part oxygen and presto, you had water. Take a man with a thunderbolt through his heart and add a woman with red hair and hazel eyes who—

Wait a minute. He replayed the mental tape.

My four-year-old son…

How had that managed to slip past him?

If she had a kid, that meant there was probably a man out there somewhere who was keeping the home fires burning tonight.

Jack glanced down at her ring finger.

Then again, maybe not.

She stumbled over the curb and he steadied her. She didn't really need steadying; he just wanted an excuse to touch her again.

"Thanks." She opened her sparkly purse and pulled out a pair of black eyeglasses, then slipped them on with a short, self-deprecating laugh. "Who was I trying to kid, anyway? I can't see three feet ahead of me without them."

And she still didn't recognize him

And he still didn't care.

He couldn't remember the last time he had seen a woman's eyes crinkle that way when she smiled. Nobody crinkled in Hollywood. He wouldn't be surprised if it was against the law. She had a funny little catch to her laughter, a cross between a chuckle and a sigh. The sound slipped past the crumbling remains of his defenses and lodged itself squarely in the center of his chest, right near his heart.

Maybe he had hit his head on the concrete, after all. There wasn't much else that could explain the way he was feeling. Take the black eyeglasses, for instance. She should have looked ridiculous with the librarian glasses and the goddess getup but, damn his luck, she didn't. Instead, the effect was so powerfully sexy that he was rendered speechless.

For the second time in less than ten minutes, he felt as if he had been body-slammed to the ground by forces he couldn't control. It took him a full twenty seconds to realize she was saying goodbye.

"...I'd feel better if you saw a doctor," she said, eyes wide with concern. "I'll pay all the expenses."

Her eyes were hazel, with flecks of navy and gold in their depths. He had never seen anything like them before. They made ordinary blue seem tired and old.

"We're on Park Avenue and I'm wearing a tux. I think I can handle a doctor's bill." Schmuck. Why did he say that? She was a half step away from giving him her name, address and phone number.

"But you shouldn't have to pay for your doctor's bill," she said. "The accident was my fault."

"What accident?" Now he sounded like a native New Yorker. "Except for the broken ribs, I'm good as new."

"Not funny," she said, but she flashed him a quick-silver smile just the same.

"You were right before," he said. "I should've watched where I was going." And there went his second chance to get her phone number.

"I should have looked before I opened the door." That quicksilver smile widened. "You're sure you don't need to see a doctor?"

"I don't need to see a doctor." Three strikes and he was out.

She flung the train of her gown over her left shoulder, and he watched as the fabric molded itself to her curves.

Did she have any idea what she was doing to him?

"Watch out for white limos," she said, and before he had the chance to pull his brains out of his trousers, she was walking away from him in what was probably the best walking-away dress on the planet, and, damn it, he wasn't going to let her go.

JULIA FELT HIS EYES on her as she attempted to glide barefoot down Park Avenue. Who could blame him for staring? It wasn't every day a man saw a woman with childbearing hips walking barefoot down Park Avenue with her Versace knockoff draped over her shoulder like a toga.

Every fiber of her being screamed for her to turn around and shriek, "It's baby weight!" but then she would have to acknowledge that the babies in question were almost five and those ten extra pounds had more to do with chocolate than childbirth.

He probably had never seen a size ten woman in captivity before, and couldn't believe his eyes. That was the thing about good-looking men. They tended to hold mere mortals up to their same impossible standards. She had liked him better before she put her glasses on and thought he was an ordinary guy.

Look all you want, she thought. Manhattan might have a ban on double-digit dress sizes, but thank God Brooklyn didn't or else half the female population would be on their way to New Jersey.

She knew what Bonnie would do. Her fearless friend would affect a major catwalk strut and give him something to look at. Then again, Bonnie didn't have childbearing hips. If Julia tried that hip-swinging Clydesdale walk, she might take somebody's eye out.

The thought of catwalking Clydesdales in Manolo Blahniks made her laugh out loud, which was when he managed to sneak up on her.

"Looks like we're headed in the same direction."

His voice, warm and supple, sounded next to her left

ear, and if she hadn't been carrying her shoes, she would have jumped out of them in surprise.

"Didn't your mother tell you that you shouldn't sneak up on women?" she asked as she picked up speed again. "Somebody should rig you up with a cowbell."

This time he was the one who laughed out loud. Okay, so he had a sense of humor, but he was still a stranger who wasn't smart enough to look both ways before he crossed the street.

He fell into step beside her. She supposed she should be grateful he wasn't walking behind her, calibrating the size of her butt, but his presence had her feeling all off balance. Maybe it was the sheer size of the man. She was used to being taller than most people she met, including the men. The sensation of looking up to a man was unfamiliar, and it made her acutely aware of the fact that she was a woman. Not a writer. Not a computer technician. Not the mother of two.

A woman.

She'd almost forgotten how it felt.

Everything about him was bigger than life. His height. His shoulders. His laugh. The rough, honeyed sound of his voice. He seemed to command attention just by breathing.

Not that she was paying any attention on a personal level, mind you. Far from it. This was strictly her writer's mind at work, mentally filing away her observations in case she ever wrote an article on Street Smarts for the Single Woman or How to Tell the Good Guys from the Bad Guys.

"For the record," he said, "I'm not following you."

His delivery was deadpan, but the sparkle in his eyes gave him away. The sidewalk beneath her bare feet disappeared and she found herself walking on air.

"You're not?" she asked, unable to match his deadpan delivery. "I'm crushed."

"The fact that we're both heading south on Park is purely coincidental."

"It's a big bad city," she said, not breaking stride. "There's safety in numbers."

"Hey, I've seen what you can do with a car door. I figure I'm in good hands."

"All I did was knock you down. How long are you going to hold a grudge?"

He pretended to look at his watch. "Another fifteen minutes should do it."

"Twelve is better."

"You sound like a lawyer."

"Not me," she said. "I'm a writer." Okay, writer-slash-computer technician.

"A writer." He sounded as if he would have been more impressed if she'd said she helped people retrieve missing e-mails from the bowels of AOL and Earthlink.

"You have something against writers?"

"It depends," he said. "You don't write for the tabloids, do you?"

What a weird question. "Last year I sold a service piece on how to buy a dishwasher."

"You're kidding."

"I'll have you know that article was reprinted by *Readers Digest.* If you'd ever washed a dish in your life you'd understand how important a good dishwasher is."

"For all you know I wash dishes every day."

"You don't wash dishes."

"You sound pretty sure of yourself."

"I sold a piece on first impressions last year to *Glamour.* My research proved that first impressions are usually right on the money."

"Not this time, Red." The man's smile redefined devastating. He made Tom Cruise look like he needed corrective dentistry. "I worked in a diner about three blocks from here when I first came to New York."

"Waiting tables?"

"That would have been a step up. Try washing dishes, pots, pans, grills, glasses, dishes, flatware, and the occasional messy patron."

"Point well taken," she said. "Maybe there's an article in that."

"Tales of a Manhattan Dishwasher?"

"I was thinking more like Five Minutes to a Clean Kitchen, but your idea isn't half-bad."

He shot her a look that made them both laugh.

So what did he do that required formal wear? Bonnie would have asked him outright, but Julia preferred to speculate.

Doctor? (Too easily distracted.) Lawyer? (Too funny.) Astronaut? (Would never fit in those little cabins.) Unemployed actor working as a seat-filler? (Now that was a possibility.)

Then again, maybe he was just a single guy on his way to pick up his date for the evening.

Julia had been out of the dating market for so long she had forgotten that single adults usually dressed up and mingled with each other on Saturday night. The more she thought about it, the more it made sense. A man who looked like that wouldn't be alone. Not in a million years. Women were probably lined up in front of his door, throwing underwear and phone numbers in his direction. Who could blame the guy if he had an ego the size of Giants Stadium?

And yet there they were, walking along in a surprisingly companionable silence. She didn't feel the need to fill the gap with chatter, and neither did he. She was even starting to get past his extreme good looks. Why hold it against him? He couldn't help being gorgeous any more than she could help having the McGraw child-bearing hips.

It just didn't make sense. She wasn't one of those gregarious types who could walk into a cocktail party and own the room. She was the typical writer-nerd, an observer, the quiet one in the corner scribbling notes. Normally she was more like her son, Daniel, slow to warm up to people because once she gave her heart it was gone forever.

Not that her heart was in any danger, mind you. It was merely a figure of speech.

A YELLOW CAB SLOWED to a crawl alongside them and Jack steeled himself for the inevitable. The driver leaned across the passenger seat and shouted "Hey!" through the open window.

Next to him the goddess frowned.

"Good to see you!" the cabbie yelled. "You need a ride?"

"We're okay," Jack called back with an easy smile. "But thanks anyway."

"Anytime," the cabbie said, then disappeared back into traffic.

"Since when do cabbies solicit riders?" She actually turned and looked after the retreating taxi.

"Maybe it's that killer dress you're wearing." He was surprised more cars hadn't stopped to take a better look.

"Nice try," she said, "but he was definitely talking to you and—ouch!" She stopped and checked the sole of her right foot. "I think I stepped on a pebble."

"You'd better hope it's only a pebble. There's some scary stuff down there."

She shivered, and her train started to slip from her shoulder. "Don't remind me."

Maybe it was the sight of her creamy shoulder sliding out from under the shimmering train of her dress. Maybe it was the look in her eyes or the way the late afternoon sun turned her mane of hair into living fire. He hadn't a clue. The only thing he knew for sure was that for the first time in years, he was exactly where he wanted to be.

He pushed away the image of a goddess in a long white gown drifting toward him across a sea of rose petals, and gestured to the shoes dangling from her wrist. "I don't know how to break it to you, but on my planet we wear them on our feet."

She feigned amazement as she rearranged the shimmering fabric. "On my planet we only wear them on special occasions."

"So you're not going to tell me why you're carrying your shoes?"

She held them up so the five-inch stiletto heels were dangling at eye level. "How far would you want to walk on these things?"

"Point well taken," he said, although he had never given it much thought. Men shaved their faces. Women walked on stilts. It was all part of one big cosmic puzzle.

She grinned up at him and they continued walking, picking up their silence where they had left it moments ago. It wasn't an angry silence or a fraught silence, but he felt off balance just the same. Every time she glanced at him he had the feeling she knew exactly what he was thinking. He felt as if the rules had changed when he wasn't looking and he was the last one to find out.

He found himself waiting for a spark of awareness, that little pop of recognition that came with celebrity, but...nothing. Not a glimmer, not a hint, not a whisper.

Some people reacted immediately when they saw him, like the little girl who had dashed into traffic earlier. Others opted for the cool approach, a nod and a smile as they drifted back into the crowd. And then there was the third group, the ones who pretended they had no idea who he was and used their indifference to let him know how little his celebrity mattered to them.

The barefoot goddess not only acted as if she didn't recognize him, he was pretty damn sure she really didn't. They walked another half block in silence, and suddenly the silence wasn't so comfortable anymore. He was starting to feel that the limo door had knocked him straight into Bizarro world.

"So do you mind if I walk with you?"

She narrowed her eyes in his direction and he was reminded again of why redheads scared the hell out of him. "Took you long enough to ask."

"I'm asking now."

There was that laugh again. "You're more like my kids than I thought. They only ask when they're sure of the answer."

"You have more than one kid?"

"Two," she said. At least this time she didn't bust him for asking. "They're twins."

And she still had a killer body. A goddess, he thought. A woman the gods loved.

"So what are they doing while you're walking barefoot down Park Avenue?"

"Probably eating pizza and watching an Olsen Twins video."

"With a babysitter?" He saw the fences going up before the words left his mouth. "Sorry. None of my business."

She didn't argue. "Most people start with the weather and then move on to the personal stuff."

"I'm flexible. We can start with the weather."

She glanced up. "Sunny and dry."

He thought for a second. "So what did you think about the last election?"

"Politics?" She shook her head. "Sorry. Too divisive."

Divisive? She probably did the *Times* puzzle in ink. His curiosity went up another notch.

"There's always religion."

"Not a good idea."

He gave his best aw-shucks shrug. "Guess that leaves sex."

They locked eyes as they waited for the traffic light to turn green. This was Manhattan. Nobody waited for the light to turn green. Once again he forgot about the fact that they were standing on a street corner in midtown Manhattan, about the curious crowd growing around them. He saw only her…saw only his future…he bent down and—

"Yo!" Another cabbie slowed to a stop in the intersection. "Your last one sucked but the wife's still crazy about you."

"Thanks," Jack called as he struggled to let the real world back in. "She said the same about you."

The cabbie roared with laughter and flashed him a thumbs-up. The crowd around them grew larger and more attentive.

The red-haired goddess looked at him and he saw her expression change. "You're famous?"

The green Walk sign appeared. He placed his hand beneath her left elbow as they stepped off the curb. "Depends who you ask."

A bright red blush spread upward from her shoulders.

"I'm sorry I didn't—I have two kids and if you're not on *Sesame Street*…"

"You don't have to apologize."

She looked so embarrassed that he was embarrassed for both of them.

"I'm two *Star Wars* prequels behind…I mean, I think the last film I saw in an actual movie theater was *Legally Blond,* and how long ago was that? I'm babbling…sorry…you're wearing a tux…you were walking south on Park…I should've figured you were heading for The Hotel."

"You, too?"

She nodded. "I'm really sorry I didn't recognize you."

"Enough with the apologies," he said as they reached the opposite curb. "My ego isn't that fragile."

"You do look familiar. I was just thinking that a second before the cab driver—"

"Let it go. It doesn't matter." At least not as much as he thought it would.

"Yes, it does. It's going to drive me crazy all night." Her quicksilver smile reappeared. "I'm sure I've seen you in something. Give me a hint."

"Fire Power at 30,000 Feet?"

She shook her head.

"Fatal Wonder? Great box office, mediocre reviews."

"Sorry."

"Heart of a Hero?"

"I told you I didn't get out much."

"Sounds like you don't get out at all. These are classics we're talking about, Red." He was laughing as he said it. "Time capsule stuff."

She shot him a dizzying look. "Sounds like your ego might be a little less fragile than you think."

He mimed a direct hit. "Good thing you don't write movie reviews. I'd be—"

"Wait a second!" She grabbed his sleeve. "Now I

know why you seemed familiar. It's your voice! Weren't you the voice of Phinneas P. Phrog in *The Greenies?*"

"You couldn't remember the one where I was a senator from Massachusetts?"

"Sorry." She didn't look sorry. She looked as if she might start laughing. "You have a fabulous voice. I knew it sounded familiar."

"I got robbed," he said. "Ebert & Roeper said it was an Oscar-worthy performance."

"The death scene with Gilda Goldfish was downright Shakespearean." Oh yeah. She was ready to laugh.

"Did you know your right eye twitches when you're being sarcastic?"

Her hand flew up to her eye and he was the one who laughed.

"Gotcha," he said. "550 million gross U.S., 827 million worldwide. My biggest film and I'm the voice of a fat frog with a derby hat and an attitude."

"You should be happy," she stated. "You have a very distinctive voice. I'd know it anywhere."

"Thanks," he said. "So what's my name?"

"Everyone knows your name."

"Yeah, but do you?"

"Don't be ridiculous."

"So what is it?" His smile was so wide it needed two faces to contain it.

"Give me a second," she said, clearly torn between laughter and embarrassment. "It'll come to me."

"You're killing me here, Red. You remembered the damn frog's name but you have to search around for mine." The last time he'd felt this happy he was still waiting for his voice to change.

"I don't work well under pressure," she said, giving

way to laughter again. "Let me run through the alphabet. It'll come to me."

"A twelve year career," he said with a self-deprecating laugh. "Awards, great box office, four official fan clubs, and she needs the alphabet to—"

They rounded the corner of Park and East 53rd Street and the goddess stopped dead in her tracks.

"Oh my God!" Her voice was little more than a whisper. "Wow!"

The Hotel was right up ahead, a gleaming modern surge of smoked glass and burnished metal. Red, white and blue searchlights scanned the sky, while screaming fans pressed up against the barricades for a glimpse of the biggest and brightest. The street was clogged with limos, Hummers, news vans, cops cars, and one lone ambulance parked discreetly up the block.

The usual suspects in borrowed finery vied for face time on the red carpet with Joan and Melissa and Star and Billy and anyone else with a microphone and a live feed to millions.

Jack had stopped really seeing any of it a long time ago. Events ran into each other, one year spilling over into the next until he could only mark the passage of time by the changing fashions.

"This is incredible," the goddess next to him breathed. "Bonnie told me what to expect but…" Her voice trailed off. "It looks like Disney on the Hudson."

He started to tell her that it *was* Disney on the Hudson, all smoke and mirrors, a theme park created for the television cameras, but the words died in his throat. She was wide-eyed as a child, completely unself-conscious in her enjoyment of the scene spread out before them, and he didn't want to be the one to spoil it for her.

Who are you? he wondered as he absorbed her unabashed excitement. A barefoot goddess in Versace who had two kids and wrote about dishwashers, and had somehow managed to get herself invited to the First Annual Reel New York Film Festival awards even though she hadn't gone out to see a movie in almost six years.

His cell phone vibrated against his hip. It was probably Clive, wondering why he hadn't hit the red carpet yet. Jack ignored it. Life was short. A chance like this—a woman like this—might never come again, and he couldn't let her go.

"Come with me," he said. "Forget whatever you were going to do and let's get out of here."

"What?!" She actually moved back a step. "Are you crazy? You don't even know my name."

"You don't know mine, either," he said. "That makes us even." He closed the distance between them. "I'll get my car out of the garage and we can drive out to Montauk for lobsters and—"

"Montauk is a three-hour drive from here."

She didn't say no. He took it as encouragement.

"It's Saturday night. I know a place that's open until eleven. Best lobsters you've ever had."

"Better than Maine lobsters?"

"Definitely." His cell phone vibrated again and once again he ignored it.

"It sounds great but—"

"It sounds crazy. I know it sounds crazy. But sometimes crazy is good. Sometimes crazy is exactly what you need."

"I can't."

He glanced down at her ring-free left hand. "Are you married?"

She shook her head. "No."

"Is there somebody else?"

"No, there isn't somebody else. There isn't even you! This is—"

"Crazy. We already agreed on that. But something's happening here and I want you to give me one good reason why we shouldn't see where it takes us."

"Where do I start? My kids. My best friend." She pushed her hair back from her face. "The fact that you're a total stranger."

"We can work out the details on the way to Montauk. Don't think, Red, just say yes." She was tempted. He could see it in her eyes. Another minute, thirty more seconds and maybe—

"What in bloody hell are you doing?" They both jumped at the sound of Clive's voice. "They're ready to close the doors."

Clive was standing on the opposite curb and it was clear he was in high dudgeon. It was also clear to Jack that something wasn't right. Clive looked paler than usual, and even from that distance Jack could see a fine sheen of sweat on the Englishman's brow.

"Was that man talking to you?" the goddess asked as Clive started toward them.

"That's Clive," Jack said. "He's my manager."

"I think he's coming over here."

Clive was bearing down on him with a thousand years of British military tradition at his back. He didn't look well. His skin was ashen and beads of sweat dotted his forehead. "You gave me your word, too, Jack. Nine minutes and counting."

"Nine minutes," the goddess said as Clive moved closer. "I'm sorry but I have to go."

"Don't!" Jack reached for her arm. "You can't—"

"I promised," she said. "I gave my word."

"Listen to her," Clive said as he glanced from Jack to the goddess. "She's clearly a person of integrity."

Unfortunately, so was Jack. He looked from his old friend to the barefoot goddess and knew that the moment for magic had come and gone.

"This isn't the end," he said, touching her wrist for an instant. "I owe you a lobster."

"I'll take a rain check," she said, then turned and hurried up the street to the employees' entrance.

"Who is she?" Clive asked as they watched her disappear into The Hotel.

"I don't know," Jack said, "but I'm going to find out."

And when he did, he intended to marry her.

CHAPTER THREE

JULIA MONAHAN, the same woman who once took two months to summon up the resolve to try a new dry cleaners, had come this close to saying yes.

Well, not exactly yes, but a very definite maybe.

Just the idea that she would consider going anywhere with a total stranger was enough to make her wonder if Bonnie had performed an extreme makeover on her personality. Could hair extensions affect your brain waves? Clearly something had changed, because the regular Julia, the one who wore sweats and T-shirts and a scruffy ponytail, would never in a million years have given a crazy idea like lobsters at Montauk a second thought.

What if that angry Englishman hadn't shown up when he did? Would she have stepped out of character and done something so totally crazy, so irresistible, that just thinking about it made her feel hot from head to toe?

The answer was yes.

A big loud enthusiastic totally unexpected yes.

The only thing that had kept her from throwing caution to the wind and running off to Montauk with a total stranger was the fact that she was the mother of two small children who expected her home tonight.

A pretty scary realization for a woman who prided herself on her practical nature. All it took was a fancy dress and impossible shoes, and a whole other Julia took over. A Julia who would run off with a man whose name she didn't even know.

Bonnie would never believe it, especially the part where she couldn't remember a celebrity's name. What had that agitated Brit called him? Jack. That was it. But Jack what?

The security guard locked the door behind her and she was herded into a narrow hallway with the other seat-fillers. Their IDs were checked by the backstage coordinator, an officious-looking woman with a headset and a mini-laptop, who then assigned them each a call number.

"Put those shoes on, 43," the coordinator said to Julia with a shake of her head. "This isn't the Grammys."

Five seat-fillers, three men and two women, were told they wouldn't be needed. A minor squabble erupted about whether or not they would be paid for showing up, and the security guard escorted them out.

While everyone was busy talking about the disagreement, Julia drifted off into the corner, flipped open her phone and texted a message to Bonnie.

MET FROG VOICE FROM GREENIES—JACK WHO??

"No cell phones in the venue," the backstage coordinator snapped at Julia.

"I'm not making a real call. I was just going to text—"

"Phones off," the woman barked. "We don't need some fool's cell playing 'Waltzing Matilda' during DeNiro's acceptance speech."

Julia powered down.

Maybe the alphabet would jog her memory.

Jack Abbott.

Nope. He was a character in a soap opera.

Jack Black.

Not quite.

"43, you're going in." The backstage coordinator loomed over Julia. "No-show guest in D-110."

"Smart move with that Versace, 43." A slender woman in black velvet snapped shut the clasp of her sparkly Judith Leiber butterfly bag. "With a dress like that, you were bound to get the first no-show. You'll be set for the night."

Julia looked up from checking the straps on her dangerous shoes. "What do you mean, set for the night?"

"Somebody famous got stood up and you're now his date du jour. You'll get face time and a seat-filler of your own. Talk about lucky."

She pulled as tight as she could on the strap, and mentally crossed her fingers that it would hold long enough for her to find her seat. The coordinator aimed her in the direction of the exit, where a young man with a shocking-pink Mohawk checked her ID number, then handed her off to a runner, who pushed her through a side door into another narrow hallway, where another woman with a headset did a quick visual inspection.

"Are those the Actors Equity Manolos?" she asked, eyeing Julia's borrowed shoes. "Lucky you."

The shoes were as famous as half the guests in the ballroom.

"Lose the glasses," the woman continued. "Too distracting."

"Sorry," Julia said, cramming them into the bag with her cell phone and comb. "I forgot I had them on."

"If you need the john, you're too late. Remember, this isn't a singles bar. I don't care if somebody yells fire— you stay in that seat until told otherwise."

Julia, who fully intended to be the first one at the exit in the event of fire, nodded solemnly.

"We need an usher, section D," the woman said into her headset, and seconds later the door opened and a small, freckle-faced girl in a black uniform appeared.

"One ten," the woman snapped, "and fast."

"This way," the usher said, and the next thing Julia knew, she was wobbling down the narrow center aisle. The air was thick with laughter and conversation, and a prickle of excitement raced all the way down her spine. He was there. She didn't know where exactly, but he had to be there.

Chandeliers glittered overhead, dripping crystal teardrops like tinsel on a Christmas tree. The air was cool and crisp as a glass of champagne, and every bit as intoxicating. The discordant sounds from the orchestra as they tuned up in preparation for the show only added to the sense of anticipation. She was quickly approaching sensory overload.

Even without her glasses some famous faces leaped out at her. Okay, so maybe she didn't know all of their names, but she knew some of them—Tom and that other Julia and Harrison and Renee for starters—and she definitely knew the voices.

One voice in particular was missing. She tried hard not to be disappointed but, to her surprise. she was. Maybe he had ditched the ceremony, after all, and was on his way out to Montauk right that very minute. She imagined him sailing past Patchogue and the Moriches, past scrub pines and farm stands and twenty-four-hour diners, on his way out to the tip of Long Island and that lobster he had offered her.

She tried to imagine what it would be like to be so spontaneous and free, but came up blank. Spontaneity and single parenthood didn't exactly go hand in hand. Children needed routine. They needed to know they could count on you to be there when they needed you, and even when they didn't. And if that meant the midnight lobster suppers had to wait ten or fifteen years, then that was the way it had to be.

Now if she could just arrange for him to ask her again when her kids graduated high school, she just might surprise herself and everyone else.

How could you feel the loss of something you never had? Her heart ached as much as if they had been longtime lovers who had decided it was time to part. How ridiculous! She didn't know his name. He didn't know hers. They had never held hands or kissed or—

Better stop right there. She had a vivid imagination, and this wasn't the place to indulge in that particular fantasy.

Still, sexual heat aside, it really was a terrific story, she thought as the usher led her deeper into the ballroom. All of the right elements were there. A cute meet. A heroine with a back story. A mystery man who sweeps her off her feet to his house on the ocean, where they live happily ever after with their two children, their golden retriever and a satellite dish.

She could see it so clearly, the two of them, still warm from their shared bed, curled up on the sofa with the Sunday papers and a never-ending pot of coffee, while their children played quietly in their rooms.

Well, maybe that last bit was a little too much, but the whole thing was so real to Julia she felt she could reach out and grab it like a ripe peach hanging from a low branch. She had a sentimental streak the size of a four-lane highway, and nothing life threw at her had been able to trample her bone-deep belief in the power of love, or dampen her enthusiasm for happy endings.

No matter how beyond reach they sometimes seemed. If she managed to pass anything along to her children, that was the most important.

The usher stopped four rows from the stage. "Second seat."

"Got it."

A dapper gray-haired man was sitting in the first seat. He nodded politely in Julia's direction, then rose and stepped into the aisle so she could claim her spot. He didn't look familiar, but given Julia's track record, that didn't mean much.

It took her a few seconds to gather up her train the way Bonnie had shown her, and settle into her seat, and she could sense the man's impatience poking through his polished veneer.

The orchestra finished warming up and the last notes from the string section drifted toward the ceiling and were swallowed up by the steady buzz of conversation.

"Your dress," the man next to her said, and she turned toward him.

"Yes?" She beamed at him. How could he not love her dress?

"It's crowding me." He pointed in the general direction of his feet, which were obscured by yards of shimmering satin.

She made an attempt to corral the offending garment before it jumped the fence again. "It seems to have a life of its own."

That was putting it mildly. There was enough fabric in the train to cover two sofas and have enough left over for a matching bedspread, and it was all trying to escape the confines of her narrow seat.

The house lights flickered.

"This is growing tedious," the gray-haired man next

to her announced. "I hope you won't be battling your costume when the cameras are trained on us."

She opened her mouth to answer, but somebody else did it for her.

"That won't be a problem. I'll take that seat now, thanks." The sound of his voice made her shiver. She would never be able to watch *The Greenies* again without needing a cold shower every time Phinneas P. Phrog was on screen.

How scary was that?

The gray-haired man disappeared up the aisle with the usher, and the anonymous movie star she had knocked flat on Park Avenue took his place. Her heart thudded so hard she couldn't catch her breath, and for a second she was afraid somebody would have to slap the paddles on her and call her back from chasing that white light.

Finally a little bell went off inside her head. "Jack Wyatt!"

"So you finally made it to the end of the alphabet." He had one of those smiles that could light up the world. A one-man electrical power plant.

She smiled right back at him. "I didn't even make it to Nicholson."

"I'm flattered." He shifted position and his left thigh pressed against her right one for a split second.

"And I'm surprised." One second he was nowhere in sight, and the next he was right there next to her, so close she could smell his skin, feel the solid warmth of his body. "I mean, what were the odds I'd be assigned to the seat next to you?"

"Pretty damn good, considering I asked for you."

Oh God! She could feel her bones melting like sweet butter on a summer's day. If she didn't know better she would think they were both reading from the same

script. There wasn't a screenwriter on the planet who
could come up with better than this.

"How could you ask for me when you don't even
know my name?"

"Lucky for me there was only one tall sexy barefoot
redhead on the premises."

Was it possible to spontaneously combust in an air-
conditioned theater? She was surprised flames weren't
shooting from her fingertips.

He seemed completely at ease in his own skin. He
was the same man here in this high-energy ballroom as
he had been when she'd decked him. He had not only
asked for her, he seemed as genuinely happy to be sitting
next to her as she was to be sitting next to him.

There had to be a catch. She had never experienced
anything like this before. The transition from friendship
to love with Danny had been as slow and natural as the
transition from girl to woman. No drama. No fireworks.
Just the sweet certainty that they were meant to be together.

She wasn't certain about anything that she was
feeling right now. This time there were fireworks and
they were going off inside her heart, rockets and
shooting stars all glittery and gold against the night sky.

He's an actor, a small voice reminded her. He made
his living being whoever he needed to be at the moment.
That should have given her pause, but it didn't. She was
too far gone for that. Colors seemed brighter. The music
was sweeter. The brush of cool air against her heated
skin was more intense.

There was probably a word for what she was feeling,
but she couldn't imagine one that could possibly encom-
pass the wild storm of emotion sweeping its way
through her heart.

Crazy.

Dangerous.

Irresistible.

And that was just for starters. She would need a dictionary and a thesaurus to even begin to describe the sensation.

The sizzle was there. She could feel it burning its way up her spine. But there was something else at work, something deeper and more all-encompassing, and it was that sense of destiny that shook her right to her core.

She shifted position and her dress erupted in the empty spaces between them.

"Is that what our gray-haired friend was complaining about?" he asked.

She peered up at him through her hair extensions as she tried to pat it back into place. "You have to admit there's an awful lot of fabric attached to me."

"That's not a problem for me."

"Just wait. In another second it'll push you right into the—"

He didn't let her finish her sentence. Instead he reached for her hand, and her breath caught sharply somewhere deep in her throat.

Suddenly she knew why people leaped out of airplanes and bungee jumped off mountaintops. This was why they risked everything, on this crazy wild exhilarating free fall without a net, for that one fleeting moment when it all came together and you could almost hear your blood singing in your veins.

That moment when a woman knew her life would never be the same again.

Crazy or not, she was in love.

JACK HADN'T MEANT to take her hand, but there was no turning back now. He didn't want to turn back, not with her gazing at him that way, hazel eyes wide with curiosity and a look so sweet and so open that the world stopped spinning on its axis and he felt himself falling for the second time that night.

The house lights flickered, then dimmed as he laced his fingers through hers. He needed to anchor himself in time and space. He needed proof this was really happening. He sensed her hesitation, that moment when he knew it could go either way, but she didn't pull away. The warmth of her palm; her slender fingers with the short, no-nonsense nails, so at odds with the sexy dress... The sense that this simple act was more erotic, more intimate than either one of them could have imagined...

That he would be feeling the aftershocks for a long, long time to come...

The orchestra launched into a rousing intro. A white-hot spotlight found center stage as the mayor of New York City walked on, to tumultuous applause.

"Welcome to the Reel New York Film Festival awards ceremony, coming to you live from The Hotel in midtown Manhattan."

The words tumbled around inside Jack's brain like Scrabble tiles. He couldn't concentrate on anything but the heady scent of her perfume, the way her hair spilled over her shoulders.

They brought up the house lights a few degrees. Camera people ran down the aisles with hand-helds aimed at the crowd as the lighting crew bounced baby spots around the ballroom. Harrison Ford was saying something into a microphone, but he might as well be speaking Greek for all Jack cared. Nothing mattered but the feel of her hand in his.

"Uh-oh," the goddess whispered. "I think my straps just broke."

He was almost disappointed when he realized she meant her shoes.

"Take them off."

"No shoes, no service."

"That was when you were a seat-filler."

"I'm still a seat-filler."

"No," he said. "Not anymore. You're with me."

Their eyes locked, and neither one of them realized they were on camera until laughter erupted around them, and they looked up to see their images magnified on the giant screen. The camera panned from his face to hers, then zeroed in on a close-up of their hands.

"Anything you want to tell us, Jack?" A smiling blond reporter angled a microphone toward him.

"Not tonight," he said, but tempered his words with the full-wattage smile that had put many a reporter off her game.

"How about you?" The reporter pushed the mike toward the goddess, who recoiled noticeably. "At least tell us your name."

The goddess's hand went ice cold in Jack's as the reporter waited for her to say something, anything, to fill live airtime. Nobody could prepare you for the first taste of the spotlight, and her deer-in-the-headlights expression awoke his long-dormant protective instincts.

"Not tonight," he said smoothly. "Tonight is about the Reel New York Film Festival."

The reporter fixed him with a baleful look, then turned toward the camera.

"We'll be back with the awards for Best Performance in a Supporting Role after this message from our sponsor." She waited, practiced smile firmly in place, until they were safely off to a commercial. "Thanks a lot," she snapped, with an extra glare for the goddess. "That won't be going on my Emmy reel."

The reporter stomped off in search of better prey, with the cameraman close behind her.

They probably shouldn't have done it, but that didn't stop either one of them. The goddess looked at him, he looked at her and they dissolved into helpless laughter. He couldn't remember the last time he had laughed so much with a woman or felt so comfortable.

"I owe you one," she said as she wiped tears from her eyes. "When she pushed that microphone toward me, I actually forgot my own name."

"First time's the hardest," he said. "After a while you get used to it."

She arched a brow. "I find it hard to believe anyone could get used to it."

"Okay," he said, laughing again, "so maybe you don't get used to it so much as you learn to put up with it."

The goddess leaned closer as the house lights dimmed. Her breasts brushed against his right bicep, and suddenly he didn't feel quite so comfortable any longer, and found himself grateful for the cover of darkness.

"By the way," she whispered as the music swelled around them, "my name is Julia."

Julia Wyatt.

THEY WHISPERED TOGETHER, they laughed, they held hands, and all because of a funky bicuspid, a traffic jam on Park and a limo with a killer door.

Maybe this was why people loved fairy tales. Maybe this was why the Cinderella story could be traced back hundreds of years through hundreds of different cultures. Sometimes a girl needed to believe there was still magic in this world, even if she knew it could never last.

Some very famous people with very familiar faces paraded across the stage to present or accept awards, and next thing Julia knew an usher, with a tall man with silver blond hair in tow, appeared next to Jack.

"You're in the next segment, Mr. Wyatt," the usher said.

He blinked like a man waking up from a long nap, then turned to her. "I'm presenting a lifetime achievement," he explained, "but it shouldn't take long."

Neither one wanted to be the first to let go. Finally she slipped her hand from his. "Go," she said, and the look he gave her made her warm all over.

The seat-filler nodded at her, then looked down at the riot of train billowing all over.

"I don't want to step on anything," he said apologetically, and waited while she shifted, gathered and rearranged the yards of luscious satin. She heard the telltale swish as the fabric dragged across the floor, and she cringed inwardly. There was definitely a dry-cleaning bill in her future.

She tried to focus on the parade of famous faces traipsing across the stage, but the spectacle was lost on her until she caught the words, "...America's number one action hero, Jack Wyatt!" and the ballroom broke into rowdy applause and wolf whistles.

He commanded attention just by breathing. He didn't raise his voice. He didn't turn cartwheels or break into a song or dance. All he had to do was stand there, and suddenly there was no place else you wanted to look.

His speech was warm and funny. He nimbly bypassed blatant sentimentality and relied instead on real emotion. Julia wanted to leap from her seat and give him a round of applause, but fortunately she restrained herself.

The award winner, a world-class director even she knew by name, rambled on for what seemed like forever.

She tried not to fidget, but her inner four-year-old was growing restless. Finally she turned to the seat-filler and asked, "How long did they say you'd be here?"

The seat-filler's smile didn't waver. He also didn't speak.

"I know they tell you not to talk to anyone, but I'm a seat-filler, too. You can tell me."

"The rest of the night," he said.

"The rest of the night? That's impossible."

"Sorry you're disappointed, but there's a lot of that going around. I'd rather be sitting next to Penelope Cruz, but those are the breaks."

Julia told herself that the seat-filler was wrong, that Jack would be back right after the segment ended, but the commercial break came and went and there was still no sign of him. Okay. Things happen. She could imagine him back there in a crush of reporters and photographers. He was probably posing for photos, giving interviews, doing all the things a celebrity at one of these award shows was expected to do. The second he could break free he would come back.

Except he didn't.

Three segments later they were about to give out the last award and there was still no sign of him. She told herself that it was nothing personal, that this was a professional appearance for him and he had responsibilities that predated their encounter, but it didn't help.

You're not in high school, she told herself, but it didn't matter. The feelings were as sharp and painful at twenty-seven as they had been when she was seventeen.

The final winner made the final acceptance speech of the evening, and all of the presenters and award winners trooped back on stage for an old-fashioned curtain call that must have strained the seat-filling resources to the max.

Only Jack Wyatt was missing.

Julia wasn't sure if that made things better or worse.

Maybe he was going to make some kind of special effects entrance and bring the proceedings to an end with a splash of Hollywood glitz and glitter. Or maybe he had tried to get back to his seat and they were holding him up until the next commercial.

Or maybe he was already gone.

If this was how it felt to have a fling, she was glad she had bypassed the experience and leaped straight into marriage. When you were flying as high as she had been these last few hours it was a long way to the ground.

The show ended and the audience began to file from the ballroom. Julia couldn't bring herself to leave. She was starting to feel like well-dressed roadkill as the glitterati muttered and climbed over her in their haste to escape to the next high-profile event. One particularly stylish starlet not only stepped on Julia's train, she kicked one of Bonnie's shoes into the next row.

For such an upscale crowd, they were surprisingly harried, and Julia found herself forced into the aisle to make way for a quartet of box office giants. She barely had time to grab the one shoe she could reach before they removed her bodily from her seat. Maybe an article on How to Act Like a Human Being would find a market in one of the trade publications.

"My shoes," she said, trying to elbow her way back into row D. "I have to find my other shoe."

An usher stepped in front of her, arms crossed over his chest. "I'm sorry, but you'll have to leave now, ma'am." Uniforms did strange things to people. You would think he was guarding the gates of Fort Knox.

"I just want to go back and get my shoe."

"I can't let you do that." He gave her a very stern look. "Security regulations."

"You don't understand," she said, as a bead of sweat popped out on her right temple. "They're my best friend's shoes and they're very expensive. I can't leave without them."

"Looks like you'll have to," said the usher, who probably bought his shoes at Payless, same as she did. "There's a lost-and-found in the lobby. File a claim and they'll see what they can do."

"But they're right there," she said, pointing toward the first row. "Not twenty feet away. It'll only take a second."

But the usher wouldn't move, and a horde of famous faces were elbowing past her, some of them muttering about selfish women who couldn't keep track of their own footwear. Her emotions were so close to the surface she was afraid she might cry and utterly humiliate herself. The usher was taking a moral stand right there in the aisle, and short of body-slamming him to the ground, there was nothing she could do.

The lobby was a whirlwind of celebrities, reporters and photographers. Cell phones rang. Flashbulbs popped. The decibel level of conversation was almost deafening. The crowd was so thick she had to literally elbow her way to the lost-and-found.

The young woman in charge looked up at her. "Can I help you?"

Julia placed Bonnie's glorious shoe on the counter. "I'm looking for the other one."

The clerk's eyes widened as she reached for the Manolo Blahnik. "Oooh," she breathed, touching the strap with deep reverence. "Could I—?"

"Sure," Julia said. Clearly the other one wasn't back there or it would have been on the girl's right foot.

"One day I'm going to have a closetful of these," the girl said. "I tried to buy some Jimmy Choos on eBay last year but—"

"The other shoe isn't there, is it?"

The girl bent down and removed the shoe from her left foot and placed it back on the counter. "Sorry." She slid a form toward Julia, along with a ballpoint pen. "Fill this out and we'll call you if it shows up."

Julia filled out the form with her name, phone number and presumed location where the loss occurred, then did another walk through the lobby. Bonnie would have been out of her mind with delight at being able to rub elbows with so many luminaries, but it was lost on Julia. There was only one face she wanted to see, one voice she longed to hear, and he was nowhere to be found.

Finally she located an out-of-the-way spot where she leaned against a pillar and watched the chaos, trying very hard not to jump every time one of the doors opened. Santa Claus was more likely to pop up next to her than Jack Wyatt, but she was, after all, an optimist.

The sparks between them had been genuine. A woman didn't need to have spent years on the dating scene to recognize the real thing. Over the last two years she had gone out on her share of setups, enough to know that no man had ever made her feel this way. She knew human nature, and what had happened between them, the deep current of destiny that had almost knocked her flat, had been as real as anything she had ever experienced.

But maybe meant to be wasn't the same thing as meant to last.

Flings had their place in the natural order of things, and her fling just happened to be the shortest one on record.

She turned on her cell phone and brought up a text message from Rachel:

11:15 OR ELSE!!!!

Which was followed by one from Bonnie:

DANIEL ATE SOAP & I'M LOSING MY MIND!!!!!

Julia closed her cell phone and slipped it back into her purse.

It had been fun to walk in Cinderella's shoes tonight, but now it was time to go home where her two beautiful children were waiting for her and would still love her long after the glass coach turned back into a pumpkin.

She flung her train over her left shoulder and headed for the exit.

CHAPTER FOUR

"SPILL," Bonnie said when Julia, back in her uniform of T-shirt and jeans, joined her at the kitchen table a little after midnight. "What the hell was going on?"

Julia pulled a container of mocha fudge from the freezer and grabbed a spoon. "Can you be more specific?"

"You and Jack Wyatt, that's what. First you text me a question about *The Greenies,* then I'm sitting here picking SpaghettiOs out of the sofa cushions while my godchildren think up ways to torture me, and I look up and there you are on screen, holding hands with only the biggest macho star in Hollywood." She leaned back in her chair and popped a handful of M&M's in her mouth. "Guess you remembered his name."

"With no help from you, I might add."

"Don't push it, Monahan. You lost my shoes. You owe me details."

"I didn't lose your shoes," Julia said as she plunged her spoon into the mocha fudge. "I only lost one of them."

Bonnie clapped her hands over her ears. "No details on the shoes or I'll be forced to eat the frozen chocolate chip cookie dough you have hidden behind the Lean Cuisines."

Julia rolled her eyes. "I thought you didn't snoop."

"I was looking for juice bars for your children."

"A likely story."

"I'm not going to let this drop, so you might as well

tell me everything. I've been seat-filling for six years and nobody's ever talked to me, and you go out there once and end up canoodling with an A-list star."

Julia made a face. "I hate that word."

"Canoodling?"

"Yes, and we weren't."

"So what is it, Jules?" Bonnie leaned across the table and peered into her eyes. "And don't lie to me. We've been friends too long for that. You look different."

That was all it took to unleash the whole story. She began with the rebellious limo door and told it all, every last bit of it, right up until the moment when she slid back into the limo for the ride back to Brooklyn.

"If you'd asked me this morning if I believed in love at first sight, I would have told you it didn't exist, but I was wrong." Julia had always believed love grew over time, that it ripened from friendship into something that could last forever. It couldn't possible explode into your life full-blown and endure.

"Did he ask for your number?"

"No, but—"

"Did he give you any way to get in touch with him?"

"I didn't ask."

"Don't hate me, Jules, but it looks to me like you were a photo op. A little eye candy to keep him from getting too bored."

"No," she said, shaking her head vigorously. "It wasn't anything like that."

"I'm not trying to hurt you, honey, but you've been out of the game for a long time. You've forgotten how it is out there."

"I never was in the game," Julia said softly. "Love isn't a game."

Bonnie groaned and buried her face in her hands.

"I didn't hear that," she said. "Please tell me I didn't hear that."

"I know it sounds crazy, Bonnie, but I've never felt this way before." The attraction between her and Jack had been fiery. She wouldn't deny that. His touch had thrilled her, but it was their easy laughter that had melted her heart.

Bonnie slowly lowered her hands and looked at her. "I know I shouldn't encourage you, but I have to admit I've never seen you this way before."

"I almost ran off with him," Julia said as she pulled another container of ice cream from the freezer. "He wanted me to drive out to Montauk with him tonight, and I swear to you the only thing holding me back was the kids."

Bonnie's spoon clattered to the floor. "He asked you to go to Montauk with him?"

Julia nodded. "Lobsters at midnight."

"This really isn't fair," Bonnie said. "The one time I don't show, and you end up being propositioned by the Coolest Man on the Planet."

"It wasn't a proposition," Julia protested.

"It wasn't a proposal of marriage, either," Bonnie pointed out.

"It was an invitation."

"To get naked."

"But not until after the lobster."

They looked at each other and started to laugh.

"Shh!" Julia warned as another wave of laughter washed over her. "Don't wake the kids."

But they were goners. They laughed until their sides ached. She had to put Kate back to bed twice.

"Life is so unfair," Bonnie said as they tucked into a piece of pineapple cheesecake Mrs. Wasserstein had sent up that morning. "If he had asked me, I wouldn't be here right now. I'd be full of lobster and smiling across the pillow at Jack Wyatt."

"So would most women on the planet," she agreed. "Believe me, I was tempted."

She got up and made them each a cup of microwave tea.

"And here I thought something wonderful was going to happen to you tonight," Bonnie said as Julia placed a steaming mug before each of them. "Looks like the lucky shoes aren't so lucky anymore."

"Something wonderful did happen to me tonight," she said with as big a smile as she could muster. "It just didn't work out the way I hoped."

"It never does," Bonnie said mournfully.

"Sometimes it does," Julia whispered. *But not this time.*

JACK LEANED FORWARD and tapped the driver of the dial-up on the shoulder. "You can let me off here."

The driver, who had been staring at him in his rearview mirror all the way from Manhattan, shook his head. "You pay for door-to-door, you get door-to-door."

"It's eight o'clock on a Sunday morning," Jack pointed out, "and this car sounds like a 747 on takeoff. I think I'd better get out at the corner and walk the rest of the way."

The driver aimed a thumb in the general direction of the back seat. "With all that crap you've got with you? You'll never make it."

"I'll take my chances."

Five minutes later, he had his arms laden with freshly baked bagels, a bag of Starbucks coffee, two dozen red roses, copies of all the New York newspapers, and chocolate milk.

A glittery, sparkly shoe with a dangerously high heel dangled from his wrist.

Last night had been a tough one, and every anxious hour showed on his face and in his rumpled clothing. He still wore last night's tux, minus the jacket, no tie, shirt open at the collar.

And his heart right there on his sleeve.

He turned right onto the street where she lived. Red brick three family houses flanked both sides of the graceful tree-lined street. Morning sunlight dappled the emerging leaves. Huge lemon-yellow forsythia bushes tumbled over porches and marked property lines. The neighborhood was peaceful and quiet in that Sunday kind of way he remembered from his childhood. At the far end of the block a woman in a pink housecoat waited while her fluffy dog took care of business. The Burberry spaniel from yesterday seemed light-years away.

The goddess lived here. *Julia.* Right here on this block, maybe halfway between where he stood and the pink housecoat lady with the fluffy dog loitered. Funny how it had taken him over thirty years to understand that old song, the one where the smitten suitor's heart soared every time he walked down the street where his beloved lived. Jack felt exactly like that, as if his heart was a helium balloon ready to burst from his chest and float up into the beautifully blue April morning sky. Just knowing she was near made him happy.

But would seeing him make her happy?

Magic was a fleeting thing. He had no guarantee that the towering sense of destiny that had embraced them last night would still be able to wield its magic in the clear, sweet light of day.

In a perfect world he would have presented the Lifetime Achievement award, taken a final bow, then picked up exactly where he and the goddess—Julia—had left off. He wanted to know everything there was to know about her. For the first time in his life he wanted to share everything about himself. A line from *When Harry Met Sally* said it all: When you've met the person you want to spend the rest of your life with, you want the rest of your life to start right now.

The last thing Jack had expected was to find himself in the back of an ambulance racing north toward Columbia-Presbyterian Hospital while he watched the only true father he had ever known being hooked up to heart monitors. Jack had scribbled a note to Julia and asked an usher to deliver it to her in seat D-110, and prayed fate would be kind to them just a little while longer.

Time moved slowly in hospitals. It was as if the forces of nature conspired to turn inward on themselves and rob you of the normal landmarks you used to navigate your way through the day. Linda and Mike made the two-hour drive in from Southold in an hour and a half, in time to see Clive before the doctors brought him in for the catheterization procedure.

The news had been good. They had managed to unblock Clive's artery before a heart attack could leave lasting damage. But nobody, not even Clive, could deny that change was in the air.

Jack left the hospital around 5:00 a.m., dazed with relief. The cool clear morning felt like a blessing. He took it as a sign. A good sign. He flipped on his cell and waited for the voice mail icon to start flashing, but nothing happened. She hadn't called, and the day no longer felt like a blessing.

He'd started walking down Broadway, and by the time he crossed into the low 100s he knew what he had to do. He flagged down a cab and minutes later he burst into the lobby of The Hotel. The night help was still on duty, and after being passed up the food chain in search of answers, he found himself at the lost-and-found counter.

Talk about irony.

"You're my last chance," he said to the young and starry-eyed attendant. "I met a woman last night during the awards ceremony and I'm trying to find out if she left a message for me somewhere." It was ridiculous. Totally crazy. The act of a desperate man. Maybe she didn't want to call him. Maybe she'd never got *his* message.

"No notes back here," the young woman said. "I've got a pair of Chanel earrings, a Prada purse, a really bad toupee and one gorgeous Manolo Blahnik."

"One what?"

"Manolo Blahnik," she said, rolling her eyes. "Don't tell me you don't know Manolos. They're only the most gorgeous shoes in the universe."

"Julia," he said, and the clerk's eyes stopped rolling as he described the shoe.

"Yes!" She looked delighted. "You know her?"

He nodded. Coherent speech was beyond him at the moment.

"I was going to hang around until nine o'clock so I could call and tell her we found the shoe, but hey, since you're here why don't I just give it to you. Believe me, there's no way it'll still be here by noon if I don't." She gave him a blatantly flirtatious smile. "You have an honest face. I think I can trust you."

She gave him the shoes. She gave him the form Julia Monahan had filled out.

She gave him his future.

And that was how America's number one action hero

came to find himself standing in front of 752 Barclay Place in Bay Ridge, in the great borough of Brooklyn, trying to screw up the courage to climb the eight steps that stood between him and the rest of his life.

"THE DOORBELL AT THIS ungodly hour?" Bonnie barely stifled a yawn as she looked up from her mug of coffee. "What goes on around here?"

"It's our punishment for staying up all night talking. Even the kids got up earlier than usual." Julia didn't bother to stifle her own yawn.

Kate and Daniel had leaped from their beds before six o'clock, filled with energy and excitement. In a moment of insanity, Julia had promised they would all go out to Kali's Place for banana pancakes that morning after church, and they had been lobbying for the earliest mass possible.

The doorbell rang again and the two women looked at each other.

"It's probably the paper boy for Mrs. W. He always rings the wrong bell."

"I have a sugar hangover," Bonnie said. "If he rings it one more time I won't be held responsible."

The intercom wasn't working, so Julia padded barefoot along the second-floor hallway, then downstairs to the lobby. She didn't have her glasses on, so all she could see was a tall, package-laden figure on the front porch, and she laughed. Mrs. W. must have sent one of her long-suffering sons-in-law out to gather up some goodies from Klechner's Bakery two blocks over, and now the poor guy was punching any doorbell he could reach.

"I'm coming!" Her feet made slipping sounds on the shiny tile floor. "One more second and—"

She swung open the door, shrieked, then slammed it shut again.

Oh God, please say she was hallucinating, and Jack Wyatt wasn't standing out there on her front stoop, bearing gifts. Please say she wasn't wearing threadbare sweats, an Aerosmith T-shirt, and her real face and hair.

The bell rang again.

He's not going away, Monahan.

She didn't want him to go away.

Open the door and face the music.

If he couldn't handle real life, there was no point to any of it, was there?

She opened the door.

IT WAS THE LONGEST MINUTE of his life. Who would've thought sixty seconds could take a man from heaven to hell and back again?

When she opened the door once more he saw the goddess and he saw the real woman, and every dream he had ever had about his future found their focus in her hazel eyes.

He put down the bags and the flowers and the ice chest and held up the glittering shoe. "Look familiar?" he asked, heart pounding so loudly he was surprised he could hear himself speak.

"You found my shoe!"

"It wasn't easy, Cinderella. I had to do some detective work."

She seemed ill at ease, a little hostile. He didn't blame her. He launched into the condensed version of the night before, including the happy ending. "I gave an usher a message to deliver to you before we left for the hospital."

She shook her head. "Nobody gave me anything."

"There was no way I could get back into the ballroom

to tell you myself. Things were pretty bad there for a while and—"

"You did the right thing," she said. "He's family. That was where you belonged."

Did she mean that or was she saying the politic thing? Jack wasn't sure. They were still too new to each other.

"I like the T-shirt," he said. "You didn't look like an Aerosmith fan last night."

Her face turned a bright shade of red. "This is the real me," she said, holding out the sides of her shirt and pirouetting for him. "Everything you saw last night was fake, including the long hair."

"I like your real hair." Shoulder-length, wildly curly, sexy as hell.

"My fake hair was better."

"I like you without makeup."

Her smile was wide as his heart. "You're just saying that."

"I'm just saying that because—"

A small, dark-haired woman appeared in the doorway behind Julia. She had strawberry-blond kids on either side.

"We're off to church," the woman said, although the twinkle in her dark eyes was anything but ecclesiastical. "And then we're off to Kali's for those banana pancakes you promised them."

A little girl with the goddess's clear-eyed gaze looked up at him. "Who are you?"

He crouched down until they were at eye level. "I'm Jack." He held out his hand. "Who are you?"

"I'm Kate and that's my brother, Daniel."

Julia placed a hand on the little girl's shoulder. "Do you want to shake Jack's hand, Katie?"

He had to hand it to her. Kate was very self-possessed and she took a moment to consider whether or not she wanted to take his hand. When she finally did and his fingers gently wrapped around her own tiny ones, he felt like he had won an Emmy, an Oscar and a handful of Tonys.

Hell, he felt better than that. He felt like he had finally come home.

The little boy was shy. He held on to the dark-haired woman's hand and peered up at Jack through a thick tangle of dark eyelashes. He had his mother's eyes, too.

"Daniel can read, write his name and address, and spell twenty-four words." The goddess's obvious pride made Jack smile. "He's working on his numbers, but six has been giving him trouble."

An elfin grin, a little boy's version of Julia's quicksilver smile, broke through his shyness.

"Onetwothreefourfivesev—" The grin widened. "—sixseveneightninocten."

"All the way to ten!" Jack hesitated. Did four-year-old boys know about high fives? For that matter, did people high-five these days at all? He held up his hand, palm toward Daniel, and whooped again when the tiny palm smacked his.

"I'm Bonnie," the dark-haired woman said "I'm twenty-eight and I've seen all of your movies."

"The Bonnie of shoe fame?" He handed her the Manolo.

"So you really are an action hero," she said, standing on tiptoe to kiss his cheek. "You braved the wilds of Manhattan to reunite my shoes, and now all's right with the world."

He liked her. There was a bite to her humor and a subtext he understood. *Don't hurt her,* she was warning him, *or I'll hurt you right back.*

He would bet his bank balance Bonnie was god-mother to Julia's children. They would be seeing a lot of each other as the years passed. He was glad she was someone he could like and respect and looked forward to the day when she felt the same way about him.

"Starbucks," Bonnie said, taking inventory of the packages spread out on the ground. "And Klechner's! How did you know about Klechner's?"

"I didn't," he said. "Lucky guess."

"He just might be a keeper," Bonnie said as Julia's throat and cheeks turned beet-red. "Not that I'm rushing to judgment or anything…."

"Mass starts in ten minutes," Julia said, "and your godchildren aren't sprinters."

"Right." Bonnie looked from her friend to Jack. "I can take a hint."

"Can we stay here, Mommy?" Daniel tugged at the hem of his mother's faded Aerosmith shirt. "This is fun."

"Hey," Bonnie said, feigning hurt feelings. "I'm fun, too, and what about those banana pancakes we promised you guys after mass?"

Clearly *pancakes* was the magic word.

"Those must be some pancakes," Jack said as the trio departed down the quiet street.

Julia didn't answer. She looked pensive. He hadn't used the word pensive in a sentence since his brief pass at a college education, but it was the only word that fit. That was the problem with surprises. Sometimes everyone involved ended up surprised, and not always in a good way.

"Look," he said, "maybe I should've called first. I wasn't thinking. I just—"

"I'm glad you're here."

He faked a big sigh of relief and she laughed, but

the truth was he could still feel the tension in the air between them.

She bent down and gathered up the flowers, the bakery bag and the Starbucks loot, and motioned for him to follow her inside. The door to the first-floor apartment quickly shut as they headed for the staircase. He had a glimpse of an older woman, in full makeup at eight in the morning, with a phone pressed to her ear.

"That's Mrs. Wasserstein," Julia said as he followed her upstairs. "She owns the building." His goddess tossed him a look over her shoulder. "I figure half the neighborhood will be camped out in front of the stoop by the time church lets out."

"And I thought the paparazzi were tough."

"There's one big difference," she said. "They love me."

"Meaning they don't want to see you hurt."

They walked into a large sunny kitchen and put the bags and cups and flowers and ice chest down on the table. She turned to face him, and the expression in her fathomless eyes made him feel the way he had when she'd rammed him in the gut with the limo door.

"They're like family to me," she said. "They helped me take care of my husband when he was dying, and they took care of me when I wanted to die right along with him. Mrs. W. was the one who took me to the hospital when my labor pains started. Bonnie was my Lamaze partner. Sara from across the street showed me how to breast-feed. They've earned the right to an opinion." Her expression softened and the sucker-punched feeling in his gut eased up.

A little.

"And what if they think you can do better?"

"I'll respect their opinions, but in the end, it's up to me and to my children."

"I married my best friend when I was twenty-two." He would lay his cards on the table, too. "She's my manager's daughter. They were my family when mine stopped giving a damn."

Julia's gaze was level. "Are you divorced?"

"Her choice," he said. "Linda's a romantic and she realized she didn't want to settle for a friend when her soul mate might be right around the corner."

"That must have hurt."

"Not as much as I thought it would."

"That's a terrible thing to say," the goddess said, but she was smiling.

"Turns out Linda was right. She found her soul mate six months after we divorced, and I'm godfather to her and Mike's three kids."

"See?" Julia's voice was little more than a whisper. "Sometimes things work out the way they were meant to."

"Like us," he said. "I wasn't going to go to the ceremony, but Clive embarrassed me into it."

"If Bonnie hadn't needed a root canal I wouldn't have been there, either."

"The car didn't show up and I couldn't get a taxi—"

"We were stuck in traffic and I knew if I didn't get out and walk Bonnie would be in big trouble."

"And that's when you slammed me with the door."

"No," Julia said as they inched closer to each other. "As I remember, that's when you ran into the door."

"And fell for you."

"And fell."

"Semantics," he said. God, she smelled good…like fresh flowers on a cool day…. "What was I saying?"

She laughed that laugh of hers, the one with the little catch in it. "We were talking about destiny."

They were inches away from each other. He could feel the heat of her skin warming the air between them. "This never happened to me before," he said. "I didn't believe things like this were possible."

"Neither did I," she said as he took her hands in his. Her fingers were long and strong. Her hands were capable and beautiful. "But here you are just the same."

"I think this is the real thing."

"It could be a fling," she said. "You never know."

"This has forever written all over it."

She longed to throw caution to the wind. She wanted to fling herself in his arms and take a chance on forever, but she had the children to protect, and that changed everything.

"I almost said yes when you asked me to go to Montauk with you," she told him as he caressed her wrist with the pad of his thumb. She was one trembling erogenous zone. "You don't know how close I came to running off with you."

"You don't know how close I came to carrying you off."

A delicious shiver ran up her spine. "I hear you're some big-shot movie star. Is that line from some movie of yours?"

"That wasn't from a movie," he said as he placed her right palm against his chest. "That was from my heart."

"This is crazy," she said as they melted together.

"You won't get an argument from me."

"We'll take it slow," she said as her hands found his arms, his shoulders, the powerful muscles of his broad chest.

"Very slow."

He pressed his lips against the side of her neck and

she almost swooned like a schoolgirl. "You and the children have to get to—" Oh! What was that amazing thing he was doing behind her ear? "—know each other."

The stakes were high and they both knew it. They couldn't build a future together unless they built it together as a family. The four of them.

"A year," she said against his shoulder. "How does that sound?"

He groaned. "Like a hell of a long time."

"Instant fatherhood might not be exactly what you thought it would be."

"I have three godchildren," he reminded her. "All under eight years old."

"Okay," she said, laughing. "Maybe you do have an inkling."

"A year is a long time," he said, looking more serious than she had ever seen him. "You might find out being with a celebrity isn't a whole lot of fun." Paparazzi. Gossip columns. Locations shoots that strained relationships to the breaking point.

She grew quiet and his heart almost stopped beating in his chest.

"That's the part that scares me."

"We'll find a way," he promised her. "Other couples have managed. We'll get advice from the best."

She smiled up at him and once again he saw a church with a long white carpet and the most beautiful barefoot bride on the planet gliding toward him.

"One year." He cupped her face between his hands.

"One year." She looked at him and saw a baby with a dimple in his left cheek and bright blue eyes.

There were first kisses and then there were First Kisses. Their lips met, then parted, then met again, quick fleeting brushes of pleasure interrupted by long looks, as if neither one could quite believe what was happening between them. He breathed in her scent. She reveled in his warmth.

"We don't want to rush things." He brushed his lips against hers.

"You're right." Was she speaking English? She wasn't sure. Her brain had shut down the moment he touched her. "Easy does it."

"We'll go nice and slow." He caught her lower lip between his teeth and she gasped with pleasure. "Just the way you want it."

She led him toward the living room and the big, squashy yellow sofa that had seen better days. "Well, we don't have to go *that* slow...."

Laughing, they fell the rest of the way into love.

CHAPTER FIVE

One year later

"YOU LOOK GORGEOUS," Bonnie said as she stepped back to admire her own handiwork. "Right down to the lucky Manolos. You look even better than you did last year."

"I'm even more nervous than I was last year," Julia said. "I don't know what that means."

"I do," Bonnie said with a knowing wink. "Your boyfriend's back in town."

"That might have something to do with it." Julia slipped on her eyeglasses and took a quick look in the mirror at the new and improved Julia. "He's not going to recognize me."

"Oh, he'll recognize you. He's only been gone for a month, Jules."

"Tell that to the kids," she said with a laugh. "They e-mail him five times a day, race me to the phone when he calls, and have worn out two DVDs of *The Greenies*." And Jack was just as bad. He sent the kids silly postcards and animated e-mails. Even better, he saw them as individuals with their own merit, not just as her children, and he treated them with respect and love.

There. She'd said it. He loved her kids and they loved him right back. Somehow during the course of the last twelve months the four of them had become a family, and the implications were enough to send her to bed for a week.

Alone.

She had asked for a year, and that year ended today. Every wonderful thing she had wished for had come true, but to her dismay she found it wasn't enough. She wanted more.

She wanted everything. The whole package. She wanted the romance. She wanted the passion. She wanted the laughter and the friendship. She wanted her kids to have a father they loved and laughed with and respected. She wanted the man she loved to love her. She wanted him to be the kind of guy who would love and protect her children if something happened to her.

And she had found all of that and more with the most unlikely man. Not another computer geek like herself. Not a stay-at-home writer who lived in his head. Not with a local boy or an online romantic. Leave it to her to fall in love with a movie star.

Jack had spent the last month in California, helping Clive set up house in a small resort community in Palm Springs. His friend and manager had had a quadruple bypass three months ago and had decided to take a major step toward destressing his life. Jack was still soft-pedaling the issue of his workload, but that was one of the many reasons she loved him. He would rather slow down his own career than hurt the feelings of the man who had been a father to him for more years than he could count.

It didn't even bother her that he had remained good friends with his ex-wife, Linda. They had visited Linda and Mike in Southold a few times and had them to dinner in Brooklyn in return, and each time it just

got better and better. Their kids had become fast
friends, even if Kate had taught Linda's three children
a few rather pungent Brooklynisms that made the air
in Southold a little bit bluer. Kate and Daniel were
spending the weekend with Linda's brood. Julia could
only hope her daughter had exhausted her vocabulary
of expletives and would move on to something less
incendiary.

This last month had unsettled Julia. She missed
Jack's nearness more than she had thought she would.
The comfort of a daily routine, the rituals of family life,
meant a lot to her. Without them life lost some of its
sweetness. For eleven months he had given every indi-
cation that he felt the same way, but what if the last four
weeks had changed everything?

Things happened. People changed, even if change
was the last thing they were looking for. Maybe that was
why he had orchestrated this very public meeting for
their first day back together. Maybe that was why he
hadn't jumped into a cab at JFK and raced the twelve
minutes to her place in Bay Ridge and swept her into his
arms the way he had in thirty nights' worth of her dreams.

It was easier to let somebody down in a public situation. He could do the whole "it's not you, it's me"
thing and she wouldn't embarrass him by sobbing her
eyes out when the camera was on them.

"What's wrong?" Bonnie touched her forearm.

Julia blinked and forced a smile. "I think I might be
having an anxiety attack."

"About tonight? You look gaw-jus, Jules. Trust me on
this."

"That's not what I'm worried about. It's Jack."

"He'll be here. His plane landed at three."

She felt her spine straighten with surprise. "How would you know that?"

Bonnie's caramel-colored cheeks reddened slightly. "You told me, didn't you?"

"No," Julia said. "I didn't tell you." She fixed her best friend with a piercing look. "I didn't know that until just now."

"Lucky guess." Bonnie, who had never looked sheepish in her life, could have passed for a leg of lamb.

"What's going on?"

"Nothing."

"You're a lousy liar."

"I'm a great liar," Bonnie said indignantly. "I'm a Broadway actress now, my dear, and don't you forget it."

Bonnie was currently understudying for the role of Velma Kelly in the long-running musical *Chicago*.

"That's acting. This is lying."

"I resent that."

"I don't care. What's going on?"

"Nothing."

"Have you been speaking to Jack?"

The interrogation was interrupted by the sound of "Here Comes the Bride" being played on a car horn.

Bonnie looked down at her watch and grinned. "Right on time," she said.

Julia ran to the window as the big white bridal limo slid into the No Parking zone in front of her house. The bluebells and doves on the side panels gleamed in the late afternoon sun.

"What is Rachel doing here?" She turned to Bonnie. "Is she driving you in to work tonight?"

Bonnie's grin was downright wicked. "Why don't you go downstairs and find out."

Her heartbeat leaped forward until she could barely

catch her breath. The two flights of stairs felt like a
marathon run. She was vaguely aware of her neighbors
gathering outside, of the dappled sunlight through the
budding trees, of the sound of city birds chirping under the
eaves of the house, but it all fell away when she saw him.

Jack Wyatt was standing near the open passenger
door to the limo.

"You clean up real good," she said as she approached.

His smile was everything a smile should be. "So do
you."

She did a pirouette. "This old thing?"

He glanced down at her feet. "You're wearing
Bonnie's lucky shoes."

Julia's heart did a little tango inside her chest. "Why
break with tradition?"

The neighborhood had grown used to having a
movie star in their midst. They liked him and he liked
them, and the protectiveness they showed to Julia now
extended to Jack, as well. By now a big white limo
drew more attention than the sight of a major film star
carrying home a loaf of pumpernickel from Klechner's.

Somehow she managed to slide herself and her dress
into the limo. Jack climbed in behind her and closed the
door, and the car glided away from the curb.

They kissed briefly, a swift touch of the lips that
left her unsettled. Something was going on, but she
didn't know what.

"You have the privacy barrier up," she said, slowly
becoming aware of her surroundings. "Rachel must
love that."

"I made it worth her while." He looked a little uncer-
tain, a little nervous, and her stomach started to knot up
in response. "Notice anything else?"

Up until that moment she had noticed nothing

beyond him and her own sense of unease. Her focus widened and she drew in a breath. "Oh, Jack!"

The jump seats were covered with roses. Red American Beauties. Snowy white ones. Butter yellow. Creamy pink. More roses than you could find at the Brooklyn Botanic Garden.

There were chocolates on a burled wood table, her favorite pecan butter ring from Klechner's, and a bottle of champagne—the wonderful flower bottle she had always coveted—nestled in a bed of ice.

She had a lump in her throat so big she could barely find her voice. "You did this?"

"Bonnie hooked me up with her cousin, but I did the rest."

"Because—?"

"Do I have to spell it out?"

"Yes." She linked her fingers through his and nodded. "You have to spell it out."

"Because I love you," he said. "Because it's been a year today and I love you more than I did when you knocked me flat with that door over there. Because I miss you when we're not together and I find myself worrying about Kate's baby teeth and Daniel's swimming lessons at the Y. I don't want to leave you at night. I want to be there when you get up in the morning and when you go to bed. I want us to give the kids more brothers and sisters, and I want to be the one who holds your hand when every last one of them graduates from college and we start nagging them for grandchildren."

She didn't even try to stem the tears that flowed freely down her cheeks and ruined Bonnie's perfect makeup job. "You spell it out pretty good, mister."

He reached into the breast pocket of his jacket and

pulled out a little black velvet box that held a million beautiful dreams inside it. "Julia McGraw Monahan, I think we've waited long enough." He opened the box and she gasped.

"It's beautiful," she said, "but I hope you did your homework. I wrote an article once about diamonds and—"

He kissed her quiet. "Will you marry me?"

She looked deep into his eyes, as far as her soul could reach, and saw her future smiling back at her.

"You know what?" she said as she held out her left hand. "I think I already have."

FOR IMMEDIATE RELEASE

New York City (July 23): Superstar Jack Wyatt confirms that he and writer Julia (McGraw) Monahan were married yesterday at his home in Montauk, Long Island. The guest list was limited to immediate family and close friends of the bride and groom. The bride's two children gave their mother away in a simple outdoor ceremony near the lighthouse.

The newlyweds will honeymoon at an undisclosed location, after which they plan to live happily ever after.

Dear Reader,

As a new year rolls around with Valentine's Day, birthdays, Mother's Day and the other gift-receiving occasions, I keep hearing, "What do you want?"

My husband likes lists, preferably on a Post-it note attached to a catalog, but the gifts I truly enjoy are the ones he can't shop for. Dinner for two, no kids, no dog. A car wash. A break from laundry. (I wouldn't mind a decent vacation to the Biltmore Inn, but I digress...)

I'd love to go back to the days when gifts didn't have price tags. (Okay, that and a bag of Dove dark chocolate hearts.) It seems like we're always rushing. This year you'll get five books from me: this anthology, a three-book Desire series this summer and in October *Forbidden Merger*, part of the Elliotts twelve-book continuity—I was able to do those because dear hubby gave me the most precioius gift of all. Time.

So...maybe he was paying attention after all. Guess I'd better hold on to him. Remember to take time for each other and for yourself.

Emilie Rose

AN AFFAIR TO REMEMBER
Emilie Rose

CHAPTER ONE

IF HE HEARD ANOTHER platitude he'd puke.

From a quiet corner Conrad Carr raked his gaze over the crowded ballroom without making eye contact with anyone. Tara would have been in her element at the glittering, designer-clad Reel New York Film Festival awards ceremony, but he couldn't wait to leave.

"For crying out loud, are they all reading from the same lousy script?" a female voice behind him said.

He glanced over his shoulder and did a double take. For a moment there... No, Tara was gone. But at first glance the resemblance between the woman serving drinks and his wife was remarkable. Upon closer inspection the dark-haired, dark-eyed, sultry bartender didn't possess Tara's cool touch-me-not elegance, and her Southern drawl certainly didn't sound like Tara's well-trained, accent-free diction.

"Your wife would be proud of you for adding another award to your collection." The bartender mimicked the head of one of the largest movie studios perfectly, and then rolled her eyes in obvious disgust. "A roomful of actors and not an original line in the place." She pointed at his glass. "Want me to freshen that?"

He glanced down at his untouched drink. The ice

had melted into a clear layer on top. Not a convincing prop. "Sure."

Their fingers touched. Static electricity sparked between them. The tumbler slipped in her fingers and she caught it with a two-handed grab.

"Oops. Congrats, by the way. An amazing piece of acting, if you don't mind my saying so, Mr. Carr. You deserved the Best Actor award." She paused with the ice scoop in her hand and a distant look on her face. "I saw the moment your saintly character decided to turn bad. It wasn't any physical thing you did. It was all in your eyes." She refilled the glass and passed it back. "Man, I wish I could act like that. One day I will."

A wannabe actress working at the post-award-show party. Not a surprise. Half the staff in the ritzy hotel ballroom probably wanted into the business. "You're an actress."

"Not that you'd notice. Right now I'm officially a former high school drama teacher looking for acting work. Bartending to pay the bills." She grimaced and then the corners of her lush lips curled upward. "But that'll change."

She had the bubbling enthusiasm of someone who hadn't been crushed by a flood of reality and rejections. An enthusiasm he'd lost. "Good luck."

"Thanks." She filled a few more drink orders.

He accepted more congratulations from his peers and choked on a few more platitudes. The bartender was right. The speakers changed, but the same dialogue replayed like a stuck record. He flicked back his cuff to glance at his watch. How much longer did he have to endure this reminder of the life he'd lost? Less than an hour. And then what? Return to a dark, empty apartment? Ride around in the limo until he was exhausted enough to sleep for a few hours without the nightmares? Neither scenario appealed to him.

A clap on his back sloshed his drink over his fingers. One of the nominees from his category weaved by his side. "What will the world do without another Conrad Carr-Tara Dean movie? So sad she's gone, old chap. What will you do without her?"

Good question. Conrad wanted his life back.

He wanted his wife back.

The drunk staggered off, fresh drink in hand, without waiting for a reply.

"Insensitive jackass," the bartender muttered behind him. "I bet you're tired of hearing that."

He found her candor refreshing. "You wouldn't believe how tired."

She passed him a napkin. "Yes, I would. I'm an identical twin. Back home nobody says my name without saying Brenna's first. It's like we're each only half a person. She's the noticeable half."

Exactly. He was only half a person without Tara. And then the rest of what the woman had said snagged his attention. Despite his desire to avoid conversation, he asked, "Why is she more noticeable?"

"Cheerleader, homecoming queen, student body president, Miss Buncombe County, real estate agent of the year…" She listed the details without a trace of jealousy in her voice. "You get my drift?"

"Got it." If this was the unremarkable twin, then her sister must be stunning. The bartender had big eyes, plump ruby lips, smooth ivory skin and masses of dark curling hair tucked into a black hairnet. Very dramatic. The camera would love her.

"Brenna's not a bad person. She's just an overachiever." She wiped down the black marble bar. "So how long are you going to torture yourself?"

"Excuse me?" He jerked his gaze away from the exit.

"You're miserable. How long are you going to stay?"

"I thought you said I was a good actor."

One brow arched. "You're not at the moment."

He exhaled and checked his watch. "Another twenty-seven minutes."

The sympathy in her chocolate-brown eyes squeezed his chest. "What is the worst costume you've ever worn and why?"

"What?"

"I'm trying to distract you from your misery. Work with me, Mr. Carr."

The smile tickling his lips surprised him. How long had it been since he'd smiled and meant it? "Gladiator. Sand in my pants."

She flashed a mischievous grin. "Well, dang. There goes my fantasy. You were wearing pants under that leather skirt?"

A rusty laugh rumbled from his chest. "Sorry to disappoint you—" he checked her name tag "—Jenna."

"I'll survive. Worst scene and why?"

"The tunnel in *Security Breach*. Bugs the size of my hand."

"I thought those were fake."

"No. They were expensive imports. We weren't allowed to step on them. They were caught and counted after each take."

She shivered. "Ick. Ick. Ick. Worst line?"

"I'm not telling. Thank God it hit the cutting room floor."

Her laugh, low, intimate and husky, slid over his skin like velvet. "Worst meal?"

"Pig's intestines in *Mountain Passage*. The smell…" He shuddered.

"Chitlins. Not a fan myself, but folks eat them back home."

For months he'd felt like a walking corpse. The bartender's silly game resuscitated something inside him. "Which is where?"

"Asheville, North Carolina." She interspersed her answers with serving drinks to the guests who found her remote location.

"Long way from Manhattan," he said once they were alone again.

"The soap opera studios won't come to us."

How long had it been since anyone had spoken honestly to him instead of kissing up? Her openness was a bright spot in what had been a very dark year. "When did you move to New York?"

Her glow dimmed. "Nine months, eleven days ago."

"And you left home because…?"

She ducked her head and straightened a stack of cocktail napkins. "Why else? I'm tired of being called by my sister's name. I want people to call *her* by *my* name for a change. Becoming the next daytime drama queen should do that, don't you think? I'll be in millions of homes every day."

"It might. But it'll cost you." He thought of the cameras shoved in his face during the dark days after he'd lost Tara. Those cameras waited outside tonight. "When do you finish here?"

"About five minutes after you end your torture session."

He wasn't ready to let her go. "Have dinner with me."

She blinked owlishly. "Excuse me?"

"Have dinner with me. Someplace quiet."

Her eyes narrowed suspiciously. "Why?"

"So you can tell me about North Carolina or teaching or anything..." He indicated the room filled with artificial smiles and faux friendships. "Anything that's not this."

Her lips parted, closed, opened again. "Like a...date?"

His stomach clenched. "Not a date. I don't date."

Her face fell. "Right. Not a date. Just dinner."

"Yes." Her disappointment made his skin prickle uncomfortably, but he wouldn't make false promises. He'd loved once. Only once. And he never intended to open himself to that kind of pain again. Losing Tara had nearly destroyed him. It had very likely killed his career.

"I'll think about it."

He tried to mask his surprise. He couldn't recall the last time someone had refused his request. "You'll *think* about it?"

"Why me?"

"Because you made me laugh." And for a few minutes she'd made him forget the gaping void where his heart used to be.

"I'm not a comedian. I can't promise it'll happen again."

That smile twitched on his lips again. "I'll risk it."

She hesitated and then, a moment later, shrugged. "Okay. But nothing fancy. I'm dressed like a bellhop, for heaven's sake, and I didn't bring a change of clothes."

"Deal. Can you get us out of here?"

"You mean sneak you out the service entrance?"

"Yes."

Hurt filled her eyes. "You don't want to be seen with me."

Damn. He needed a good script. He kept saying the wrong thing. "I don't want to be followed by the press."

Her reluctance couldn't be more obvious. "Okay."

"Do you have a car?"

Her brows shot up? "In New York City?"

"Right. I'll have the limo meet us—"

"A limo? I thought you wanted anonymity."

"You have a better idea?"

"Yes. The subway. At two in the morning it'll be almost empty."

The lights blinked twice, signaling the end of the gala. He waited while Jenna pocketed her tip money and closed out her station.

Tonight he wanted to escape the demons chasing him. Soon he'd have to face his agent and admit the truth. Conrad's gift, his talent, had been buried with his wife eighteen months ago. He couldn't fulfill his contract. His career was over.

IT ISN'T A DATE, Jenna Graham reminded herself. *Just dinner. In the middle of the night. With one of Hollywood's highest paid actors.* Conrad Carr, her all-time favorite movie actor and the star of more than a few of her private fantasies, had asked *her* out. It seemed surreal.

The tiny, candlelit Italian restaurant on Manhattan's Upper East Side was romantic enough to make even her—a nascent cynic who'd recently sworn off love—

sigh. Who knew such places existed or that they served melt-in-your-mouth manicotti at two in the morning?

Tonight was a rare gift, and she intended to savor every second and file away every detail about him for future reference. Sable hair, cut short with just a hint of curl. Straight brows, dark slashes above serious hazel eyes flecked with gold and green. Luscious lips; full but not feminine. Strong, angular jaw. Broad shoulders. If she closed her eyes she could picture Conrad bare-chested in his gladiator costume, her personal favorite. Yum.

"What made you want to teach?"

Reality nudged fantasy aside. She lifted her eyelids and focused on the man who was becoming more real and more likable with each passing moment. "I love watching the kids catch the acting bug. It's like a light igniting inside them, you know? On stage they can be anyone. Tongue-tied boys can be witty and eloquent. Awkward, unpopular girls can become bold divas who rule the set. It's like showing them how to overcome their worst faults."

"It's make-believe."

"Believing in yourself has to start somewhere. Why not from the safety of someone else's skin?" Her own drive to act had derived from her need to step out of her sister's shadow.

"You love it and yet you left it behind."

She dragged her gaze away from the wedding ring on his long-fingered hands. His wife was dead, but he still wore the ring. "It was time to practice what I preached."

After nine months of rejections she was beginning to think the old adage, "Those who can, do; those who can't, teach," might apply to her. Good thing she enjoyed bartending.

"Are you taking acting lessons?"

"Not anymore. My roommate bailed. I had to cut expenses. But enough about my boring life. What's your favorite location?"

"Montana," he answered without hesitation.

She shuffled through her mental catalog of his movies—she'd seen them all—and couldn't place one in that state. "I expected you to say Fiji or Morocco."

"Montana's home. I don't get to visit often."

"I can imagine. What led you to acting?"

He shrugged. "Pretty much what you've just described. I didn't want to be me. The town drunk's stupid kid."

"Stupid? You?" The man was brilliant. Every magazine she'd read—and she devoured dozens of them—said so. But none of what he'd said meshed with the articles she'd read about him.

"Learning disabilities. I learned to fake it early."

"I—I don't remember reading that."

He swiped a hand over his face and pushed his plate aside. "I've never told anyone the truth. In fact, I shouldn't have—"

She covered his fist with her palm, and that same spark zapped her as the last time she'd touched him. "I won't tell."

The heat of his skin seeped into her. He turned his hand over and captured hers. Her pulse faltered. Jenna gulped at the impact of his intense gaze and firm, warm grasp.

"Thanks, Jenna." Current traveled from her fingers to her arm and shoulder. It sank through her torso to puddle low in her abdomen like a summer heat wave shimmering on asphalt.

"Come home with me, Jenna."

Her breath hitched. "W-what?"

His jaw muscles bunched, then relaxed. "Please. It's been a hellish night. I don't want to be alone."

A hellish night? Yes, it probably had been. Conrad Carr and Tara Dean had been Hollywood's hottest couple. Their romance both on and off screen had been legendary. Conrad had won the Best Actor award tonight for the last movie he'd made with his late wife, and she'd posthumously won Best Actress. Seeing her image flashed repeatedly on the big screen for each of the film's five nominations must have been difficult for him.

Jenna studied his face and didn't get any slimy I-want-to-jump-your bones vibes back. Conrad was alone and lonely. He needed a friend. And Jenna was a sucker for lonely outsiders. How could she refuse his invitation?

CHAPTER TWO

"SO…I GUESS BLACK is your favorite color?" Jenna hesitated on the step leading into Conrad's sunken living room.

He reexamined the space, curious to see what she saw. From the thick, black carpeting to the leather sofa and smoked-glass tables, there wasn't a speck of color anywhere to relieve the unrelenting *blackness* of his hideaway other than Jenna's red coat. Even the walls were pewter-gray.

She hugged her arms and shifted on her feet, no doubt wondering—as did he—why he'd brought her here. Surely he could handle the remaining hours before dawn alone without breaking into a cold sweat? Unlikely, if the past was an indicator.

Her curious gaze met his. "I thought you lived in Bel Air."

"I bought the apartment last year." He flicked on the overhead track lighting and then a pair of lamps. The light didn't do much to brighten the room. "May I take your coat?"

She handed it over. "Where are your other awards?"

The fabric carried the warmth of her body, and her scent—more woman than perfume—enveloped him as he laid the garment over the back of the closest chair.

"They're in California." He'd fled the house he and Tara had shared, leaving behind all of their personal effects, the art, the souvenirs, *the life* they'd collected together during twelve years of marriage. He couldn't bear the thought of returning without her, but he was expected to do so in four short weeks.

Jenna crossed the room and pushed back the vertical blinds covering a wall of windows. "I'll bet the daytime view of Central Park is beautiful from this high up."

He shoved a hand through his hair. Was it? He hadn't noticed. "Probably. Would you like a drink?"

"Sure. I'll have whatever you're having." She released the blinds and smoothed her hair self-consciously.

She'd removed the hairnet—a uniform requirement, she'd said—before leaving The Hotel, the trendy new establishment where the gala had taken place, revealing the kind of loose, waist-length coffee-colored curls a man loved to get tangled in. That he'd noticed her hair and her generous curves surprised him. Was he attracted to Jenna? Impossible. His libido had died along with his talent. Hadn't it?

Surprised by the hum in his blood stream, he retreated to the kitchen. For six months after Tara's death he'd numbed his pain with alcohol. He hadn't taken a drink since he'd woken up facedown on the bathroom floor and realized he was repeating his father's mistakes. Sure, he carried a glass at parties. The prop was part of pretending he was enjoying himself. But he never drank more than a sip to perpetuate the pretense. Not only did he have to worry about becoming a drunk like his father, booze loosened the iron control Conrad had clamped on his emotions. God help him if that control ever snapped.

He didn't want to fall into that black hole of despair again. He might not be lucky enough to crawl back out a second time.

He found a bottle of champagne on ice and a tray of hors d'oeuvres in the fridge. Evidently, his housekeeper expected him to celebrate tonight. And he probably should. If he couldn't pull his act together, at least he'd end his career on a high. As Tara had.

The thought released a flood of acid in his stomach. He refused to act again if he couldn't deliver another award-winning performance. He didn't think he had one in him.

Conrad Carr washed up at thirty-five.

He extracted two flutes from the cabinet, snagged the champagne bucket and the food and returned to his guest. He found Jenna kneeling beside the mountain of scripts he'd been ignoring, much to his agent's disgust.

Blushing guiltily, she dropped the script in her hands and rose abruptly. "You have an impressive collection of scripts. Have you read them all?"

"I've skimmed a few." They all reminded him that he'd have to start over with another costar. Without his irreplaceable Tara. He unloaded his haul on the coffee table. "Sit. Please."

She settled on the sofa. He sat beside her, opened the champagne and searched for words to fill the silence. No luck. He focused on the cork instead of the smooth flesh above a strip of white lace revealed by the slight gaping of her blouse.

"I've never had Moët & Chandon. Are you sure you want to waste a seven-hundred-dollar bottle of champagne on me?"

She knew her wines, but that was probably part of her job.

"I don't consider it a waste." It wasn't a line or a come-on. And he wasn't flirting. Was he? Certainly not. But he had to admit the optimistic bartender fascinated him. She smiled up at him through her thick lashes, and his chest muscles constricted.

"Thanks. So...what do you want to talk about? Surely you heard enough downhome tales over dinner to bore you silly."

He could listen to her exaggerated hillbilly stories all night. She reminded him of the girls he'd known before leaving Montana for the artificial world of L.A. Natural. Unassuming. Admirable. Honest. He poured the champagne and passed her a glass. "Tell me about your auditions."

She grimaced. "What's to tell? I was passed over for a feminine hygiene commercial. A good thing, because I really don't want to be known as the tampon lady for the rest of my life. I've gone for several daytime drama auditions—mostly walk-on roles— but no bites yet. I've been an extra in a couple of crowd scenes with B-list stars. My agent says I'm too Italian looking. *Puhlease,* I don't have a drop of Italian blood in me."

"Maybe you have the wrong agent. Did you ever hear that a bad agent is worse than no agent?"

She nodded. "Yes, but without recent acting experience on my résumé he was all I could get. I haven't been on stage since college."

The movement of her lips mesmerized him. Her mouth was full and sexy. The turned-up corners hinted that she could show a man a good time—laughing or loving. Heat pooled in his groin and his heart thumped heavily against his ribs. He lifted his gaze and stared into her deep, dark eyes.

My God, he *was* attracted to her—to her enthusiasm, to her infectious smiles and her self-deprecating humor. He shrank back from the shocking physical awareness. It wasn't personal or emotional, he assured himself. The desire to procreate was a basic survival instinct, like hunger for food or thirst for water. All were natural signs that he hadn't died with his wife.

Jenna sipped her champagne and then lowered her glass. "Is something wrong?"

"No." Her nearness brought a flood of moisture to his mouth. He washed it down with a gulp of champagne and then set the glass on the table. Too risky. "What do you have lined up next?"

"I have bartending gigs lined up four nights a week through The Hotel. No cattle calls or no auditions, though. But I could get the call any day now." She sounded as if she believed it.

"You're too beautiful to stay unemployed for long."

She gasped and then wet her lips. "I...thank you, Conrad."

He wasn't looking for a relationship. His heart would always belong to Tara, but he couldn't ignore the magnetic pull any longer. He leaned forward and touched his mouth to Jenna's. A charge shot through him on contact with her soft flesh. Her lips parted. He tasted champagne on her tongue, and his body jump-started to life.

But he wasn't ready to feel again—not pleasure or pain.

He lifted his hand to push her away, but his fingers glided over her silky skin to tangle in her hair and cup her nape.

And he couldn't find the strength to let her go.

CONRAD LIFTED HIS HEAD and Jenna was afraid to breathe, afraid if she did she'd awaken from this wonderful dream where the sexiest man on the planet found her amusing and attractive. Slowly, reluctantly, she lifted her heavy eyelids.

Desire and curiosity, but not regret, burned in Conrad's eyes. He took her champagne and set it aside. Her nails bit into her palms and her heart raced. Her breath shuddered in, then out. He cradled her face in his hands, traced her cheekbones with his thumbs and then he kissed her again. *The man knew how to kiss.*

She lost herself in the hungry possession of his mouth, the tangle of tongues and the steam of his breath on her cheek. She reveled in his taste and his strength when he banded his arms around her and pulled her closer to the body she'd secretly lusted over for years. She hadn't come here for this, hadn't dared to dream that one day she might meet Conrad Carr or that he might be as attracted to her as she was to him.

His hands stroked her back, her waist, and then he scraped his thumbs beneath her breasts. She quivered and forced air into her forgotten lungs. He cupped her, and her nipples tightened and pushed into his palms. She wasn't a virgin, but she trembled like one. His hair was soft beneath her questing fingers, his jaw raspy and warm. He captured her hand and turned his face into her palm to trace an erotic design with his tongue. *Wow.*

He eased back until his gaze met hers. "I want you, Jenna."

Her stomach knotted. With nerves. With need. She'd never slept with a man she didn't believe herself in love with, but none of her past relationships had caused this inundation of sensation or this consuming need. If she let this chance pass by without exploring the powerful effect he had on her, she'd regret it forever. "I want you, too, Conrad."

His nostrils flared and satisfaction flashed in his eyes. He lifted his hands to the buttons of her blouse. She had a flurry of second thoughts. Should she stop him? No. He needed someone tonight, and she'd never felt more desirable in her life—a balm she desperately needed after her last humiliating encounter with a lover.

She shoved his tuxedo jacket off his shoulders, released the knot of his black bow tie, and then reached for the onyx studs fastening his shirt. She dropped them on the table. The clatter of gold on glass echoed throughout the room. The fabric of his shirt parted to reveal a broad, hair-spattered chest. Living, breathing reality far exceeded the larger-than-life image on a movie screen. She let her fingers explore his hot, supple skin, and took pride in the sharp whistle of breath he sucked between his teeth. A tingle traveled from her palms to her belly.

He whisked her blouse away. She mirrored the action, but Conrad didn't give her time to admire his chiseled physique before he traced the lace edges of her bra with unsteady fingers. She relished the evidence of his need. And then he flicked the front clasp open, shoved aside the cups and scalded her with his palms. He teased her nipples with the pads of his thumbs until she whimpered, and then he dipped his head to sip from her breast. The heat of his mouth, the swirl of his tongue and the gentle nip of his teeth sent her hunger spiraling out of control. She clutched his hair, scraped his back with her nails and bit her lip to keep quiet.

The searing press of Conrad's chest on hers contrasted with the cold leather sofa against her back. He stretched out beside her with one hard thigh nudging the part of her aching for his attention. She pressed against him, wanting, needing more. His hands grazed her belly, swept under the waistband of her slacks, and then the button and zipper gave way. He delved his fingers beneath her panties and found her wetness. He stroked her with a master's touch, drawing her higher and tighter with each pass.

She savored the taste of his skin, the roughness of his cheek against hers, the passion of his mouth on her nipples, her ribs and her belly. He removed her shoes and then her pants and panties with sharp, jerky movements. Cool air swept her legs.

She fumbled with the fastening of his slacks, released him from his snug briefs and shoved the fabric out of the way. He kicked his clothing aside, and then the hard, hot length of his legs tangled with hers, and his arousal branded her thigh. She arched against him, but he pulled away with a hiss of breath. His tongue delved into her navel, and then his breath steamed the knot of need between her legs. He feasted on her with the ravenous appetite of a starving man, mercilessly pushing her higher and faster than she'd ever climbed before.

She shook with the effort to slow things down, to delight in each moment of this fantasy come to life, but he hurried her along. Her knees bent. Her back bowed. Pleas for relief slipped past her lips. And then ecstasy shattered her. Conrad gave her scant seconds to catch her breath before driving her up and over the edge again, and then his lips grazed a molten trail upward.

A trace of reason invaded her brain. "Wait. Condoms."

Conrad froze above her. He swore. And then he stood—all bunched muscles, fisted hands and naked, aroused male. Without warning he scooped her into his arms and carried her down a darkened hall. He hit a wall switch with his elbow. Lamps clicked on. His bedroom. Also black. He set her down beside a wide bed and jerked open a bedside table.

"Thank God," he muttered, withdrawing a box. He shredded the condom box while trying to open it.

"You'd better let me do that." Jenna selected a packet from the pile and applied the protection over his thick erection. His teeth clamped shut with a click. The tendons of his neck stood out. Next time she'd linger and explore the length and breadth of him, but now she wanted him too much to dally, and he looked near the breaking point. *For her.* The knowledge sent a fresh wave of heat surging through her.

His muscles turned rigid at her touch. She licked his knotted jaw and then one tiny beaded nipple. He groaned, ripped back the black silk duvet and tumbled her onto the cool sheets. A hot, hungry man and an impossible fantasy united to fill Jenna with a yearning so intense she thought she might die from it.

He devoured her mouth with a carnal kiss, hooked her knees with his arms and slid into her so slowly, so deeply her breath whooshed out in a moan. She lifted her hips to meet his thrusts, and gasped for air as he pounded into her like a man driven beyond his limits.

The scent of their loving embraced her. His breath scorched her neck. The taste of him lingered on her lips and tongue. The muscles of his back, buttocks and thighs bunched and shifted beneath her fingertips. She relished each gasp and groan she elicited from him, and the payback as he evoked the same from her with his ravenous mouth, talented hands and powerful thrusts. Desire wound tighter and tighter inside her until she thought she'd scream. And then she disintegrated into a cloud of sensation so intense and gratifying every cell in her body hummed with satisfaction.

Conrad surged on with his eyes closed and his face a mask of passion. She traced the lines furrowing his brow, swept the width of his shoulders and raked the length of his spine, reveling in the knowledge that Conrad Carr, movie star, wanted her, Jenna Graham, a nobody.

His body clenched. His head fell back. He shuddered. "Tara," he groaned as he climaxed.

Jenna's cloud of contentment evaporated. She crashed to the ground in a painful heap.

Déjà vu.

CHAPTER THREE

JENNA'S FISTS BEATING on his chest knocked Conrad out of paradise. He pushed himself up on straightened arms. "What's wrong?"

"My name is Jenna." Her face was pale, her eyes anguished.

"I know that."

"You called me *Tara*."

Damn. "I'm sorry."

"Let me up."

He didn't move. He had to explain. "Jenna, I—"

She shoved him and twisted and squirmed frantically beneath him, disengaging their bodies. The corners of her eyes looked suspiciously damp. "Let me up, damn you."

Carr, you are an ass. He rolled off her. "I knew who you were."

"That's what he said, too." She snatched the sheet up to her chin, swung her legs over the side of the bed and hugged herself.

Studying her hunched spine, Conrad cursed himself for hurting her. He reached out to smooth her tangled hair, but lowered his hand before making contact. She wouldn't welcome his touch now. "Who?"

"My fiancé." Her voice carried a shipload of pain.

"He called you by another woman's name?"

"My sister's." She ripped the sheet off the bed and swaddled herself in it, leaving him exposed in more ways than one. "Turns out he'd wanted her all along, but since he couldn't have her he decided to settle for me—the faded carbon copy."

Double damn. Her words at the gala now made perfect sense. What kind of fool would think she was a faded copy? Jenna was warm and sexy and vibrant, so different from Tara's serene—

No, he would not think about Tara or the fact that he'd just had sex with a woman other than her. Not now. When he was alone he'd open that can of worms and dig around.

"I'm sorry," he repeated.

"Me, too." Jenna headed for the hall, dragging the sheet with her.

Conrad sprang from the bed. He ducked into the bathroom to discard the condom and snatch his robe from the back of the door. He arrived in the living room in time to see her drop the sheet and reach for her panties, her back toward him. Even in the midst of catastrophe he couldn't prevent the kick in his pulse at the sight of her long legs, naked bottom and the indention of her waist. Curvy. Womanly. Tara had been reed thin.

Don't go there.

"Jenna, don't leave. Not like this."

He heard a sniff and she swiped at her cheeks. His insides clenched in agony. He'd hurt and betrayed her. Unintentionally, yes, but pain was pain. He ought to know. He'd wallowed in it for months.

He laid a hand on her shoulder. "Please."

She jerked out of reach and, backing away from him,

snatched up her blouse and stabbed her arms into the sleeves without her bra. Every jiggle of her round breasts hit him with a fresh punch of desire, proving the first time hadn't been a fluke. She misaligned the buttons in her haste to cover up.

"I want to be an actress, not a stand-in for another woman."

It's just sex, Carr. You are not getting emotionally attached. But her silent tears eviscerated him. He tunneled his hands through his hair and fought to check the reaction. "You're the first woman I've been with besides my wife in fourteen years. I screwed up."

She paused, holding her pants in front of her like a shield. Her throat worked as she swallowed, and then she lifted pain-darkened eyes to his.

"So did I." For the first time all night he heard defeat in her voice.

Fix this. But he didn't know how. He'd just devalued a woman in the worst way possible. How could he right that wrong? "Don't go. I need your help."

She fastened her pants. "Yeah, right. What you need is a grief counselor. And a decorator. You didn't crawl into the coffin with her, Conrad, but this place looks like it."

He flinched. Direct hit. The apartment was a black hole in which he'd sealed himself off from light and life. He never opened the blinds, and he rarely ventured outside. His only visitors were his biweekly housekeeper, a monthly personal trainer and when unavoidable, Sid, his agent, who'd left the condoms six months ago along with the edict to "snap out of it."

Jenna looked left and right, searching for her remaining articles of clothing. Conrad retrieved her bra from the floor behind the sofa and passed it to her. She took it without touching him, shoved it in her pant's pocket and bent to pick up her shoes.

"I need you, Jenna. You revived my libido. Maybe you can do the same for my career."

She stopped with one shoe on and the other in her hand, and eyed him incredulously. "Your career? You've won fifteen acting awards in ten years. You don't need me."

He fisted his hands and ground his teeth, bracing himself to bare his soul. "I've lost the gift."

She snorted. "Sure you have. Last night's award proved that, didn't it?"

He massaged the muscles knotting in his neck. "I haven't been able to work since…in eighteen months."

Her skeptical expression eased. Slightly. "Why?"

"I don't know. I…just…can't." Each word bit like the slice of a razor. Until now he hadn't voiced his fears to anyone.

Her dark brows puckered. "But the scripts…"

"I can't read more than a few pages and then I—" He raked a hand over his face. She'd think he was crazy, and hell, he probably was, but what did he have to lose? "And then I want to crawl out of my skin."

The rigidity of her shoulders softened and sympathy replaced the wariness in her dark eyes. "You have stage fright."

"Impossible."

"You're out of practice and you're so focused on what could go wrong that you won't let yourself succeed."

"Does that line work on your students?"

"Most of the time. Because it's true." Her lips quivered in a sad smile. "The first play of every school year is the same. Everyone's a basket case—including me. But you've failed already if you don't try, Conrad. Remember your successes, and you'll be fine." She shrugged on her coat and headed for the door.

Desperation swelled in his chest. He didn't know why he couldn't let her go, only that it was imperative that he convince her not to give up on him. "I'll pay you."

She called over her shoulder, "I don't want your money."

"Then I'll introduce you to my agent and help you make the connections you need to land an acting job." An offer he'd never made before. And shouldn't have made now. What was he thinking? He didn't even know if she could act.

She paused with her hand on the doorknob, and he knew he had to talk fast.

"Please, Jonna. I have four weeks to get it together, and then I either have to report to the studio to start the project I left hanging eighteen months ago, or retire. Right now, there's no chance that I can pull off that movie."

She turned slowly. "I don't get it. How can I help? I'm just an out-of-work actress."

"You're a drama teacher. Teach me how to act again."

"A *high school* drama teacher, not a professional acting coach. I'm a nobody, Conrad. Not even a blip on the radar."

"Which is why this could work. I can't use somebody in the business who might talk to the tabloids. You're my last chance." He hated the desperate edge to his voice.

Her expression slowly changed from disbelief into resignation. She huffed out a breath. "Sure. Why not? I can't make a bigger fool of myself than I already have, can I? But this goes both ways. If I help you rediscover your talent, then you have to help me refine mine. I'm not looking for a handout and I don't want your money, but I obviously need help. I'm learning fast that in this business it's not what you know but who you know."

Conrad nodded and joined her in the foyer. "Deal."

She ignored his outstretched hand and opened the door. "I'm going home. I need sleep."

"It's 4:00 a.m. Let me call the limo."

"No, thanks. I'll take the subway."

He hadn't felt responsible for another person in ages and didn't want to now, but he couldn't shake the feeling. The sentiment rattled out of hiding with rusty, clanging awkwardness. He reached over her head and shut the door again.

"The subway's not safe for a woman alone at this time of the morning. Let me have the doorman call a taxi for you."

Her gaze met his and he was struck again by her warm, vibrant beauty. His pulse rate doubled and the urge to kiss her and drag her back to his bed hit him low and hard. Her breath hitched and her eyes widened. He suspected he wasn't the only one remembering how good it had been between them.

She stepped out of reach. "Okay, but I'm waiting downstairs."

Victory surged through him. He'd won the argument and her assistance, and she'd made him feel like a man again. Sex was an itch he hadn't missed, but one he now looked forward to scratching frequently with Jenna. "Can we start this afternoon?"

Her mouth set in a firm line and her chin lifted. "Sure.

Fine. But I don't believe in sleeping my way to the top. You'll have to promise that from here on our relationship will be strictly businesslike. No more sex."

Conrad exhaled. He'd found one part of his life that hadn't gone to hell, and she wanted him to ignore it. But what choice did he have? "Agreed."

SHE WAS AN ACTRESS, dang it. How hard could it be to pretend that for a few precious hours Conrad Carr hadn't made her feel like a leading lady? His leading lady.

She'd spent her entire life in another woman's shadow, and here she was volunteering for more of the same. But Conrad was a master actor. With his help she could improve her craft, maybe even become a star, and finally, *finally* outshine her outgoing twin. Risky gamble or just another dumb decision? She'd made her share of each.

Jenna knocked on Conrad's apartment door Sunday afternoon. He opened it, and the powerful attraction she'd felt for him last night hit her like a city bus. Her mouth went dry and her skin tingled in anticipation of his touch.

Wise up. In his mind, he wasn't touching you.

His black V-neck sweater revealed a tuft of dark curls. Gray slacks molded his lean hips and thighs. The old adage "When you're nervous picture your audience naked" assumed an entirely different meaning when she'd not only seen him naked but had touched, tasted and thoroughly reveled in his nakedness.

Don't just stand here gawking. Take charge. Just as you would in a classroom. There was no chance of getting past the embarrassment and hurt from last night, so she brazenly ignored both and forged ahead. "Hi. Let's get started."

Hazel eyes, more olive-green than sparkly gold today, examined her face. "Did you get any sleep?"

Don't be nice, she whined silently. *I want to stay angry.* "Yes. Thank you. And now I'm ready to work. You'd better be."

She barged past him, crossed to the windows and yanked open the black blinds. Light flooded the room. She caught his wince. "I don't know where to start, but I do know you don't need the basics. Your talent is there."

"I'm glad one of us thinks so." He shut the door, shoved his hands in his pockets and joined her beside the coffee table.

"Look, I've seen every film you've ever made too many times to count. In fact, I used *Unconscionable Sin* as a teaching tool in my classroom." It was the only movie he'd made without a romantic subplot, and therefore, it didn't have steamy love scenes that the school would ban. "You know how to act. We just have to find a way to oil your hinges."

She gestured to the pile of scripts. "Where do you want to begin?"

"I don't care. About last night—"

"Forget last night." She lifted the top script and shoved it at him. "Read. If we're going to read these together then I'm going to need a copy of each script."

He ignored the pages rattling like fall leaves in her hand. "I can't forget."

His raspy whisper made her pulse race and her hands shake harder. "You have to, because it's not going to happen again."

"Jenna, other than the first glimpse I caught of you at the gala, I never once mistook you for Tara. Your coloring is all you have in common, and even then—"

"I refuse to have this discussion." She dropped the script on the coffee table, paced back to the window and tried to appreciate the million-dollar view of Central Park. If he insisted on rehashing what had happened she'd slap her hands over her ears like a petulant child and hum.

"Tough," he rumbled into her ear.

She started. How had he crossed the room so silently? The fine hairs on her body rose with the awareness that only an inch separated them. If she leaned back she'd press into his chest, into the strong arms that had held her. Temptation pulled at her, but she fought it. *Get over yourself. You're here for the benefit of your career. And his.*

He braced his arms on the window on either side of her, caging her in before she could move away. "I needed you last night. Your candor and your humor. You kept me from wallowing in my own bad company. I've done too much of that lately."

"Right. Well, you're welcome." She ducked beneath his arm and put the width of the room between them.

"Dammit, Jenna, would you let me—"

She held up her hand like a traffic cop, stopping the flow of words. "I don't want to hear excuses or polite lies."

And she didn't want to get her hopes up. No matter how fantastic making love with him had been it was a mistake, and Jenna tried not to repeat her mistakes. The ring on his finger was a sign she shouldn't have ignored. He still loved his dead wife. "In fact, if you mention last night again I'll walk out that door and never come back. Now, shall we begin or do I leave?"

His jaw shifted as if he were chewing on the words she wouldn't let him say. "Just like that? No warm-up?"

She gave him her best *you've-got-to-be-kidding-me* look. "I hardly think you need to practice being a tree. You've had years to master the basics."

He shoved a hand through his hair. "Have you had dinner?"

"No. Quit stalling."

"It takes time to get into character." His frustration couldn't be clearer. Neither could his avoidance of the task. She'd become familiar with both through her students.

She propped her hip on the back of his leather sofa. "How do you usually get into character?"

"I read the script. I research the character's background. If possible, I walk in his shoes."

Suddenly she knew exactly what Conrad needed. She popped off the sofa, snatched up the script and scanned a few lines to refresh what she'd read last night while he'd been out of the room. "Lucky for you this guy lives in Brooklyn. Get your coat."

Stillness overcame him. "What?"

"We have a few hours of daylight left. We're going to Brooklyn. I'm familiar with the area the screenwriter describes. In fact, I live there."

He had refusal stamped all over him. His expressive face was one of the things she loved about him. *About his acting,* she amended.

"That's not a good idea."

If Conrad had sealed himself off from the world, then finding his talent might be as simple as making himself a part of that world again. And going to

Brooklyn would get her out of the intimacy of his apartment. Perfect. "How long has it been since you walked down the street like a regular guy?"

"Last night when you dragged me three blocks to catch the subway."

"That doesn't count. How long has it been since you took a Sunday stroll, people watched or bought a hot dog from a street vendor?"

"Are you kidding?" he asked, aghast.

"No, I'm not. It's time to come back into the land of the living, Conrad. Get your coat."

"You'll regret this."

"Regret taking a walk on a beautiful, sunny day? Impossible."

"Jenna, there's a reason I ride in limos."

"Yes, to seal yourself off from life. I don't want to hear your excuses."

His jaw took on a granite edge. "You want life. Fine. You'll get it. But don't say I didn't warn you."

CHAPTER FOUR

"WHY DIDN'T YOU WARN ME?" Jenna panted by Conrad's side in the dimly lit, back-alley restaurant.

A few dark curls had escaped her long braid to tumble around her flushed face and cling to the damp sheen on her forehead. She looked very much like she'd looked in his bed last night—before he'd opened his big mouth. His pulse thudded rapidly and it had nothing to do with his recent sprint. She pressed one hand to the cherry-red top stretched over her breasts. The other clutched his like a lifeline. Oddly, he didn't want to let go.

"I tried to." The urge to protect Jenna from the fans had ambushed him. He didn't know how to define the relationship between them, but he didn't want it destroyed by the media before he had a chance to figure it out. So he'd grabbed her hand and run. "When I go out I get recognized by one fan and then ten and then—"

"May I help you?" a soft-spoken hostess asked.

Jenna flinched and blurted, "No."

"Yes," Conrad said simultaneously. "We need a taxi. There's twenty bucks in it for you if you can flag one without letting the crowd out there know we're in here."

She looked out the window and then back at him. "Yes, sir. Oh, you're…you're *him.*"

"Yeah." He didn't have to watch TV to know his face had been plastered all over the screen before, during and after the award ceremony. The press liked to replay the tragic story of Tara's death ad nauseam. Each report drove a dagger of guilt through Conrad's heart. He'd convinced Tara to do the film. If he hadn't…

Jenna tugged his hand, drawing him out of the past. "We can't go back out there."

"Unless they'll allow us to sneak out the back door, we'll have no choice." The mouth-watering aroma of Chinese food penetrated his senses and his stomach growled. How long had it been since he'd had an appetite for anything? *Besides Jenna.*

He removed his sunglasses and stuffed them in his pocket, tugged off his baseball cap and then turned back to the hostess. "Do you have a table where we can eat without being disturbed?"

The hostess bowed. "Yes, Mr. Carr. We would be most honored to serve you."

He flashed his best smile. His rusty muscles protested the movement. "Thank you."

She turned away to pick up menus. Jenna elbowed him in the ribs. "Stop it."

"This way, please."

"Stop what?" he whispered as he followed the woman into the bowels of the building.

"Melting women with that smile."

Her waspish comment made his lips twitch. He shouldn't be so pleased that she liked his smile. And then it hit him. He'd smiled more in the past twenty-four hours with Jenna than he had since Tara became ill.

Their journey ended in a private dining room with a long table. "Will this be acceptable?"

"It's great," he assured the hostess. She distributed the menus and departed as soon as they sat down.

Jenna looked up from her menu. "I'm sorry. I had no idea what I was getting you into when I suggested a walk. I should have known better. I mean, I read the gossip rags religiously."

He shrugged. "We would have been fine if that one lady hadn't gone ballistic."

"So how do you walk in a character's shoes if you're going to be mobbed within five minutes of stepping from the cab?"

"One, I use a car service. Two, most of my films are shot on foreign soil where I'm not as easily recognized. Three, I limit most of my outings to familiar restaurants and shops. And four, sometimes I wear a disguise."

Her gaze skidded over his face. "I can't believe anyone would miss your chin. It ranks right up there with Clooney's and Pitt's as sexy and recognizable."

A waitress slipped into the room to take their orders before Conrad could label the discomfort caused by the knowledge that Jenna considered George and Brad sexy. He suppressed the sensation. Whatever it was, it didn't matter. His interlude with her was temporary. Jenna was a self-professed career-driven woman, and he'd had his fill of those.

"If you never leave the apartment, then how do you keep in such good shape?" she asked after the waitress left.

"You think I'm in good shape?" More than his pride

swelled at her comment. She might want to ignore the physical side of their…friendship, but he didn't. And he intended to remind her of their fireworks often, and maybe convince her to break that no-sex rule.

Her lips flattened and she gave him a look guaranteed to censure even the most unruly student, but her cheeks pinked.

"I have a gym in my second bedroom and a personal trainer who comes in once a month to keep me from slacking off."

"I can't imagine being cooped up all the time, never walking in the park or browsing through a bookstore. That's not living, Conrad."

He hadn't sealed himself away until recently. Before Tara's death he'd been an active outdoor sports nut. But his old hobbies held memories—memories he couldn't face. "I don't miss as much as you'd expect. Still want to be famous?"

Jenna hesitated only a few seconds. "Yes. When will you introduce me to your agent?"

Her question reminded him why she was here. Like Tara, she had a burning need for fame. Did she derive any pleasure out of his company at all? Without a doubt, she'd found pleasure in his bed until he'd screwed up. A woman couldn't fake that flush, the fluttering pulse or the wetness waiting for him. But was it for him, the man, or Conrad Carr, the movie star?

"When I think you're ready."

Anger sparked in her eyes. "Now wait a minute—"

"That's the deal. Take it or leave it." He hoped like hell she didn't call his bluff, because he wasn't ready to let Jenna go yet.

"I'VE NEVER RIDDEN in a limo before." Jenna stroked the leather upholstery and studied the man across from her. He looked as if he rode in limos every day. Which he probably did. One phone call had brought a driver from the car service he routinely used to the back door of the restaurant.

Once she became famous she'd have to get used to being sealed off behind tinted windows, but for now... She pushed the button lowering the privacy glass between the passenger compartment and the driver.

"Ma'am?" the driver asked.

"Hi. I just want to see where we're going." And she wanted a third party to break up the sexually charged atmosphere. Her mind insisted on replaying what had happened when she'd gone home with Conrad last time, and when she tried to stop that train of thought it shifted tracks, creating a list of wild things to do behind the dark windows on the long, wide seats.

Getting Conrad out into the real world wasn't going to be easy, but the thought of being locked with him in his apartment until he deemed her "ready" to meet his agent gave her heart palpitations. If she wanted to stay out of trouble—and out of his bed—she needed a lesson plan she could stick to. She had dozens of exercises to cure stage fright, if that's what Conrad had, but she was beginning to have her doubts. None of her old lesson plans covered helping a man find his way back to the land of the living.

Pedestrians barely glanced at the long black car. It hadn't been that way when they were walking. Jenna distracted herself from the length of Conrad's sprawled legs brushing against hers by reliving the horrible scene. Despite his baseball cap and sunglasses he'd collected a crowd of followers like the Pied Piper. They'd peppered him with questions, which he'd answered without slowing his pace. A screech had been their only warning before an overzealous fan launched herself at him almost as if she were trying to rip off a piece of his clothing as a souvenir. Pandemonium had broken loose.

Conrad had wrapped his fingers around Jenna's, leaned closer and whispered, "Run."

If he hadn't found that hidden restaurant… Jenna shuddered. So maybe fame had a teensy downside.

"Would you like us to drop you off at home?" he asked.

"You're not getting out of work that easy. You mentioned a classic movie collection over dinner. I'd love to see it. I adore old films." She wasn't ashamed of her fourth-floor walk-up, but the mob scene had begun a few blocks from where she lived. She'd rather go back to Manhattan and take the long subway ride home than face that again.

Minutes later Conrad closed the door to his apartment, sealing them into a dark, intimate cocoon. Maybe this hadn't been a good idea, after all. If she were staging this production she'd cue the romantic music at this point. "So…the movies?"

"This way." She followed him down a short hall on the opposite side of the den from his bedroom. Through an open door she spotted a gym. The second door yielded a treasure trove.

"Wow." Jenna entered the room. Bookcases soared from the floor to the ten-foot ceilings on three of the four walls. Closed window blinds lined the fourth. But this room looked lived in, whereas the sterile living room and bedroom didn't, and it smelled of Conrad. A single leather club chair and ottoman had been angled to face a big-screen television and a state-of-the-art stereo system.

"Music, books, movies." Conrad pointed to each loaded shelf sequentially.

She dragged her fingers over a cookbook collection and then the DVD cases. "You don't go out into the world. You bring the world to you."

He shrugged out of his jacket, and instantly her thoughts somersaulted back to her shoving his coat off last night. "Sometimes it's easier that way."

"Which is your favorite movie?"

He slid a well-worn case from the shelf.

She blinked in disbelief. He'd chosen a movie with an alcoholic hero who'd been redeemed in the end. Was his choice a coincidence or did it have something to do with his father? *"True Grit?"*

"I like cowboys and the code of the West."

"And yet you've never done a western."

His jaw tightened. "Cowboy flicks rarely impress critics."

"Does every film have to impress the critics? Haven't you earned the right to do films you enjoy?"

He opened his mouth and then closed it again. "Good point."

"Are there any westerns in the script pile?"

"Probably not. My agent knew what kinds of movies Tara—" He turned away and shoved the film back on the shelf.

Conrad's wife had been a huge part of his career. As much as it had hurt Jenna to be called by the other woman's name, she was convinced that getting past Conrad's problem meant talking about his dead wife. "Tara what?"

He shoved a hand through his hair. "She only liked projects she believed stood a chance of winning awards."

"But Tara wasn't nominated until the last film."

"No." He sighed. "And that…frustrated her."

"Her characters were always the beautiful foil to your meatier parts, but she never went deeper than superficial supporting roles until your last movie. It was her best work."

He clenched his fists by his side. "If not for that damn role Tara would still be alive."

"What do you mean?"

"Tara was bitter over being ignored by critics. As soon as I read the script I knew it could be the role of a lifetime for her and a chance for her to win the critical acclaim she craved, so I pushed her into accepting the part."

"With the way the movie turned out I'll bet she was glad you talked her into the role."

His gaze held Jenna's for a long, tense moment. "No, she wasn't. In the end she couldn't handle how rough she looked in a couple of the clips. She begged me to convince the director to let her go back on location to reshoot those scenes. I knew it was a mistake, but I wanted her to be happy. I used my clout and he agreed. The crew left, but I stayed behind to work on the preliminaries for my next film.

"They were stuck north of nowhere for a week because of weather. Tara became ill before they even started filming. She thought it was a virus and refused medical treatment because she didn't trust what she called backwoods doctors. She died before I could get there with her personal physician." His voice broke. He swiped a hand over his jaw and took a bracing breath. "And I, the person she trusted the most, told the director to use the footage she hated because it was, as you said, her best work.

"So I killed my wife, Jenna, and then I betrayed her."

His defiant gaze dared her to disagree, but how could she not? Jenna's throat ached with unshed tears.

"No, Conrad, you didn't betray her. You gave her exactly what she wanted, but didn't have the courage to seek."

CHAPTER FIVE

"TRY THE NEXT SCRIPT." The lessons weren't working. He couldn't do it. His gift was gone. Frustrated, Conrad flung the pages onto the coffee table.

Jenna rubbed the pleat between her eyebrows. "There's nothing wrong with this script or any of the others we've read and discarded over the past ten days."

He paced the length of the room, wanting—*needing*—to retreat to his study, shut the door and play loud music. Better yet, he could go into his gym and work out his frustrations. "I don't feel the character."

"That's because you're holding back."

Her patience astounded him. His mood had deteriorated over the past week, but Jenna had maintained her calm. Not once had she gone into histrionics when he lost his temper. He and Tara would have been at each other's throat by now or more likely, not speaking at all. "I'm giving it my best shot."

Jenna perched on the arm of the sofa and crossed her legs. Each day she arrived dressed in bright colors. The color du jour was fuchsia. From her breast-molding sweater to her snug, pink, hip-hugging jeans, she looked like a splat of paint in his colorless world. And when she went to work at The Hotel she left color behind in a forgotten hair ribbon, the red glass fruit bowl she'd parked on his kitchen table because she liked to snack while she worked, or the flowers she'd bought from a street vendor and scattered throughout his apartment.

"I've seen your best shot, Conrad. This isn't it."

Day after day she'd pushed him mercilessly. Right to the edge. He'd come close to losing control several times. But he couldn't afford to lose it. "The script sucks."

"Actually, the script is brilliant, and one of these days you ought to shoot it, but it's probably not the best project for you right now. Have you considered doing a film that doesn't have a female romantic lead? All of these—" she gestured to the stack "—resemble the films you made with Tara. Maybe you should call your agent and tell him that when he comes to meet me you'd like him to bring some westerns."

Right, and then he'd have to answer Sid's "how's it going" and "when are you coming back to work" questions. No thanks. Conrad hadn't called his agent because he didn't have any answers. He'd done so much ducking and diving he ought to take up boxing.

"You're hardly qualified to give me career advice." He wanted to swallow the rude words as soon as he said them, but Jenna didn't appear to take offense.

She pursed her lips and tilted her head. "Are you trying to pick a fight again? Because you should have learned by now that you can't get out of work by snarling at me."

Guilty as charged. His ears burned. How had this woman he barely knew invaded his head so deeply and quickly? He'd tried every trick he knew to distract her, but she was an odd combination of relentless pit bull and optimistic cheerleader. "No, but you're not willing to work off tension in the only way that would benefit both of us."

As quick as a lightning strike, the air between them crackled and popped with sexual tension. Because each script contained a romantic subplot, there'd been several emotionally charged scenes between them as they read their lines, but in those instances Jenna read hers from across the room or with a half-eaten apple in her hand as if she believed keeping both hands occupied would prevent them from acting out the stage directions—specifically the kisses.

He wanted her so badly his teeth ached.

"Sex won't solve your problem," she said in a placating tone.

It would sure as hell solve one of them. He couldn't sleep. He tossed and turned each night in frustration, his body tight and itchy and triggered. When he closed his eyes he pictured Jenna, her ivory skin bare on his black silk sheets, her round breasts waiting for his touch, her dark curls glistening—

That jerked Conrad up short. He hadn't had a nightmare since he'd met Jenna. Wet dreams, yes. Nightmares, no.

Tara…he hadn't dreamed about his wife in over a week. The thought both saddened and relieved him. He couldn't forget Tara any more than he could fall for Jenna. In less than three weeks he would return to the West Coast. Jenna would stay in New York. Even if distance wasn't a factor, he'd never let himself love another woman. Too dangerous.

Tension knotted between his shoulder blades. "Don't you need to leave for work?"

Why did she smile like that—as if she'd figured him out—when she should be telling him to go to hell for his bad attitude and for wasting her time? "I have another hour. We can read over the scene again. This time I want you to go for the emotional punch. The hero's been through hell. He's lost his job, his family and his home."

He found her passion for acting sexy. She threw herself into the role and *she* didn't hold back. She wasn't the most talented actress he'd ever come across, but she was the most enthusiastic.

She'd shown the same enthusiasm in his bed. And just like that his brain deferred to a more insistent part of his anatomy, as it had numerous other times this week. He'd liked it better when his sex drive was as numb as the rest of him.

Just because he couldn't love Jenna didn't mean he wouldn't sleep with her again if she'd lift her no-sex ban. If he could shake this damn fascination with her then he could concentrate on the job at hand—rediscovering his lost talent. Assuming it was there to be found.

He crossed the room, cornered her against the sofa and then lifted his hand to tuck a wayward curl behind her ear. He let his finger drift over the pulse fluttering at the base of her neck. She might pretend to be unaffected by the attraction between them, but that little indicator gave away her true reaction every time. She wanted him. Why fight it?

"I don't want to do the scene again." He pitched his voice low, deliberately implying what he'd rather be doing.

Her breath hitched and her cheeks flushed. She swallowed and leaned away from his touch. "Does this role hit too close to home for you? Is that why you're afraid to channel the character's emotions?"

Dammit. He fisted his hand and let it drop and then stepped back. How did she keep doing that? Heading him off at the pass. Derailing him when he was spoiling for a fight or some sex.

She stood and laid her hand on his forearm. "I know you're scared."

"I'm not scared." The knee-jerk denial sprang from his lips. It was a lie and they both knew it.

"But it's okay to be afraid. There's nobody here but me. What's the worst that can happen?"

He'd turn into a damned emotional train wreck, that's what. And if that happened he'd end up just like his worthless, drunken father, living in a cabin in the middle of nowhere and drinking himself into a case of cirrhosis. Conrad jerked his arm away from the heat of her hand. "I'm done for the day."

"Conrad, you'll never beat this if you keep walking away."

"I'm not walking away, dammit." But he was, because if he didn't, the emotions inside him were going to erupt like Mount St. Helens volcano.

"Prove it. Read the scene with me. Please. One more time."

Anger and frustration vibrated through him. He considered snatching up the script and hurling the words at her along with the fury and fear building inside him. But he slowly, painfully drew back behind the walls he'd constructed.

"See yourself out." He retreated to his gym, ripped off his shirt and wrestled on his boxing gloves. His fist hit the punching bag with a satisfying smack, followed by another and another.

A hard rap preceded the door opening. Jenna stood on the threshold with her hands on her hips. Conrad paused midswing. He couldn't handle more of her prodding right now. "What?"

"You can hide in here for the rest of the afternoon if you like, but when I return tomorrow we're going to work on that scene until you get it right. You can do this, Conrad. But you have to stop running first." She shut the door before he could argue.

Running? Dammit, he wasn't running. Conrad took another swing at the bag. Was he?

BEING A BITCH *is exhausting.* She'd rather try to convince a cast of jocks to dance the *Nutcracker* than torture Conrad.

Jenna stepped into the elevator and tried to get into character by suppressing any sympathy she felt for him. It wasn't easy. As an actor he'd been her idol, but as a man… Her heart ached for the wounded soul who struggled to keep his feelings bottled up while she pushed and nagged and basically made his life miserable in an attempt to break through his emotional block. It was painful to watch. But he was so close, and if she could maintain the harsh taskmaster role a little longer she could bring down his walls. Stage fright would have been so much easier to cure.

The elevator glided open on the top floor with a quiet ping. She traversed the plushly carpeted hall, past the richly stained wainscoted walls, heading for Conrad's door. The contrast between her budget building and millionaires' row was too vast for description.

What trick would Conrad employ to get out of working today? His diversionary techniques thus far had been amusing, frustrating and dangerous. When she backed him into a corner he either fed her—a meal he cooked himself—picked a fight or turned up the sensual heat until she thought she'd burst into flames. Pretending to be unaffected was her best acting job to date. She didn't know whether to shake him or wrap her arms around him and comfort him.

Fool. You're doing it again. Falling for a man who loves someone else. If you have a single functioning brain cell left you'll run before you get hurt.

No, she wouldn't fall for Conrad, but neither could she afford to walk away from this fight. Her pride was at stake. She would either land an acting job before her money ran out or return home a penniless failure. Only she didn't have a home anymore, because she'd sold her house and her car and used the equity to finance this adventure. She'd have to move in with her parents until she got on her feet again. Not an anticipated event for a twenty-six-year-old woman used to her independence.

Chances were the situation with Conrad would get uglier before it improved. Could she handle that? Ugly emotional scenes—real ones, not scripted ones—had never been her thing. She'd run from the last one rather than stay and face the humiliation of being second best. But she wouldn't run this time, because she truly admired Conrad's talent, and she found the possibility that he might not make another film intolerable. Besides, she needed his help to get her career going. But working with him was a bigger challenge than she'd ever faced. He pushed her as much as she pushed him.

Squaring her shoulders, Jenna rapped on his door. Seconds later a blond-haired, blue-eyed, goateed stranger opened it. "Hello. Is Conrad..."

Hold it. The color was different but the shape of those long-lashed eyes looked familiar, as did the classically straight nose, the seductive lips and the broad shoulders encased in a nondescript gray jogging suit. And then there was his scent. Citrus and spice. Armani, unless she missed her guess. "Conrad?"

His chest fell. He stepped back and motioned her inside. "Can't fool you, can I?"

She entered his apartment. "What's with the disguise?"

"We're going out."

"We need to work on the scene."

"Maybe later. You seem to think my life is lacking because I don't walk in the park. Today we're touring Central Park."

She'd expected him to try to avoid the emotionally charged scene, but getting him out of his hideaway was a positive step, so she let him get away with it. "Okay, but you owe me a carriage ride."

"Tourist." His smile took the sting out of the word. He smiled a lot when he was teasing and tormenting her, but this one looked relaxed and genuine instead of practiced or calculated. "Dump your stuff and let's go."

Jenna deposited her tote bag in a chair and followed him out the door. As soon as they stepped from the building he shoved his hands in his pockets, rounded his shoulders and effortlessly assumed the role of tourist. She kept pace beside him, marveling that no one could possibly recognize him through his disguise. The famous movie star had vanished in plain sight.

Five minutes later he'd chosen a path into the park. "What exactly do you expect me to do now that I'm here?" he asked.

"People watch. Brenna and I used to pick people at random and try to figure out what they did and where they came from by the way they dressed and carried themselves. Of course, we were romantic, starry-eyed girls at the time, so we tended to see a lot of spies and exiled princes." She smiled at the memory and felt the tug of loneliness. She and her sister were competitive, but they'd also been each other's best friend for their entire lives. It wasn't Brenna's fault their father's junior partner preferred her.

Despite the late spring sunshine, the park wasn't crowded on a weekday afternoon. A few joggers and bicyclists passed, and a spattering of preschoolers and their mothers or caregivers dotted the grass.

Conrad indicated a park bench. He waited until Jenna sat down and then settled beside her and draped his arm along the back rail. Her senses went on full alert at the brush of his biceps between her shoulder blades. The desire to put her head on his shoulder nearly overwhelmed her.

A ball bounced in their direction. Conrad caught it and rolled it back toward its three- to four-year-old owner. The boy beamed and kicked the ball again. Conrad grinned and volleyed it back, only to have it returned. The game continued for about fifteen minutes before the mother called, collected the boy and his ball and departed.

Conrad looked more relaxed than Jenna had seen him thus far. "You like children."

"What's not to like?" He returned the kid's goodbye wave. "My brother was about his age."

Another surprise. "I didn't know you had a brother."

"I don't. He died when he was three. I was twelve."

"I'm sorry." She'd come to love the brief glimpses into his life that he shared sparingly.

He shoved his hands in his pockets and stared off into the distance. "It was a long time ago."

And he'd managed to keep it out of the tabloids. Amazing. "What happened?"

"The car slid off an icy road, down a bridge embankment and into a partially frozen creek. Mom died instantly. Tommy didn't. He died of hypothermia before they found the car."

Her pulse skittered in alarm. "Were you with them? Was your father driving?"

"No. It was just Mom and Tommy. Dad started drinking after the accident. He blames himself for not finding the car in time to save Tommy."

Compassion squeezed her heart. "How sad. It was just you and your father from then on?"

He met her gaze, but hesitated. A parade of emotions tumbled through his eyes. He had the most expressive eyes of anyone she'd ever met. "Yeah. Just me and Dad."

She wanted to ask him to explain his bitterness, but she didn't. One thing she'd learned this week was that she couldn't pry information out of Conrad. If he wanted her to know more he'd tell her. "I would have expected you and Tara to have children, since you like them so much."

He stood and started walking. Jenna kept pace beside him. "We were barely twenty-one when we met. We thought we had plenty of time. And then career issues got in the way."

"I know the feeling. At the rate I'm going I probably won't have children, either."

"You like kids?"

Jenna rolled her eyes. "I'm a teacher. Of course I like children."

"The two don't necessarily go hand in hand."

"For me they do." She laced her fingers through Conrad's, stopping him on the sidewalk. "You would have been a great dad and still could be one day."

His fingers tightened. He met her gaze. Even though he wore a disguise, her heart skipped a beat at his nearness. "Not going to happen for me, but thanks. You, on the other hand... Jenna, don't get so caught up in your career that you miss out on what's important."

He dragged a finger along her jawline and her breath hitched. His gaze focused on her lips. Jenna was certain he'd kiss her right in the middle of Central Park, and as foolish as that might be, she wanted him to because this wasn't a game. He wasn't dodging a difficult scene. He'd given her another glimpse at the man inside, and she felt closer to him than she had an hour ago.

He lowered his head and his lips brushed hers. The fake beard and mustache tickled and aroused simultaneously. Kissing the man wasn't the same as kissing the movie star. This time more than hormones and hero worship swirled through her blood making the touch of his lips and the taste of his tongue twice as arousing. Twice as risky. She liked the man behind the Hollywood image too much, and heartache would be her only reward if she continued down this path. She stepped out of reach and prayed she could find the strength to continue resisting him.

Conrad lowered his hand. "Ready for that carriage ride?"

CHAPTER SIX

HOW LONG HAD IT BEEN since he'd been just a guy on a date? So long that Conrad had forgotten the energizing rush of teetering on the knife edge between awareness and the uncertainty of how an evening would end.

He knew how and where he wanted his day to end. With Jenna in his bed. With him deep inside her. Convincing her she wanted the same thing wouldn't be easy.

"You don't have to work tonight. Let me cook for you." He followed her into his apartment, closed the door and leaned against it. The sun had kissed her nose and cheeks, and the wind had teased tendrils of hair from the yellow ribbon tied at her nape. Conrad itched to comb the tangled strands with his fingers. Her excitement over the carriage ride still sparkled in her eyes.

"The chef's specialty this evening is beef tenderloin with chipotle potatoes." The Creole accent rolled easily off his tongue—something it wouldn't have done before a relaxing walk in the park, a carriage ride and a hunt through the local bookstore.

Jenna hesitated, worrying her bottom lip with her teeth. "On one condition. You do the scene and you give it one hundred percent."

His stomach took a bungee jump off the Brooklyn

Bridge. He didn't want to sour a good day with failure. "After dinner."

"Before dinner or no deal. We're running out of time."

Clawing panic replaced his appetite. He ducked back into suave Creole mode and bent to kiss the back of her hand, hiding behind a character the way he had since his teens. "If you insist, *chère.*"

When she tried to pull away he turned her hand in his and pressed an openmouthed kiss into her palm. He heard her breath catch and pushed his advantage. Nudging back the sleeve of her yellow sweater, he sipped a string of kisses along the blue veins of her wrist and forearm. Her fragrance stirred his senses and his pulse drummed in his ears.

Her fingers curled and then unfurled to cup and caress his chin. He cursed the fake beard and adhesive blocking direct contact. He craved her healing touch on his flesh.

She lifted his jaw, tilting his head until their gazes met. Her breath came in pants through parted lips, and more than sun exposure flushed her cheekbones, but the resolve in her eyes told him his seduction diversion hadn't worked. "Conrad, stop."

He straightened. "You want me." And God help him, he wanted her like an addict needs a fix, like an alcoholic needs a drink.

"I can hardly deny that, can I?" Her honesty always surprised him. "Every day we play this game, but I have a job to do, and you're not helping either of us by getting us off track time and time again."

He ought to be ashamed of himself for his cowardly evasions. But he wasn't. He knew the consequences if he let the two-fisted grip on his control slip, so he searched for another way out the predicament. "Let me get rid of this disguise first."

He turned to leave, but Jenna caught his hand and pulled him back. She planted both hands on his shoulders and held him with a firm grasp. He could see by her set expression that she'd tired of his games.

"Leave it. Maybe it will help. This evening you're not Conrad Carr. You're Peter James. Your family is gone. Your home has been burned to the ground by your worst enemy. You're on the run because you've been framed for cheating and murdering your business partner. Peter—" she addressed the character, not him "—you have nothing left to lose and the only one who can help prove your innocence is me—your partner's widow."

Jenna picked up the script and shoved it into his hand. "Convince me."

Conrad's gaze locked with hers, but she'd already assumed her own character's distrustful mask. His lifeline had been cut, his escape route sealed. His skin seemed to shrink two sizes and the muscles alongside his spine knotted. Even the blond wig compressed his skull.

"'You've robbed me, Peter James, robbed me of the one thing I valued most.'" She fed him his cue.

All he had to do was get through this one scene and then Jenna would leave him alone. He closed his eyes and tried to block the tension invading his limbs. But he couldn't. Loss, pain, betrayal and desperation pulled him under, restricting the airflow to his lungs.

"I didn't do it, Ellie. I didn't betray my family or yours…." The lines from the script came out flat at first, but then something clicked like a key in a lock. The cylinders turned and the words poured out in the agonizing, jerky plea of a drowning man. Peter's despair welled up, suffocating him, but Conrad kept choking out dialogue until there was nothing left on the page.

Silence echoed in the room when he finished. The script fell from his fingers. Drained, he dropped to his knees, planted his hands on his thighs and sucked one lungful of air after another.

Jenna knelt beside him. She cupped his face and waited until he found the strength to lift his eyes. Tears streaked her cheeks. "That…was…brilliant."

He couldn't still the tremors racking him, couldn't stop the pain ripping open his chest as all he'd lost—his mother, his brother, his father, his wife—consumed him in a flood of excruciating memories. Jenna's arms enfolded him, and then she pulled his head to her shoulder. She rocked him, soothed him, while he fought a losing battle to regain control.

Gentle fingers brushed away the blond wig and then peeled off the latex and fake facial hair. She kissed him on the forehead, the nose. "You did it, Conrad. You've broken through the wall and rediscovered your gift."

The pride in her voice and her eyes anchored him. The gentleness of her touch pulled him free from the whirlpool trying to suck him under. He clung to her. And then her mouth covered his and she breathed life into his dying soul.

Her lips strengthened and reenergized him. Blood pumped through his veins, reviving him, healing him. Desire washed away the bitter taste of fear. He cradled her face and brushed the tears from her cheeks with his thumbs. "Thank you."

She covered his hands. "You're welcome."

Her lips were damp from his kisses, from her tears. He bent and kissed her again. Gratitude gave way to hunger, heavy, insistent and undeniable. But he'd tried to distract her with seduction too many times this week already. He had to make sure she understood this time wasn't a diversion, and since she was the one who'd established the no-sex rule, breaking it had to be her decision. "Jenna?"

Her mouth quivered into a siren's smile. "Make love with me, Conrad."

Elation swelled his chest. Slowly, he rose and pulled her to her feet. Hand in hand, he led her to his bedroom. Each brush of their shoulders along the way jolted him with an electric charge. This time he wouldn't let Jenna down. This time he'd make damn sure she knew he was aware of whom he held in his arms. He owed her that much and so much more.

He'd broken down and it hadn't killed him. His life and career weren't over. Because of Jenna. His good luck talisman. His savior. And soon, his lover.

SHE'D MADE A MISTAKE. A colossal and devastating mistake. She'd fallen in love with Conrad Carr—another man for whom she could never be more than second best.

Jenna closed her eyes against the painful discovery and let Conrad banish her panic along with her clothing. The brush of his hands against her waist, the whoosh of her sweater over her head and the sweep of cooling air over her hot body chased away her fears, replacing them with an aching desire. He didn't love her, swore he *couldn't* love her, but he could make her feel like his leading lady. Temporarily.

Was she foolish to hope that one day his feelings would change?

Hot and moist, his mouth covered her breast, drawing a response from deep inside her. Her fingers tangled in his hair, holding him close, encouraging him to work his magic. He removed her jeans, sneakers and socks with urgent yanks and impatient tugs. His hands mapped her skin, finding and titillating her pulse points and then her damp center. He stroked her into a knee-dissolving frenzy, and held her on the brink of ecstasy for endless seconds. Her legs quivered and she had to grasp his broad shoulders or she'd collapse at his feet.

"Jenna." The warmth of his breath teased her beaded nipple.

She forced her heavy lids open. As soon as she met his passionate gaze he sent rapture undulating through her.

Once the quakes stopped he rose to stand beside her and his big bed. Without breaking eye contact he shucked his shirt, kicked off his shoes and shed his pants and socks. She threaded her fingers through his chest hair, and his breath whistled through clenched teeth. This time, she wanted to savor the length and breadth of him and to explore the power of his body. She curled her fingers around the silky column of his thick erection.

"Jenna." His voice, half plea, half groan, encouraged her. She stroked from the base of his shaft to the slick tip, tasted him from one flat nipple to the other. His fingers tunneled into her hair. He yanked her close to devour her mouth. His chest burned her breasts. His thighs spliced hers, making her want to rub against him. With her hands trapped between them, her movements were limited, but she tried to make her touch as arousing for him as the caress of his big hands was to her. Judging by his thrust against her palm and the guttural sounds from his throat, she succeeded.

He jerked his head back and groaned, "Enough," and then he opened the bedside table drawer, extracted a condom and offered it to her. Jenna took it from him and glided it over his rigid flesh. He ripped the coverlet back with enough force to send it sailing to the floor. Jenna smiled at his zeal, scooted onto the cool sheets and lifted her arms.

Conrad paused to remove the last of his disguise—the colored contacts. She could have told him it wasn't necessary. Her soul would recognize his no matter what disguise he wore. He stretched out beside her, braced himself on one elbow and gently undid her hair ribbon. He combed the tangled strands across his pillow and then captured a lock and used it to paint erotic patterns over her breasts. His eyes—she loved his expressive eyes—watched each stoke as if everything about her, even her hair, fascinated him. His total concentration on her pleasure was an aphrodisiac beyond compare, and Jenna squirmed with need.

Conrad dipped his head and strung hot, openmouthed kisses from the hollow beneath one ear to the other. She tried to drag him nearer, but despite his earlier haste, now he wouldn't be rushed. He sampled and sipped, laved and nipped until she thought she'd go out of her mind. She twined her legs through his, savoring the tickle of his rough leg hairs against her smooth skin.

By the time he moved over her she was beyond control. "Please, Conrad, please."

He filled her with a single deep thrust. She gasped at

the pleasure, at the fullness, at the rightness of having him in her arms, her body. Her heart.

She didn't have to wonder who he thought of while they made love, because his gaze held hers, and when the pleasure overwhelmed her and she couldn't keep her eyes open any longer he whispered her name in her ears and against her temple.

Tension spiraled, lifting her higher and higher, until the stage collapsed beneath her and she tumbled head over heels into ecstasy.

"Jenna," he groaned against her lips as he joined her.

She couldn't love him more than she did right now, with their hearts pounding in unison, their rasping breaths mingling and their bodies still joined. But that love was bittersweet, because in today's soul-baring performance Conrad had made her doubt her goal of becoming famous. Nothing, certainly not the endless cattle calls and auditions, had given her the thrill or satisfaction she'd felt the moment she saw Conrad become his character.

He rolled to her side and pulled her into his arms. Jenna laid her head on his chest and listened to the slowing of his heart. What if she wasn't meant to act? What if teaching was her true vocation? What if she didn't have star quality?

No, she had to practice what she preached and believe in herself. With Conrad's help and an introduction to his agent she *would* make it happen. Otherwise, she'd never become famous enough to step out from Brenna's shadow, and she'd spend the rest of her life being the dull twin.

But now the stakes were twice as high. She loved

Conrad, but he was used to glamour and glitz and Hollywood starlets. Plain old Jenna Graham would never do. If she wanted any chance with him, then she had to become a star.

But how could she win his heart when he still wore another woman's wedding ring on his finger?

CHAPTER SEVEN

"SO YOU'RE READY TO WORK again and you're claiming this woman—a woman who needs my help finding a job—is responsible," Sid said from the sofa.

Conrad turned away from the window in time to see his agent fill his palm with a rainbow of jelly beans from the jar Jenna had left on the coffee table. Jenna's odd snacking habits brought a smile to Conrad's lips. "Yeah."

He should have known that as soon as he called to say he was ready to return to work Sid would catch a flight to personally deliver the latest version of the script.

Conrad checked his watch again and looked out at the sidewalk below. No Jenna. She'd been scheduled to work a lunch shindig at The Hotel today, but she should have been here by now. After a second week of working with her he'd begun to look forward to reading with her, cooking for her, talking to her, sleeping with her.... His heart slammed against his ribs.

"Remind me to thank her," Sid said around a mouthful of candy. "But letting another actress ride your coattails is a bad move. Last time it worked out. This time…"

Conrad pivoted back to Sid. "What are you talking about?"

Sid shrugged. "Tara latched on to you because she saw what I saw—a man destined for the top. She became a star because you became a star."

Sid made it sound as if Tara had used him. "I loved my wife and she loved me. You should know that, since you introduced us."

"Smart move on my part. Tara was more experienced, and you were so damn wet behind the ears when you hit town that you needed somebody to show you the ropes. But face it, pal, most Hollywood matches aren't made in heaven. You got lucky last time. This time think short-term. When you come back to L.A. we'll find a slew of starlets to warm your bed and keep you happy. It's free publicity and fun, too." Sid sent him a ribald wink. "This Jenna chick's served her purpose of getting you back in the game. Let her go and move on."

Conrad couldn't conceive of wanting anybody else in his bed anytime soon, and hearing Sid cheapen his relationship with Jenna made him want to go a few rounds with his punching bag. Or Sid's face. Strange, since he and Sid had always gotten along. His agent was brutally honest—a trait Conrad admired. Usually.

"I never said anything about Jenna other than that she was coaching me."

"Didn't have to. When a man's getting some there's a spring in his step—a spring you didn't have three weeks ago. Don't go falling in love. Your career can't handle more time off. Besides, the studio will sue our *assets* off if you fail to fulfill this contract."

"I'm not in love with Jenna." The automatic denial flew from his lips. *No way was he in love.* The fizz in his veins was the excitement of discovering his career wasn't over. Jenna had shown him that he could channel his painful emotions without being swallowed by them or using booze to numb them. That didn't mean he was willing to risk his heart again.

"Glad to hear it's only lust. Then you won't mind packing up and moving back to Bel Air. I'll call the house-keeping service and have the house readied for you."

His stomach knotted. "I want to see Jenna settled in a job first."

Sid joined him by the window. "Conrad, we're running out of time. If you don't report by the end of next week we're in default. We've had all the extensions they're going to grant."

A weight settled on his shoulders. Sid was right. As much as Conrad disliked the idea, he'd have to say goodbye to Jenna soon. Getting his career back on track and returning to Hollywood had been the plan all along, but as the time to leave drew nearer he liked it less. "I won't let you down."

"Glad to hear it. But now it's time to say your goodbyes." He reached in his suit coat pocket and withdrew an envelope. "These will help. Two tickets to a Broadway opening tonight. I've made dinner reservations for two at Balthazar afterward. Catch a little face time with the press, and let 'em know you're back. Make sure she gets some attention, too."

"Jenna deserves more than a casual brush-off."

"I'm sure you'll come up with something."

A tap on the door made Conrad's heart stutter. Jenna. He crossed the room and opened the door to her bright smile.

"Hi. Ready to flex your acting muscles, cowboy?"

Her soft, intimate voice sent heat spiraling through him. She'd asked the same teasing question every day for the past seven days. They'd developed a routine of working on the scripts for a few hours and then tumbling into bed and not surfacing until hunger or her need to go to work forced them out. That wouldn't happen today. Damn. He opened the door wider. Jenna looked past him and her smile wobbled.

"Come in and meet my agent." Regret twisted inside him. He wasn't ready to say goodbye. But what choice did he have?

ACT III, THE BEGINNING of the end.

Jenna had known the curtain would eventually fall on her time with Conrad if she couldn't breach the walls around his heart. He'd given one hundred percent to his acting this week, but he still held something back from her. She'd known the risk going in, but she hadn't expected the failure to win his love to hurt so much.

Thankful for once for her sister's beauty pageant castoffs, she smoothed the beaded black silk designer gown over her hips with unsteady hands. Tonight she would literally walk in her sister's shoes and in Tara Dean's shadow.

Sid Raye's sputtered, "Damn, she looks enough like Tara to be her baby sister," had been a slap of reality in the face. She could pretend all she wanted that Conrad saw *her,* Jenna Graham, when they made love, but facts were facts. She did resemble his dead wife. Did Conrad see beyond the shared coloring?

The buzzer nearly startled Jenna out of her spike heels. Conrad had arrived. Her heart raced and a lump rose in her throat. She crossed to the intercom and pressed the button. "Yes?"

"Jenna, may I come up?"

With a heavy heart, she hit the button to release the front gate, unlocked both dead bolts, pulled open her door and waited. Conrad's steps echoed up the stairwell long before he came into view. He stopped on the fourth floor landing and his gaze raked over her. Passion flared in his eyes. "You look stunning."

She wanted to believe he meant it. Self-consciously, she touched a hand to the clip holding her curls off her face. "Thank you."

The climb hadn't even winded him. He looked so handsome in his tux that he took her own breath away, and made her heart ache. The last time he'd worn his tux she'd taken it off him….

"May I come in?"

He hadn't visited her apartment before. She doubted he'd be impressed with her homey flea market finds, but she stepped back and motioned for him to enter. Her chintz furniture, which had suited her cozy Asheville cottage perfectly, looked out of place in this modern, boxy space.

His gaze locked on the brass bed visible through her open bedroom door, and his nostrils flared. Then he turned his hungry eyes on her. "I have half a mind to say to hell with dinner and the show and spend the evening here with you."

Her knees weakened and heat shimmied over her skin. She'd love nothing better than to cast off her borrowed finery and join him beneath her hand-stitched quilt. "Sid wouldn't like that. He's expecting you to court the cameras tonight."

"The exposure will benefit both of us. Tomorrow he's going to call your agent and tell him, in his words, to 'get off the pot.'"

"That sounds like him." She'd spent less than an hour with Sid Raye before he'd hustled her out the door to get ready for tonight, but that had been more than enough time for her to see that Sid was as devoted to his client as a momma bear to her cub, and he'd let nothing stand in the way of Conrad's career. It was equally apparent he viewed Jenna as an encumbrance to be shed.

Conrad reached into his tux pocket and withdrew a small box. "This is for you."

The goodbye gift—another sign that their time was limited—chipped away another piece of her heart. Her hands shook as she plucked off the white ribbon and folded back the silver paper. She opened the black leather box and found a delicate gold filigree carriage pendant suspended on a thin gold chain. A diamond twinkled in each tiny spoked wheel. "It's beautiful."

Conrad extracted it from the box and fastened it around her neck. The scrape of his fingers on her nape sent a shiver of awareness dancing down her spine. "I want you to remember that day. I know I won't forget it."

The day he'd had his breakthrough. The day she'd realized she'd fallen irrevocably in love with him. She blinked furiously to hold back her tears, and firmed her lips to conceal the telling quiver. *Jenna Graham, you will get through this evening without wearing your breaking heart on your sleeve.*

"Thank you."

"I owe you, Jenna, more than I can ever repay." And

then he lifted her chin and kissed her, so tenderly that she wanted to burrow into his arms and cry her eyes out. But she didn't.

She squared her shoulders, gritted her teeth and stretched her lips into a smile. The next four hours might be the toughest of her life, but she would survive them. "We'd better get going."

He looked as if he wanted to say more, but then shook his head. Seconds later he whisked her down the stairs and into the waiting limo. Tension filled the car like an extra passenger seated between them. The teasing banter she'd grown to love over the past week was conspicuously absent.

Finally, Jenna couldn't stand it. "This is it, isn't it?"

Conrad covered the fists she'd knotted in her lap with one big hand, and met her gaze, but the shadowy interior concealed the emotions in his eyes. "I have to be on the set by the end of next week, but I don't have to leave right away. We have four more days. Sid brought the script for my next film. I'd like you to take a look at it."

Her stomach plunged at hearing her fears confirmed. Four short days to store up a lifetime of memories. And he wanted her to help *with work*. He'd said nothing about missing her or dreading their parting. The pain of the omission nearly engulfed her. But that was her fault. Conrad had made no promises. She was the one who'd made the mistake of thinking about forever.

Jenna swallowed the hurt and tried to smile. "I wish you well, Conrad. I really, really do."

He cupped her jaw, but before he could respond, the limo stopped and the driver announced they had arrived. Conrad lowered his hand. Jenna looked out the window and gasped. A red carpet—just like the ones she'd seen on TV—led from the curb into the brightly lit theater. A crowd formed a wall on each side of the golden-roped path. A uniformed stranger opened the limo door.

"Whatever happens, keep smiling," Conrad said before he climbed from the car and waved to the fans. He turned and extended his hand to her. Jenna blinked at the change in him. Energy, charisma and confidence rolled off him in waves. Her lover was gone and Conrad Carr, the movie star, had taken his place.

Her mouth dried and her stomach clenched. *Opening night jitters. Get over it. If you want to be a star then you'd better get used to this kind of spectacle.* She stiffened her spine, widened her smile until her face threatened to crack, and forced herself to step into the bright lights like a diva sailing onto the stage.

Conrad looped her arm through his and angled her toward the cameras. Flashbulbs popped in rapid, blinding succession.

"Who's the lady, Conrad?" one reporter called.

"Jenna Graham. My acting coach. My friend." His tender smile nailed her to the carpet as what seemed like a hundred flashbulbs blinded her.

"Is she Tara's replacement?" called another voice, but Conrad ignored the question and guided Jenna down the carpet and into the theater. Suddenly, she was part of the glittering, star-studded event instead of watching from behind the bar. She tried not to gape or crane her neck, but everywhere she turned she spotted another famous face. Movie, television and soap stars milled around her, and because she was with Conrad they accepted her into their midst. *Wow.*

And then her gaze met Conrad's and her smile faltered. His trademark grin might fool others, but his eyes revealed the truth. He wasn't enjoying this. He was *enduring* it.

"We don't have to stay," she whispered in his ear.

Surprise flickered across his face, but then his jaw turned resolute. "The show's about to begin. Let's find our seats."

The play was dazzling, the music superb, but the knowledge that Conrad would rather be somewhere else dampened Jenna's enjoyment of the evening. Or did he wish he were *with* someone else? She'd read dozens of accounts of him and Tara attending Broadway openings, so it had to be Jenna herself who'd ruined the evening for him.

By the time the play ended her face ached from faking merriment she didn't feel. She just wanted to crawl back into her apartment and pull her quilt over her head, but as she'd told her students countless times, you can't walk off the stage when a performance goes bad. You have to brazen it out until the final curtain falls. You owe it to your audience. You owe it to yourself. Her pride demanded she suck it up and get through this evening.

The most important lesson she'd learned tonight was that no matter how good of an actress she became she could never be Tara Dean.

CHAPTER EIGHT

CONRAD HAD WHAT HE WANTED. His career back. His life back. His face on the front page of the entertainment section and a damn good script to play with.

So why wasn't he happy?

He swigged down his coffee and battled grogginess caused by lack of sleep. The nightmares had returned for the first time in weeks. But instead of dreaming that he couldn't get to Tara and Tommy—in his dream they were always together—in time to save them, he'd dreamed of Jenna telling him to kiss off because she was a star now and no longer needed him.

Sid's suggestion chafed like new boots. Was Jenna using him to further her acting career? And if she was, why did that bother him? It had been their original deal. When had her...*friendship* become so important to him? But if career help was all she wanted from him, why had she offered, when she'd realized he was miserable, to leave the opening and skip dinner at a restaurant known for its celebrity clientele?

And how in the hell could a woman he'd known just over three weeks read him so well? She'd pegged him the night they'd met, he recalled. Even after twelve years of marriage Tara never had looked past the smile plastered on his face. His wife would have been so enthralled with being seen by and seeing the show biz elite that she never would have noticed his discomfort with the artificial atmosphere. He liked his privacy. Tara had loved the Hollywood hype. He'd wanted their home to be an oasis where they could get away from the "show" part of show business. She'd wanted a house in Bel Air where she could entertain, and she'd wanted their home listed on the tourist maps. She'd won.

Was Jenna more turned on by the Hollywood image than the man? But if bedding a famous actor was her goal, then why had she sent him home last night after dinner instead of inviting him to join her in that big brass bed? Confused by the mixed signals, he scraped a hand over his jaw. Why did he care? This had always been a temporary arrangement.

He parked his elbows on the kitchen table and studied the picture of him and Jenna taken outside the theater last night. Her smile couldn't be wider, and she couldn't possibly look more beautiful.

"Conrad finds solace with Tara look-alike," the caption read. He shoved the paper aside in disgust, but the one beneath it said almost the same thing. He'd found six papers outside his door this morning—compliments of Sid, no doubt—and they all spouted the same garbage. Damn reporters.

Jenna wasn't Tara. Two women couldn't be more dissimilar. Why was he the only one who saw beyond the superficial similarities of coloring and height?

Tara had been career focused and driven. In her mind, appearances and climbing the ladder of success weren't just important, they were the only thing that mattered. She'd taught him more about the business than anyone, and he'd loved her, loved her vivaciousness and her single-minded determination to succeed against all odds.

Jenna, on the other hand, was genuine and generous. She was as tenacious as Tara, but in a different way. Being happy meant more to her than being the most lauded. He'd lost count of the times she'd told him that if he couldn't love what he did then he'd better find something else to do. Her joy in the craft had reminded him why he loved acting, and he owed her for pulling him out of the darkness and back into the light. She'd become his good luck charm and he wasn't ready to let her go.

He couldn't love her without reservation the way she deserved, but he could repay her generosity by giving her the glitz and glamour of Hollywood. There were soap studios in California. He'd use his clout to give her a leg up the ladder.

He scrubbed the back of his neck. He'd only thrown his professional weight around once—the time he'd convinced the director to let Tara reshoot the scenes—and that had backfired. Tara had died. He shrugged off the discomfort. That wouldn't be the case this time. He wasn't sending Jenna off to a remote location. He was inviting her into his home.

Would she move west if he asked her? If being a star was what she really wanted, she would, and Jenna swore stardom was her goal.

Years with Tara and Sid had taught him that you wouldn't get anywhere in life if you didn't learn to ask for what you wanted. Conrad picked up the phone and punched in Sid's cell phone number.

"I want Jenna with me in California," he said without preamble as soon as Sid answered. "Make it happen."

JENNA CONSIDERED CALLING and telling Conrad she couldn't work with him anymore. Wouldn't a clean break be less painful than chiseling away small pieces of her heart over the next four days?

Someone knocked on her door and her pulse faltered. She fingered the carriage pendant and debated ignoring the summons. She wasn't expecting anyone and her neighbors were all at work. It had to be Conrad. But why hadn't he sent the car the way he had every other day this week? Why was he an hour early, and how had he gotten into the building without her buzzing him up? He'd probably smiled that woman-melting smile and conned some unsuspecting female into letting him in.

She couldn't face him yet. She looked awful, with her eyes all swollen and puffy from a crying jag last night, and her hair a tangled mess. But what did it matter? They were finished anyway, and hiding never solved anything. She yanked open the door and gaped. Her sister stood outside with an overnight bag in her hand.

"Brenna. What are you doing here and how did you get in?"

"Surprise. Someone downstairs thought I was you. Story of my life." Her sister barged into the apartment. "You look like hell this afternoon, but you looked gorgeous in my dress last night. I nearly fell out of bed when I saw a clip of you and Conrad Carr on that late night entertainment show you love so much. I can't believe my twin is dating a movie star and I'm the last to know. What's up with that?"

"Come in," Jenna said sarcastically. She needed a dose of Brenna's take-no-prisoners attitude in the worst kind of way.

Her sister dropped her bag and plopped down on the sofa. "Don't mind if I do. So what's going on, and why do you keep choosing losers who are hung up on someone else?"

The jab slid quickly and painfully between her ribs. Besides Conrad, Brenna was the only one who knew the whole embarrassing truth about Devin. How had she guessed that Jenna was repeating her mistake? "Conrad's not a loser."

Brenna dragged a pile of newspapers from her tote bag and spread them across the coffee table. "Have you seen the papers this morning? I bought a pile of them at the airport. The good news is your gorgeous face is all over them. The bad news is they're all saying Conrad Carr has found a body double for his dead wife. Didn't Devin, the jerk, teach you anything? Guys are so damn shallow. They can't see beyond the wrapper."

Jenna winced at the mention of her ex-fiancé, but it was a wince of embarrassment, not pain. It surprised her to discover that thinking about Devin didn't hurt at all. She was over him. "Devin Tew is history."

"Good. Now look, I know Conrad is a gorgeous piece of man and you've had a crush on him forever, but c'mon, Jen, where's this going?"

Nowhere, Jenna silently admitted. *Absolutely nowhere.* "He needed a friend and a drama coach."

A manicured nail tapped the top page of the paper.

"In these pictures you're not looking at him like he's your friend or your student. You're looking at him like you could eat him up and come back for seconds."

The camera had captured that special smile Conrad had bestowed upon her right before they'd entered the theater, and her besotted reaction to it. Brenna was right. At that moment Jenna would have done anything for him, but that was before she'd realized that he was miserable *with her.* Until then she'd held on to some far-fetched dream that he would discover he couldn't bear to leave her behind.

She'd always told her students you can't do more than your best. Well, she'd tried her best to win his heart, and failed. Wasn't it time to bring the curtain down and close the show? The idea made her heart ache. When she considered life without Conrad, Jenna started to shake. She sank down on the sofa beside her sister and put her head in her hands.

"Oh God, Bren, I've done it again. I've fallen for a man who loves another woman."

And the story came tumbling out. From the exhilaration of their first nondate, to the collapse of Conrad's emotional walls, the carriage ride and falling head over heels in love with the man behind a movie star's face. She skipped the part about him calling her Tara, because if she revealed it, Brenna would tear him apart. Since their playground days her sister had been more than willing to defend any slight—real or imagined. Jenna, on the other hand, tended to avoid conflict.

Brenna shoved the tissue box into Jenna's lap. "Okay, I'm going to be big-sister honest with you now."

Jenna straightened and dread curdled in her stomach.

Brenna was only older by ten minutes. When she pulled out the big-sister jargon, whatever followed would be about as much fun as a bikini wax.

"I'm furious with you for letting Devin drive you away from teaching. You loved that job and those kids. If you hook up with a movie star, you're kissing your dream job goodbye. Can you live with that? Because you shouldn't have to give up something that makes you happy, Jen."

"My dream now is to become a soap actress."

Brenna snorted. "Oh *puhlease*. You can lie to our parents if you want, but please don't lie to me or to yourself."

"What makes you think I'm lying?"

"Because I read your e-mails. Not just the stuff you wrote, but the stuff you didn't write. You used to gush for hours about your students. The same way you did about Conrad's progress a few minutes ago. You haven't gushed about anything else since leaving home."

"I could love daytime drama if I found the right part," she retorted defensively, despite her own growing reservations.

Brenna looked ready to explode. "Do you have any idea how hard it is to be your sister? I had every teacher in school tell me I wasn't as good a student as you. I've spent years trying to outshine you, Jen. I've bounced from career to career, trying to be the best at something, *anything,* and what do I have to show for it? Nothing. A few plaques on the wall. A damn pageant sash I can't wear anywhere, and an empty bed. No boyfriends, no children and no life outside of my freaking job, which I *do not love.*"

Slack jawed, Jenna stared. Until now she'd viewed her sister's success with envy. Brenna seemed to have it all, but apparently appearances were deceiving. "But you were always the center of attention, and you're doing great at your job."

"C'mon Jen. Don't be as dumb as me. Until this year you were the together twin, the one who knew she wanted to be a teacher since we were twelve years old. Don't screw that up now, all because of a well-hung guy."

A shocked laugh burst from Jenna's chest. "I never said Conrad was well-hung."

Brenna sighed. "Right. Whatever. Is he?"

Jenna grinned. "Extremely."

"When do you see lover-boy again?"

Jenna darted a panicked glance at the clock and bolted to her feet. Too late to call and cancel now. "He sends his car service to pick me up every day. It should be here any minute and I'm a wreck."

"So go take a bath and pull yourself together. A ten-minute ice pack wouldn't hurt your eyes."

"I don't have time."

"Are you or are you not worth waiting for? Take your time. Big sis will handle everything."

CHAPTER NINE

"THANKS, SID. I'm sure she'll accept. I'll call you back with confirmation as soon as I talk to her." Conrad disconnected.

The knock sounded right on time. His pulse quickened the way it did every time Jenna arrived. He sprang to his feet, eager to share his good news.

He opened his door and the words halted on his lips as he took in the downward curve of Jenna's lips and the hard glint in her brown eyes as she looked him up and down. Odd. Conrad examined her more closely. The woman on his doorstep looked like Jenna. She had the same luxurious curls, but she wore a stylish black pantsuit, instead of the colorful informal clothing Jenna preferred, and her features and figure lacked the sexy softness of Jenna's. Not Jenna.

"You must be Brenna."

One dark brow arched. She nodded and offered her hand. "And you're more than just a pretty face, Conrad Carr."

He briefly shook her hand and searched the hall behind her. No Jenna. He released her, but not without first noting that the spark of attraction that arched between him and Jenna was missing. "Where's your sister?"

"I imagine she'll show up soon."

What did that mean? Had she ducked into the coffee place across the street for a cup of her favorite amaretto blend? A few days ago she'd confessed that she bought a cup each evening when she left his place to drink on her way to The Hotel. "Would you like to come in?"

"Don't mind if I do." She stalked past him. Even her walk was different. Jenna's enthusiasm carried her from place to place with a spring in her step. This woman moved like the U.S. Coast Guard cutter *Polar Star*, slicing the most direct path through the ice. Conrad had visited the ice-breaking ship to research one of his roles.

Glancing left and right, she crossed the room and then turned on him. "What do you want from my sister?"

"Her friendship, her coaching."

"No, dummy. Long term."

Taken aback, he tried to mask his surprise at her bluntness. "Are you asking what my intentions are?"

"Yes, I am."

"Isn't that a father's job?"

She whipped out her cell phone. "Want me to call him? He may be a lawyer now, but we're mountain folk and we take care of our own. He'd probably castrate you for sleeping with his precious baby girl without the blessing of a preacher. So, I'll ask again, what do you want from Jenna?"

The mere thought of marriage slammed the doors around Conrad's heart. He didn't know what to make of this woman or how to answer her questions. He felt as if he'd shown up on set after learning the wrong day's lines.

"It's not a trick question. Is she a stand-in for your wife like the papers said, or not?"

"Of course not. Jenna is…Jenna." He needed a script.

"And what do you have to offer her?"

Conrad had no experience with family interviews. Tara's parents had been divorced and disinterested. "If she'll move to California with me I'll help her get her acting career off the ground."

"Personally, not careerwise. I mean, jeez, you're secondhand goods, Carr. Besides the obvious—" she indicated his body with a flip of the wrist "—why should she settle for you?"

Dumbfounded, Conrad blinked. "You're about as subtle as a tank."

"Jenna is the subtle one. She can milk something out of you and you won't even feel the squeeze. Her students loved that about her. I'm a steamroller. Why waste time when I can just get to the point? Which you are dodging, by the way."

No wonder Jenna felt invisible. Her sister was pushy as hell. She advanced on him like a circling shark. He held his ground and braced himself for the next bite.

"Since you seem to be at a loss for words, let me recap. In return for sleeping with you, you're going to reward Jenna with an acting job. A revival of the casting couch, isn't it?"

He ground his teeth in frustration. "There are no strings attached to my assistance. It was the deal Jenna and I forged originally. And for your information, my agent has already arranged for her to have a bigger and better part than anything Jenna has hoped for thus far."

His words clearly did not impress Brenna Graham. She looked disgusted and…sad? "One, I don't think she'll move to California with you, and two, you're completely missing the point. How are you going to make Jenna believe she's the most important person in your life—even more important than your dead wife? Because she deserves that and if you can't give it to her then you need to let her go."

Whoa. "You have the wrong idea about Jenna and me."

Someone hammered on his door. Conrad had never been more grateful for an interruption.

"For a guy who's supposed to be smart, you're as dumb as a rock. You're breaking her heart, you moron."

A part of him recoiled from the possibility of an emotional entanglement and the consequences. For him to break Jenna's heart there would have to be more than friendship involved. That hadn't been part of their deal.

He yanked opened the door and relief poured through him. "Jenna. I'm glad you made it."

Her worried gaze darted from him to Brenna and back again. She stepped past him and glared at her sister. "You stole my ride."

Brenna shrugged, showing no trace of shame. "Yes, I did. I needed to talk to lover-boy, and since I didn't know where he lived the best thing to do was pretend to be you. It didn't get tricky until I tried to get the apartment number out of the guy downstairs."

Conrad studied the two women, intrigued by the similarities, but even more so by the differences. How could anyone confuse them? Hadn't that been Jenna's reason for wanting fame?

Jenna's face darkened, but whether in embarrassment or anger, Conrad couldn't tell. As hard as he had tried, he'd never been able to agitate her, but her sister had done an admirable job.

"Brenna, as much as I would love to have your support right now, I'd rather you take a hike," she said.

"Gotcha. Perhaps Mr. Carr will be kind enough to volunteer his driver to give me a limo tour of Manhattan."

Eager to get rid of her and find out what exactly was going on, Conrad picked up the phone and made the arrangements. "Done. Kyle is waiting downstairs."

Conrad's knotted muscles didn't unkink until the door closed behind Brenna, and then he turned back to Jenna and tension fused his vertebrae all over again.

JENNA DIDN'T KNOW WHETHER to laugh, cry or just hang her head in shame.

"Was that some kind of test to see if I could name the twin?" Conrad asked with a half amused, half confused smile.

"No. I got out of the shower and looked out the window in time to see her getting into the car. So…did she fool you?"

"No. You don't look anything alike."

She couldn't deny the pleasurable punch his statement delivered. Did that mean he could see beyond the superficial coloring she shared with Tara? "Our DNA says differently."

"Your eyes and mouth are different, and you're…" he shrugged "…softer."

A smile danced across her lips. *He was paying attention. That had to mean something, didn't it?*

Don't get your hopes up.

Even though she was certain she didn't want to hear the answer, she had to ask, "What did Brenna say?"

"She seems to think you won't be interested in

moving to California with me to take the part Sid has landed for you in my next film."

"Your next film?" Jenna parroted in amazement. "You pulled strings. For me?"

"A few. The actress who replaced Tara is pregnant with triplets and on bed rest for the next five months. She's backed out. Sid suggested you for the part. You'll have to do a screen test, but it's a formality. The part is yours if you want it. I know it's not daytime drama, but after this role you should be able to work wherever you want, and there are soap studios nearby in Studio City and Burbank."

He crossed the room and took her hands in his. "I'm leaving in three days and I want you to come with me, Jenna."

Her heart raced like a hummingbird's. The man and the career she thought she wanted were hers for the taking, but glamour, fame and outshining her sister had lost their appeal. What she wanted was love.

"What about my apartment? My job?"

"You won't need either. You can live with me."

The bottom fell out of her stomach. "In Tara's house?"

"Bel Air is convenient to the studios."

She pulled her hands free and paced to the window. "You want me to fill Tara's role in the movie, move into her house and sleep in her bed."

His jaw flexed and a cautious light entered his eyes. "We can get new furniture or move to a different room. The house is huge."

Brenna was right. Men were clueless. "You haven't even taken off her ring."

He glanced down at the wedding band, his expression clearly saying, *What does that have to do with anything?* And then his shoulders stiffened and he met her gaze with a touch of panic in his eyes.

Her chat with her sister had cleared up quite a few misconceptions, including the reasons behind Jenna's misguided quest for fame. Even if she were willing to compete with the ghost of Tara Dean, Jenna no longer wanted to be an actress. She missed her students and the excitement of pulling an amateur stage production together. She missed seeing that light click on as young actors developed poise and skills that would carry them long after they stepped off the stage. She was born to be a teacher, but a high school drama teacher would never be glamorous enough for a movie star.

But that didn't look like love in Conrad's eyes, and surely, no man would be crass enough to propose with another woman's ring still on his finger. Maybe she was putting the cart before the horse. "Let me get this straight. You're asking me to move in with you as what?"

He shifted on his feet. "A friend."

She waited in vain for more. "A friend. With benefits."

His brows lowered. "What does that mean?"

"Friends with benefits. That's what my students called it when friends have sex together, but there are no strings, no romantic ties. No love."

"Is it a bad thing to care for the person in your bed?"

Only if one cares more than the other. If it were possible for a heart to break in two, then Jenna's just had. "I'm sorry, but I can't accept your offer and I can't fill Tara's shoes."

She made her way to the door and opened it, but paused on the threshold. "Have a great life, Conrad. I wish you the best. But I can't be your friend anymore."

CHAPTER TEN

GONE. AND SHE WASN'T coming back.

The good news was that Jenna wasn't using him to further her career. But something about the look in her eyes as she'd said goodbye had gnawed a crater of emptiness in Conrad's chest that hadn't healed in the two days since she'd left. Where was the sense of relief he'd expected? He'd dodged an emotional bullet. He wouldn't have to deal with losing someone he cared for again.

He paced his apartment, circling the glass coffee table covered in Jenna's things. The red fruit bowl, her lavender raincoat, a lime-green hair clip, her jar of multicolored jelly beans. As soon as he returned them he'd have his life back. Exactly what he wanted. But the future yawned like a big, black hole. Without Jenna's belongings there wasn't any color in his apartment. Or in his life.

She'd made him feel healthy and whole again. In fact, she'd made him stronger both as a man and as an actor, and she'd given him a reason to look forward to each new day. She'd seen him at his worst and loved him anyway. His heart slammed against his ribs and his muscles locked with shock.

She loved him. That was the look he'd seen in her

eyes when she'd said goodbye. And he'd hurt her. Again. The ache in his chest consumed him. The idea of caring too deeply scared him spitless, but losing her, never seeing her again, terrified him more.

And then it hit him. He'd fallen in love with Jenna Graham.

He'd been so busy guarding his heart that he hadn't realized Jenna had stolen it that first night, when she'd reached out to the man hiding behind the mask and turned a miserable evening into a memorable one he would always treasure. He couldn't name another person who saw him so completely or read him so accurately.

Soul mate. So that's what it meant.

His gaze dropped to the wedding band on his finger. Brenna was right. He *was* a moron. He'd tried to wedge Jenna into his old life, when what he should have been doing was forging a new life with her.

Could he convince her they belonged together? He wanted her by his side permanently, and standing here wasn't going to accomplish that goal.

Thirty minutes later he sat in the limo, stuck in a traffic jam three blocks from Jenna's apartment and around the corner from the last fan ambush. The car hadn't moved in ten minutes. Impatience crawled through him. He checked his watch. If she had to work today she'd be leaving her apartment in an hour. "I'm getting out."

"Sir?" his driver asked.

"I'll walk the rest of the way." He shoved open the car door and closed it on Kyle's protests. Within minutes Conrad had gathered a following of fans. His heart pumped and his palms dampened—not because of the crowd peppering him with questions about where was he going and what was he doing in Brooklyn, but because he had to talk to Jenna. He stopped on the stoop of her building and faced his fans, knowing whatever he said today would be in tomorrow's tabloids.

"I'll level with you, but in return I need you to give me some space. I'm going to ask the woman I love to give the moron who let her down a second chance." He juggled his armload of Jenna's things and hit the call button with his elbow.

"Yes?"

Elation and relief spread through him at the sound of her voice. He hadn't missed her, but was he too late for them? "Jenna, let me in or I'm going to start giving away your jelly beans."

Ten seconds of silence ticked past, and with each one the knot of dread in his gut tightened. He hated to push the button again and, in front of an audience, beg her to let him come up, but he would if he had to. The entry signal was the sweetest sound he'd ever heard. Air whooshed from his lungs. One of the fans reached past him and opened the gate. "Good luck, Conrad."

"Thanks." The gate clanged behind him. Conrad climbed the stairs. Jenna waited by her open door. The hurt in her eyes hit him like a fist in the gut, and then he noticed the pallor of her face and the shadows under her eyes—shadows similar to the ones he wore.

"I brought your stuff." He winced at the lameness of the excuse. She gestured for him to enter. He took two steps forward and stopped. Piles of boxes lined one wall. Adrenaline surged through his veins. "You're packing. Did you change your mind?"

She folded her arms over her chest, stretching her peach-colored sweater over her breasts. "About going with you? No. I'm going home. Just drop that stuff anywhere."

"What happened to your dream of becoming a soap star?"

She shrugged. "I woke up."

He wanted to grab her and hold her, but first he had to tell her how important she was to him, how much he needed her in his life. Yet the words tangled in his head the way they always did when he was uptight, and he couldn't straighten them out. Damn learning disability. That's why he preferred to read somebody else's words. Scripts made sense.

He set her stuff on the sofa and shoved his hands in his pockets. He opened his mouth and closed it again when words failed him.

"So…thanks for bringing my things. If there's nothing else, then I need to get back to my packing."

Conrad couldn't move. He needed powerful words, but emotions choked him. He couldn't lose Jenna.

"Is something wrong?" she asked.

He exhaled slowly. "Nothing that can't be fixed by you coming to California with me. I need you, Jenna. Make a life with me."

She backed away. "I can't be what you want me to be."

"The newspapers are wrong. I'm not looking for a replacement for Tara. I'm looking for someone who knows I hate openings and award shows and doesn't mind if we skip a few. I need someone who wants me to do movies I'll enjoy and not just the ones that will please the critics." He closed the distance between them. "I need a life partner who'll stand beside me, not because I'm a symbol of her success, but because she loves me."

Jenna ducked her chin and closed her eyes, wishing this moment would end. Why was Conrad doing this? Couldn't he spare her this one humiliation? "I never said I loved you."

He lifted her chin. A tender smile curved his lips and softened his eyes. "But you do."

She jerked her chin out of his grasp. "No, I don't."

Instead of looking hurt by her lie, he grinned. "You're a decent actress, sweetheart, but you're a lousy liar."

Her breath hitched. "I'm not cut out to be an actress. I'm going home because I love teaching and I never should have quit."

His hands curved over her shoulders. "I want you to do whatever makes you happy. If that means teaching, then we'll buy a house in California, New York or even North Carolina—wherever you can find a job. As long as there's an airport so I can get to work and back home to you again, we'll make it work, Jenna."

He'd said all the right things except the one she needed to hear the most. "You had a perfect marriage. I could never measure up."

"You're wrong. I did love Tara, but my marriage wasn't the fairy tale Sid and my publicist made it out to be. Tara and I didn't have children because she needed to be the center of attention. She didn't want to take time out of the spotlight or risk ruining her figure. But when I make a promise I stand by it, and I convinced myself that if we didn't have kids then I'd never have to face the agony of losing one."

He lowered his hands and clenched his fists by his side. The anguish in his eyes made Jenna's throat hurt.

"Jenna, I've told you things about my past, about my family, that I've never told anyone. Not Sid. Not even Tara. But I didn't tell you all of it." His chest expanded on a shaky breath. "When my mother and brother died, I had no one but my father left. I loved him, but he was so lost in his grief that he couldn't love me back. He drowned himself in booze to numb the pain.

"After Tara's death I did the same thing. Then one day I woke up lying facedown in a pool of vomit on my bathroom floor. I realized that I'd become my father. A drunk. I disgusted myself. I poured out all the liquor in the house and vowed I'd never drink again and never love anyone again."

Her heart ached for him. A tear burned a trail down her cheek and a lump rose in her throat. She pressed a hand to her lips to hide their trembling.

One corner of his mouth tilted upward. "And then you came along. You found me at rock bottom, but instead of leaving me there, you hoisted me up, and I fought you every step of the way. I tried every dirty trick I could to run you off, but you wouldn't let me. *You* believed in me when I'd quit believing in myself. Because of you, I'm a better man than I was before." He lifted a hand to stroke a tear from her cheek. "I need you, Jenna."

He *needed* her. But he didn't love her. It wasn't enough.

"What would it take to convince you to change your mind? I'm a wealthy man. You name it and it's yours."

She covered his hand with hers and nuzzled her face into his palm. Her heart missed a beat. She pulled his hand away and examined his bare fingers. He'd removed his wedding ring. "I don't want your money or your mansion or a part in your movie. All I want is a man who loves me."

He inhaled sharply. "I do love you, Jenna."

His words stole her breath. She searched his eyes and her heart swelled, but she was afraid to trust what she saw. "How can I be sure that you're seeing me instead of her? And how do I know this isn't gratitude or a rebound romance?"

"This has nothing to do with looks. It's the way you make me feel that I can't let go. And you'll know that I love you the same way I know you're not still in love with what's-his-name, your ex-fiancé. You can see it in my eyes and feel it in my touch when we make love. You're the only woman in my life, Jenna, and the only woman in my heart."

He carried her hand to his lips and kissed her knuckles and then dropped to one knee. "Marry me, Jenna Graham. Build a life with me, and I promise I'll prove my love every day."

Emotion welled inside her, spilling over in hot tears. Conrad's expressive eyes had always been her favorite feature and right now those beautiful hazel eyes promised everything she'd always dreamed of, but never believed she'd find.

"I love you, Conrad, and nothing would make me happier than building a life with you."

Dear Reader,

Have you ever met people so into their own lifestyles and ideals that they think everyone else should share them?

If not, you're about to. Ex-lovers Lindsay Kenyon and Gavin Harvey, the heroine and hero of my story, both think they've found the key to happiness in the way they live their lives—on separate coasts. It takes about a hundred pages for them to figure out the true key to happiness is each other.

I love movies and have a few special favourite "oldies" from the so-called golden age of cinema. Stars like Cary Grant and Katharine Hepburn, Jimmy Stewart, Barbara Stanwyck. Is it me or don't they make them like that anymore? Gavin and Lindsay definitely reminded me of a leading man and lady from that age, when dialogue was everything and who'd ever heard of special effects?

I hope you enjoy their story!

Isabel Sharpe
www.IsabelSharpe.com

IT HAPPENED ONE NIGHT
Isabel Sharpe

To fellow author Shannon Hollis, who opened
my eyes to the surprisingly wonderful world of Chickens.

CHAPTER ONE

THIS WAS WHY SHE'D LEFT the biz.

Lindsay stepped out of the taxi, which had been inching tediously closer to the door of The Hotel, where the Reel New York Film Festival awards ceremony was due to start in half an hour. Her plane from Burlington, Vermont, had been delayed, and she'd had to change into her fancy gear in the back of the cab on the way from LaGuardia Airport. Either that or make her entrance, two years after she'd left L.A., in plain black cotton pants that probably cost less than most attendees' dental floss.

She'd have left the cab earlier on and walked, to get here faster, but who wanted to shove through the crowd of onlookers jostling for closer views, peering down the length of red carpet for the arrival of their latest favorite star?

Ex-Hollywood screenwriter Lindsay Kenyon was going to disappoint them. Vastly.

She paid the driver and stepped out into the surprisingly soft early-April air, thinking about the possible snow predicted for her little town in Vermont, so she wouldn't have to think about the rows of curious and disappointed faces turned toward her. They hadn't a clue who she was. Screenwriters weren't household names like actors, and Lindsay wasn't even here for a nomination for her own work, but to accept the Best Supporting Actress statue on behalf of her friend Tara Cooper, off finishing a shoot in Australia. If Tara won. Which Lindsay was almost selfish enough to hope she didn't. Emerging from this cab with several hundred eyes upon her was bad enough. The thought of standing on stage being skewered by quadruple that many made her shudder.

Two years earlier, she would have craved that attention. Or at least been more practiced handling it. Not anymore.

She walked the length of the red carpet, smile frozen on her face, attempting grace on high heels she was no longer used to, and discreetly hiking up a hem dangerously close to the pavement. If she tripped, she was turning around and going back to Vermont immediately. Already the whispers were reaching her; *Who's that? I have no idea.* A few cameras flashed, obviously from optimists who thought if Lindsay became famous someday, they'd have her photograph from way back when and could sell it on e-Bay.

She reached the door, nodded to the black-uniformed man opening it, and slipped into the chic lobby, grateful to be safely inside.

Except once she checked in, dumped her bag with the concierge and rode the escalator up to the lobby outside the hotel's ballroom, nothing felt safe about the inside. Bodies everywhere, decked out in extreme splendor of sometimes questionable taste, seeing and being seen, babbling, shrieking, booming, darting around like hummingbirds, milling like ants, swarming like bees. Flocking like chickens? Maybe that was more like it.

Either way, she could happily say she didn't miss the razzle-dazzle stressfest a bit. Not one bit.

She stood by the top of the escalator, taking in the scene, breathing deeply, thinking of her day yesterday, spent sitting dreamily on her enclosed back porch with the view of green hills and distant mountains, sun streaming through the windows, laptop in her lap, utterly contented even though no words seemed to be coming on chapter four of her brilliant debut novel. In fact, no words had been coming for a week or two now. And she wasn't sure she liked any of the ones that had come so far….

A body nudged—no, shoved her out of the way. An icy glare was directed at Lindsay from perfectly made-up eyes, "Excuse me" was hissed through chemically whitened teeth.

Lindsay recognized the woman, who was obviously pretending not to recognize her. Marlie. A bit-part actress with enormous…other parts, who had perfected at least one role: The Hanger-On. Strange how the least successful sometimes carried around the largest prima donna attitude. She'd been something of a last straw in Lindsay's decision to leave L.A., the business and Gavin. It wasn't that he'd done anything with Marlie; Lindsay trusted him completely. It was that he never told Marlie to go away, either. Not her and not anyone else who wanted his time and energy and talent. In the end there was not enough of him left for their relationship.

Feeling even more off balance and now slightly ill, Lindsay moved away from the escalator, trying not to skulk along the wall, but wishing she could. Who to talk to? Where to break in and how? Or should she even bother? She felt utterly disconnected from the crowd. People here and there were familiar, but distantly, as if she was observing her past in a crystal ball.

She didn't belong here anymore. Besides cab drivers and airline employees, the last person she'd had a conversation with had been her neighbor, Frank Weller, whom she'd asked to keep an eye on her pet chickens, Frieda and Freia. Frank thought a succinct phrase every minute or two was plenty of chatter. Right now she agreed with him.

A tall tuxedoed man with short dark hair walked past, face averted. Even though she knew it wasn't Gavin, she couldn't help the adrenaline rush. He'd be here, of course, up for Best Screenplay for his movie *Doing What Comes Naturally*. She'd known that when she'd agreed to come on behalf of Tara. Some part of her must be a sicko masochist to court a reunion, even a brief one, since she was on her way back to Vermont in the morning. Even a glance or two across a crowded room... But then, you didn't rip someone out of your life after nine years as friends, five of those years as lovers, without fallout. It had been a full year in Vermont before she'd stopped expecting him to show up at her door, having recognized the error of his continuing L.A.-worship, swearing he couldn't live without her, begging to let him move in and start a new life her way....

"Lindsay?"

She jumped, then steeled herself, turned, and felt her hasty airport burger dinner starting to work backward. Besides Hanger-On Marlie, Alexandra DuBois, née

Alex Woods, was another blond, big-mouthed, two-faced, reason Lindsay had chucked Hollywood and moved away.

"Alex!" She forced the requisite amount of enthusiasm into her voice and performed the expected air-kiss, thinking she preferred eau de cow patty to the choking scent enveloping Alexandra, and the honest suspicious treatment of outsiders by Vermont natives to all this fake affection.

"I can't believe you're here! I thought Maine had swallowed you alive." She smiled, displaying another in a roomful of frighteningly white smiles, which made Lindsay wish she'd thought to paint her own teeth a horrifying yellow. Maybe black her incisors out entirely.

"Vermont. I moved to Vermont."

"Oh?" She spoke with a careful combination of scorn and disinterest, while fussing with her droopy, red satin sleeve. Obviously she'd mixed up the state names up on purpose. What a charmer. "Well anyway, I knew I recognized that dress."

"Yes, I wore it to the Oscars two years ago." Lindsay admitted it, head up, proudly. She'd risen above such childish score-keeping and what a damn relief that was.

"Oh yes." Alex eyed Lindsay's royal-blue silk dubiously. "I thought I'd seen it somewhere else. Or on someone else. So Gavin's here. Of course you know that."

Of course she did. What's more, she managed to keep her expression pleasant while her throat tightened traitorously. Darn it, she was over him, she was over the whole thing. She could go a week at a time now without thinking of him…more than a few times a day. "Yes, I look forward to seeing him."

Alex's heavily shadowed blue eyes, which had been traveling the room, searching for someone more interesting, snapped back and held Lindsay's, making her fight not to step away. "He's going to win tonight. I can feel it."

"Oh?" Her throat tightened further. Winning was all Gavin wanted. Awards, contracts, nominations, options, people's good will and approval... And if he won the award, he'd win for the one script he'd written without her, though she'd helped him brainstorm the concept at the beginning. But her heart hadn't been in it somehow, another more urgent signpost along her pathway toward realizing they had to leave L.A. or be destroyed. Only he hadn't been able to see that.

"No chance of the dynamic duo staging a reunion?" Alex's eyes were still fixed on Lindsay in that peculiar stagnant way of people with very little brain.

"None." She cleared her throat and gestured to the thinning crowd. "Well. Looks like everyone's going in. Great to see you, Alex."

"Same here." Alex laid a perfectly red-manicured set of chilly fingers on Lindsay's arm. "If I see Gavin, I'll tell him you're looking for him."

She swished away in a shimmer of satin, to spread the news that Lindsay was back and pining for Gavin, or that Lindsay was back and determined to ruin Gavin, or that Lindsay was back and had turned lesbian over Gavin, leaving Lindsay with *I'm not looking for him* still stuck between her lips.

Fine. Lindsay had changed. Become deeper and more content, endlessly more content. Did she expect everyone else to have changed also? Depth and contentment would dry up and blow away in the harsh sunlight of the L.A. film scene.

She filed into the gently sloped auditorium, to find buzzing excitement palpable in the large cream-and-burgundy room. Huge pots of flowers adorned the stage, and projected replicas of the Reel NY award statues glistened tantalizingly on enormous twin screens. TV cameras waited on either side, and doubtless more were positioned expectantly in the wings and farther back in the room.

An usher peered at her ticket and swept off to show her to her place. Lindsay sank into the burgundy plush seat thankfully. Stage one complete. Now all she had to do was sit here, read the speech Tara had written if Tara won, and go back to her room. Tomorrow she'd be on a plane home to her wonderful, peaceful, nonshallow, non-appearance-worshiping life in Vermont, and her first novel, and that would be that.

Except she became aware of a persistent disturbance in the bodies around her, and some pretty pointed whispering, which caused her to glance to her left, where she recognized Bill Angleterre and Cheri Draxmer, who were good screenwriting friends of Gavin and hers. She smiled and waved and noticed them glancing to their left, so she glanced farther…and *bang* into the dark eyes of Gavin Harvey, who she'd once been sure was the love of her life.

She barely had time to register the thrill shooting through her chest and traveling to all extremities, before the lights lowered, the music blared, spotlights circled the crowd. All signals to turn her attention to the stage.

Only her attention wasn't turning. And neither was his. And instead of the sweet rush of fondness she'd prepared herself for, she experienced a wild stampede of longing and anger and warmth and pain, as if she'd walked away from him yesterday instead of a year and a half ago.

Okay. Breathe. Probably natural, given that they'd been together for so long. Four years of friendship and five as a couple, most of those years wonderful. Dynamic. Exciting. Passionate. They lit fires in each other unlike anyone she'd ever...

Ahem.

She gave him a small finger-wave and a half smile, and wrenched her eyes to the stage, where the mayor of New York City was starting the ceremony. Oh, Lord. She'd barely be able to concentrate hard enough to recognize Tara's name if she won.

Half an hour later, however, she had no trouble recognizing Gavin's. Nor could she contain the proud tears springing to her eyes as he strode toward the podium, stooping here and there to accept quick congratulatory handshakes or hugs from friends seated in the audience, clearly reveling in the moment.

The writing had been nearly everything to her. But this—this type of Big Public Success—had been nearly everything to Gavin. And that drive, nurtured in the poisoned atmosphere of Hollywood, had eventually torn them apart.

He mounted the stairs with easy grace to continued applause. Everyone loved Gavin. What was not to love? Handsome, dynamic, intelligent...

And obsessed with getting to the top, to the point where he was willing to sacrifice the woman he loved, sitting now in the audience drinking in the sight of him, eyes and

heart brimming in equal measure. She was so happy for
him. So proud. So…determined not to go there again.

He reached the podium, grinning, breathless, triumphant, and proceeded to give a quick speech of thanks
and acknowledgment that had the audience laughing
and sighing right there with him. She kept her eyes
glued on the big-screen image of his face, projected for
the room to see. He looked tired, and thin. Was he
eating? She used to have to remind him to when they
were working full tilt on a script…

Not her problem anymore, was it.

"…and finally." His voice thickened. He ran his
index finger along his nose. "I'd like to thank my longtime partner and best friend, without whose help and encouragement this script would have remained under my
mattress for the rest of time. Lindsay Kenyon."

Lindsay sucked in a breath that nearly choked her.
Damn it. Damn it. She clapped so hard her palms
burned, following his exit stage right through tears that
made him look as if he were swimming. If she cried any
more and Tara won, she'd look like a bag lady accepting the award. Already she had on about a quarter of the
makeup of any other woman in the room.

Somehow she made it through an endless, dull, claus-
trophobic eternity until Best Supporting Actress was
called, the nominations read by Nicole Kidman in her
musical Australian accent.

"And the winner is…Tara Cooper for *Take Me to
the River.*"

Lindsay struggled up to the stage—not tripping again,
thank God—and read the sappy speech Tara had given
her. The lights burned into her eyes; the crowd was a

restless mass of heat and movement. She wished so fervently for her peaceful, white wooden farmhouse in the middle of hilly farmland and forests and grazing pastures, she could almost sense its cool air and greenery.

"Lastly, she thanks her parents, who made everything wonderful in her life possible." The crowd thundered; Lindsay smiled, lofted the statue briefly, took off stage right, posed for an endless round of backstage photographs no one would want to see without Tara in them, and headed for the exit, bursting with relief.

Done. Her trip here was done; she'd accomplished what she came for. Any possible doubts she'd had about her new life compared to this nuthouse were gone now. She'd even seen Gavin and survived, though she still felt a little bruised. But alive, by God yes, and ready to get the hell out of this mini-reproduction of Tinseltown and head back to reality, to the peace she'd come to—

"Lindsay. Hello." The deep voice as familiar as her own came from over her left shoulder and brought with it an unwelcome certainty.

Anything resembling peace was going to have to wait until she got back to Vermont.

GAVIN COULDN'T STOP grinning. Damn, what a night. The trophy—hell, he loved the trophy; he'd been living for a chance to hold this trophy. But more, Lindsay was back. Back where she belonged. Looking pale and thin and depressed—what the hell had she done to herself in that cow pasture she'd moved to?—but she was back. He knew she couldn't stay away.

Though he had to admit it was a year before he'd stopped expecting her at his door every day, her tears, her inevitable admission that she'd made a crazy mistake, that he and their partnership were in her soul and how did she think she could ever leave part of her soul behind?

Maybe that confession would come tonight, as soon as her notoriously stubborn pride allowed it. Why else would she be here? Not from a burning desire to stand on stage and show off someone else's award, not if he knew her, which he did, inside out.

She was back. And if she needed prodding to admit she was back to stay, then he was her guy.

"It's great to see you." He wanted to grab her in a huge bear hug, but people were watching, and he was here with Kaytee this week, so he embraced Lindsay casually, shocked at the bird-bone feel of her.

"You too, Gavin." She glanced away, blushing, which, thank God, put some natural color in her face, then looked back up at him with her dark, deep eyes, making his heart pound as if it had stopped for the last year and a half. In spite of her weight loss and general pallor, she was still beautiful. An Audrey Hepburn-like delicacy that belied her stubborn determination and tough skin.

Figuratively tough. He knew firsthand that her skin was anything but.

"How long are you in town?" He waved over her shoulder at someone he should know, uncharacteristically not caring that he didn't. He wanted to see as much of Lindsay as possible this week while she was here. To make sure she knew why she'd come back tonight, even if she hadn't figured it out yet. And during that time, he wanted her to look over the pitch he'd worked out for the script they'd talked endlessly about writing together after he convinced her it was the way to go—the rewrite of the Hepburn, Grant, Stewart oldie *The Philadelphia Story*. He had a meeting in L.A. at the end of next week to pitch it to John Saxman at Universal Pictures. If it went well—finally, the big time.

But the pitch still needed…something. And when Lindsay had shown up today, it hit him like a bolt of lightning that what it needed was her.

"I'm leaving first thing in the morning."

He blinked. "For where?"

She gave a small coy smile. "Back home."

To California. He couldn't stop his grin. She'd had enough farmers and cows and country living. He'd known she couldn't survive it long. "You need a place to stay?"

She looked genuinely baffled. "Why would I need that?"

"You said you were coming—" He stopped, then let his breath out in a sigh. Home. Not L.A.

"Home is Vermont now, Gavin." Her voice was gentle, like that of a parent to her child, not the merciless teasing of the Lindsay he knew. Maybe she was depressed? Their battles and sharp banter were legendary, and he missed them like crazy.

"Hey, you two, back together again?"

"No." They spoke the word together and turned their backs on Izzy Thornton, a Joan Rivers wannabe who'd reported too much of their breakup in daily rags.

"Oh? Where's Kaytee?" She asked Gavin, but immediately slid her rodent eyes to Lindsay, looking for a reaction.

Bless Lindsay, she gave none.

He took Lindsay's elbow and steered her away from Izzy, then dodged another reporter, a few well-wishers he really should have spoken to, another reporter, and finally ducked through a doorway into a cable-and-duct-filled hall that must be part of the tech area and led who knew where. "So when are you leaving?"

"I'm heading back first thing. Who is Kaytee?"

"A…friend."

Her sharp glance told him he might as well have skipped the pretense. "How nice for you. Where are we?"

"No idea." He put his hands on his hips. "Actually, you're not leaving tomorrow."

"No?" She turned to him, eyebrow arched, the first show of her familiar spirit. "What am I going to be doing?"

"Spending time with me."

"How thoughtful of you to let me know."

"You're welcome."

"I didn't say thank-you." Her eyes narrowed. "What would your…*friend* think?"

"She doesn't usually bother."

"Bother getting jealous?"

"Bother thinking." He smiled and was rewarded with a tiny twitch of her pretty mouth. "I'll pick you up at eight. We can have breakfast and talk about the rest of the week."

"My flight home is at eight-thirty." She moved to the door they'd come though.

He blocked her. "Change it."

"I can't afford to." She moved right.

"I'll pay." He blocked her again.

Again her eyebrow raised. "I wasn't referring to money."

"No?" He took a step closer, amused to see her stiffen. "What then?"

"I need to get back to my novel. And I need to feed my chickens."

He could only stare as she brushed past him and through the door. Those were the very last words he would ever imagine coming from Lindsay Kenyon's lovely lips.

"Your chickens?" He caught the door behind her and followed her out. Or in, depending on where they were and whose point of view one took.

"I only left them enough lay crumble for the weekend." She sailed down a hallway, then stopped. "Where is this?"

"Here." He chuckled to himself. She never had a sense of direction worth a damn. "Enough lay who?"

"Food. Where do we go from here?"

"That's what I want to ask you."

She glared at him, then caught the sound of the crowd down the hall behind him, and pushed past.

He followed again, biding his time, happy playing her little I-do-so-love-Vermont game, feeling his lust for life rising the way it always did when he was—

"Gavin!" A huge slap on his back made him nearly drop his statue. Bob Franklin. Oh goody. Backstabbing Bob, who'd done everything he could to take credit for Gavin's last script until an up-and-coming independent studio turned it down after a long hard look, and suddenly Bob never had anything to do with it. "Congratulations, buddy. Lindsay, great to see you, babe. Glad to have you back."

She eyed him coldly. "I'm not back, I'm just here."

"Oh. Okay." He clearly missed the difference, but Gavin got it, all too well.

"She has crumbled chickens to go home to." He couldn't get past the idea of Lindsay in back-country Vermont. He'd pictured her in the same kind of technology-enhanced luxury she'd slavishly enjoyed in L.A. with him.

"That's swell. Hey, there's Laura, gotta go. See you two at the party?"

"Sure." He gave a hey-ho-buddy salute, wishing he could just punch Bob in the nose instead.

"I'm not going."

Gavin snapped his salute toward Lindsay and let it droop. She wasn't going? His victory party, his chance to revel in this achievement that would make him visible to the big studios, and only enhance his chances at the pitch meeting at the end of the week? She didn't want to share it with him?

"Why not?"

"I'm tired and I want to go to bed."

Panic clawed at him. "You're not…are you ill?"

"Tired." She shot him a teasing glance. "It's what happens when you spend too much time awake."

He stared at her, fear adrenaline still rushing. Her eyes were ringed with fatigue, but clear. She wasn't hiding anything. He'd know. "You're sure?"

"Gavin, trust me, I've never been healthier."

Did they not have mirrors in Vermont? He wished he had a picture of the old Lindsay in his wallet to shock her into realizing how she looked. But Kaytee had found the one he kept there, and, understandably, asked him to remove it. Which he had, feeling as if he were removing one of his internal organs.

"Come on, Lindsay, you used to be the life of the party."

"No, Gavin, that was you."

She was right. Lindsay preferred quiet small gatherings to the big blowouts. He liked intimate gatherings, too, but for sheer adrenaline-pumping fun, give him a drink in his hand and a big crowd to work. Granted, he needed longer to recover than he had a decade ago, but he didn't let that stop him.

"I can't change your mind?"

"Could you ever?" She smiled then, and he welcomed it like a surprise ray of sunshine on a cloudy miserable day.

"Never. So you go to your room and sleep and I'll go to the party and have fun?"

"That's the plan. Good night." Her eyes softened. "It was wonderful to see you again."

"I'll see you in the morning."

Those softened eyes rolled in exasperation. "I have a plane to catch in the morning."

"So you keep saying."

"Good night, Gavin."

He kissed her on the cheek, wishing he could aim lower and center, and chuckled. She wouldn't leave. He knew exactly how to get her to stay.

He wouldn't allow her to go back to Vermont any earlier than Thursday, the day he flew back to L.A. He needed her here all week to work on his—*their*—story, the pitch and the treatment.

And judging by the wan, waiflike look of her, Lindsay needed him even more.

CHAPTER TWO

SHE WAS CRAZY. She had to be completely crazy. Instead of on her way home to Vermont, where she could unwind playing with her beautiful silver laced wyandottes, Frieda and Freia, then get a decent night's sleep, she was sitting here in her room at The Hotel—only in New York could you name a hotel The Hotel and have it be terribly chic—waiting for Gavin to come by for breakfast. Her plane was probably boarding now, bound for Burlington, passengers escaping the chaos and noise and claustrophobia of the city for the sweet forested hills of the Green Mountain State.

She wasn't going to be on it. She hadn't even rescheduled her return.

Why? Besides being crazy? Two reasons. One, Gavin was working on The Script. Over the five years of their romantic partnership, their co-written scripts had been optioned six times and made into movies three, all by small studios to critical acclaim, but not much box office revenue.

This script, this rewrite of *The Philadelphia Story,* was the script of their hearts. Well, Gavin's heart, mostly. Lindsay's dream was to do a rewrite of her favorite, the 1934 Clark Gable-Claudette Colbert comedy *It*

Happened One Night, the movie she and Gavin had watched the night they'd finally become lovers.

But she loved *The Philadelphia Story,* too. Who didn't? They'd dreamed big dreams, planned endlessly, fought like wild animals, and only ended up finishing about a quarter of it. Other projects always seemed to interrupt, and since money in the bank was vital, especially to Gavin, it became their "someday" project, back when they'd thought they had their lives to live together.

Last night, as she'd been lying awake, listening to sirens and shouting in the street, thinking of her feather bed and down pillows, and open windows that let in sounds and smells of nature, Gavin—or someone—had quietly shoved the pitch and treatment for the script under her door.

She'd stayed up much later than was good for her, certainly later than she was accustomed to these days, reading and rereading. Taking notes, frowning, laughing, sighing. Then afterward, she'd spent even longer staring up at the ceiling, her mind spinning through possibilities.

Damn, he was good. The script would be good. Unfortunately, it could be better. And doubly unfortunate, she'd been able to figure out how. Triple that misfortune then, because worst of all, she found herself itching to get at it, expose its cracks and weaknesses, fill them and bolster them, tear out the rot and replace it with good strong showy prose. A hunger for creativity that she hadn't felt in way too long.

Try as she might, her stalled novel and her beloved chickens were no match for her Pandoralike curiosity and passion when it came to this project. How far could it take him?

And yes, she was touched that he felt he needed her creative input. As long as she remembered that he'd go back to doing his Gavin thing in L.A. and she'd go back to doing her Lindsay thing in Vermont, and they were no longer Hollywood's Dynamic Duo.

The second reason she wasn't on that plane was Gavin himself. No, not like that, though of course she'd probably die still drawn to him. But frankly, he looked like hell. He'd lost weight, he had dark circles under his eyes; his usual relaxed confidence had taken on a jittery edge that wasn't flattering.

Of course, it was all relative. He could still make any random group of women drop to their knees and worship. But Lindsay knew him inside out, and he was not happy. More than that, she knew why. He needed his own Vermont, his own version of what she'd found. He needed to get out of L.A. and its crazy incestuous moral and spiritual roller coaster, and settle somewhere calming, someplace where pressure would be only the healthy, inspirational variety that came from characters and scenes gamboling inside his head. He needed space, he needed freedom, he needed healthy living. To sit under a shady maple, watching chickens peck and neighboring cows graze, while he ruminated on his own—

Three sharp knocks sounded on her door.

After three skipped beats, her heart settled into a steady too-fast rhythm as she went to open the door.

"Hi." She grinned at him, keeping tight hold of the doorknob as if she needed it to steady herself.

As if.

"Hi." He smiled and winked, and she was very glad for the doorknob. The pig. He had no right to take her breath away and appear so unaffected himself. He was wearing a shirt she'd given him, white with a thin-lined plaid of muted greens and blues and browns, which set off his face and eyes and dark hair and…well, yum. If only he would put about five pounds back on and get some sleep…

She really owed it to him, to their past, to try and get him to slow down.

"Ready?"

"You bet." She started to explain what she had in mind for breakfast, but he was already moving down the hall.

"Where are you going?" She had to hurry after him to keep up.

"There's a great brunch place around the corner, a few blocks up, serves every flavor omelet you can think of. Crowded, and we'll need to wait in line, but—"

"No." She stopped and folded her arms.

"—it will be worth…" He turned his head, noticed she wasn't next to him, and swung the rest of the way around, to face her ten paces down the hall.

High noon. Time to duel.

"No?"

She shook her head and pointed at the doorway they'd just left. "Room service."

"Oh?" He started walking with a slow swagger down the hall, head cocked to one side, looking at her through narrowed eyes as if trying to figure out who she really was. "That's what you want? For your one short week in the city? To stay in the hotel and have room service?"

"Yes." She lifted her chin, trying to pretend his prowl wasn't making her just a tiny bit weak-kneed. "We need to talk, we need quiet, we need time."

"True, but—"

"Room service, thumbs-up. Crowded restaurant, thumbs-down."

He stopped a foot away. Too close in the softly lit hall. "Since when do you turn down chances to be in the thick of things?"

"Since I got cured."

"Of?"

"The need for pressure, insomnia and constant overstimulation."

"And now?"

"Now I have open spaces and nine hours of sleep and naps and—"

"*And* naps? Are you sure you're not ill?"

"I'm sane. I have leisure and beauty and peace and—"

"Chickens."

She held her head up and squeezed her folded arms tighter. "Yes. Chickens. Chickens are very intelligent and affectionate animals."

"They are." His tone was clearly skeptical.

"Who think I've been eaten by a predator while I'm not there, and are probably anxious, so let's go back to my room to have breakfast and get this done."

"Hmm." His mouth twisted in an I'm-not-giving-in expression she knew way too well. "I had my heart set on taking you out."

Lindsay took a tiny step closer so they were nearly touching. She wasn't above playing dirty when necessity called, though it had been a long time since she'd had to. "I read the pitch. And the treatment."

"And?" He tried to act casual, but she saw his jaw tighten.

She shrugged. "I know what needs to happen."

"You do." His eyes flashed with excitement. "What?"

Lindsay smiled slowly. "We need to talk, we need quiet, we need time."

"Oh, for…" He shrugged, hands up in surrender, and sighed. "Room service."

She smiled sweetly. "Why, thank you, dear."

"You are *so*…" He rolled his eyes and mumbled something she was probably glad she didn't catch. "…welcome. Lead on."

She led him back to her room, threw her plastic card key on the wooden nightstand next to the bed, turned and realized with a jolt that they were alone for the first time in well over a year.

In a bedroom.

"So." She gestured to the room service menu. "Let me guess. Mushroom omelet with cheddar, no onions, double pot of coffee, grapefruit juice?"

"You got me." He chuckled. "And for you, granola, fresh fruit, orange juice, yogurt and also a double pot of—"

"Uh-uh." She waggled her finger. "Tea. Single."

"Tea?" He gaped. "Single?"

"I sleep now at night. Amazingly, that's what nights are for. You should try it sometime."

A knock at the door was followed by a low call, "Room Service," which she could not have timed better if she'd scripted it herself. "That'll be breakfast."

He gave her a dirty look. "I've been had."

"Not the first time."

"Not the last." He said the words in a mournful tone and winked as she walked past to open the door for breakfast.

Damn. She didn't like the way she felt so hyped up. It couldn't be healthy. Didn't they say stress was the number one killer? Lindsay wanted to live a long life. She had things to do, books to write, days to spend blocked in front of her comput—

Oops. Days to spend enjoying the life she'd embraced wholeheartedly.

The studly young room service attendant set up breakfast, shooting more than a few glances at Lindsay, who beamed at him when she saw Gavin starting to fidget. Easy payback for him scrambling her serenity so easily with a wink.

"Thank you…" she peered at his name tag "…Raoul. Very nice. We'll eat well."

"You're welcome, Miss Kenyon. *Any* time." He bowed and backed out, smiling at Lindsay, bless his hunky heart.

"Well." She gave Gavin a cheerful grin and sat at the table. "*My* appetite has been whetted."

He made a low growling sound. "Would you like me to call him back and leave?"

"Hmm…" She pretended to consider, and he growled again. "Jealous, dear?"

"Oddly, yes."

Her smug expression dropped off her face and something real and warm and sweet threatened to take its place. *Oh no. Ohhh, no no no no no.* Mr. Charmer. Mr.

Pleaser. She'd have none of it. His script was at stake, he came here from the Land Of Ingratiation and Butt-Kissing Manipulation, so much a part of him he used it sometimes even when he thought he was being genuine. While she'd graduated to a place where genuine was the only option and she much preferred it.

She was not falling for the act. Or him. Definitely not him. Not again.

"So. The script." She put her napkin in her lap and dipped up a spoonful of strawberries, yogurt and granola.

"Yes." He leaned forward over his omelet, unrolling his silver from its linen, and she tried very hard to keep her mind on what she wanted to say about *The Philadelphia Story,* and keep her mind off of what it felt like to look at him over a breakfast table again. Maybe the crowded restaurant would have been better…

"I really like what you've done with it, how you've updated it, made the Katherine Hepburn character into an Ivy League workaholic. But…oh, who are you thinking of to play her—Cate Blanchett?"

"I was thinking Nicole Kidman."

"Yes, either one."

"So…" He gestured impatiently, chewing a huge bite of omelet. "You like the character, but…"

"What bothers me about the script and the pitch is the same thing that bothers me about the movie. You have this woman, the Hepburn character, pursued by her ex, Cary Grant, who deep down she is still crazy in love with…."

Her voice thickened and lowered. Yogurt must have coated her throat. She cleared it harshly.

"You okay?"

"Sure. Fine." She coughed and thumped her chest. "Ducky."

"You were saying?" He affected a look of total innocence. "About the woman whose ex comes back into her life, who she is still, deep down, crazy in love with?"

"Yes. Her." Not jumping, not taking the bait, not reacting. "And him. The Cary Grant character—let me guess, George Clooney?"

"Absolutely."

"The movie spends so much time developing the chemistry between Katherine Hepburn and the Jimmy Stewart character, the other man who shows up in her life, that when she ends up with her ex again, sure, we're rooting for her to, but only because he's sooo..." She sighed rapturously. "So Cary Grant."

"I see." Gavin stopped attacking his omelet and she made a mental note to recommend yoga or some other stress reduction exercise, so he'd stop bolting his food. Bad for digestion. "You think she should spend much more time reconnecting with her ex."

"Yes." Lindsay took another bite and chewed carefully. Was she getting herself in trouble here? It felt like it. "The two of them need more of those great scenes, with all that fabulous chemistry, to remind them and to show the viewer how much they're meant to be together."

"Yes, I think they do need more time together. Because they are meant to be together."

His eyes were entirely too warm. She resisted the juvenile urge to bend back her spoon and make a nice pink yogurt splat between them. "We need to see more of how strong their personality pull is, how they complete each other, even while they're struggling to work out the issues that drove them apart."

"Namely, that she was intolerant of what he was trying to do."

Forget flinging yogurt. Now she wanted to bite and scratch. "*Namely,* that he was intent on destroying himself and therefore their relationship, and she couldn't help him until he wanted to help himself. All she could do was kick him out before he dragged her down with him."

"But they get a second chance."

"Uh, yeah." Stating the obvious now. He'd better not be hinting at what she was starting to think he was hinting at. "Only after they recognize what went wrong and change."

"Gotcha." He took another huge bite of omelet, chewed too fast and swallowed too soon. She spooned up a strawberry, bit half and waited for him to speak. Frankly, she didn't see how he could eat at all. She wasn't sure she'd even manage her strawberry half. Why hadn't she seen when she was reading the script how many ways the story could be applied to them?

"Take the scene where Kate Hepburn comes home drunk from the office party, driven by Jimmy Stewart." She did polish off the strawberry, appetite returning, and dug in for another bite. "Who d'you have in mind for Jimmy Stewart's character?"

"John Cusack."

"Mmm, good one. So she's sleeping it off in the car, and there's that incredibly tender shot where Cary Grant lays his head next to hers on the back of the seat. They talk briefly and that's it. The movie cheats us out of more, and I think your treatment does, too."

"Okay. Let's work that." He gave his trademark devilish smile, got up, went over to the bed, sat beside it, laid his head on the edge and patted the spot next to him. "Come here. Beside me."

Oh yeah, good plan. Emotional suicide was her favorite way to spend time. "Let's talk this one out."

"You afraid to get close to me?"

"Of course not." She laughed unconvincingly. "Absolutely not. I just think—"

"Prove it."

"Fine." She ground her teeth together and got up from the table. Gavin thought best when he could put himself into the physical realm of a script. He and Lindsay had acted out countless scenes before.

But this wasn't before. This was now.

She sank to her knees, rolled sideways onto her butt and put her head a good foot and a half from his.

"Come on." He smirked and patted the spread two inches in front of his face. "We wouldn't even be in the same shot."

"Right." She wiggled six inches closer and nearly shrieked when his hand moved to cup the back of her head and brought her face to within an inch of his.

"There."

She smiled weakly. Oh crap. He smelled so good. He looked so good, in spite of the dark circles and too-prominent cheekbones. He was still the most handsome and sexiest and most exciting man she'd ever known—ten years since they'd met in their freshman year at UCLA.

After four years as friends, they'd moved on to being lovers just like that. They'd been watching *It Happened One Night*. She'd sighed when it was over, turned to share the fun, and found him looking at her as he'd never looked at her before, not by any stretch of her imagination. Even stranger, she'd responded exactly the same way, as if a bolt of lust stretched out from the video and zapped them both.

Dangerous remembering…

"So."

She had to swallow to speak. "So?"

"Any ideas?"

Oh, he was damn good. Of course, the logical fix for the scene would be a kiss, maybe accidental, maybe only halfway so. She blocked the sight of his lips and stared at his nose instead. Except even his nose was sexy to her.

Ideas? Plenty. But she'd only tell him the ones involving the script.

"The lines of dialogue should be expanded, stretched. The lovers should start the scene a foot apart, where I was before, and gradually—"

"Ex-lovers."

"Ex." Her "oops" smile barely made it onto her mouth. "Gradually come closer, just casual movements as they speak their lines, nothing dramatic until they're as close as we are now."

"Yes." His voice dropped to the low, tense range that indicated he was excited about an idea. "I can see it. It's great. Go on."

"Then when they're this close, they should start saying the lines of dialogue glancing down, briefly focusing on each other's lips." She didn't focus on his. She knew them, the masculine shape, their taste, their warmth…. *Talk, Lindsay. Keep talking.* "Then…some clincher line admitting they have feelings for each other. Skirting around the issue, though, maybe couching it in some dialogue that can have a double meaning, so they're apparently discussing something else, but what they're really after is how they still feel about each other. Then at the perfect time they look into each other's eyes…."

She looked up into his eyes and forgot what she was going to say. Or where she was. Or who she was.

But she sure as hell remembered him. Way, way too much about him.

"And then?" His voice was a slow, soft murmur.

"Um…" Her mind was blank, gone, erased. She was only aware of his deep brown eyes, his scent, his mesmerizing presence, which she'd spent the last year and a half trying to banish from her consciousness. Apparently unsuccessfully. Way unsuccessfully.

"I know what happens next." He whispered the words.

"What?" She seemed to be whispering, too, even though she hadn't planned to

"He does what he's been dying to do since the second he laid eyes on her again after their year and a half being apart." A slow smile spread his mouth, which seemed to be sliding even closer to hers. "He kisses her."

CHAPTER THREE

"No." Lindsay jerked back. "No. He absolutely does not kiss her."

Gavin lifted his head from the bed, feeling as if he was struggling to wake from a dream. The lines had started to blur early on as to whether he and Lindsay were talking about the characters in the script or each other. He'd pressed the confusion to his advantage, intending to turn the conversation around to where he could begin to show her how her newfound life was dulling and suffocating her spirit.

But when she'd laid her head so close to his and looked up with those tired, sad eyes, such an avalanche of tenderness had engulfed him, he'd crossed over completely. What script? Who?

He loved her. What kind of idiot did he think he was, imagining he was over her? Or that he ever could get over her? How could he ever have taken up with Kaytee? Lindsay was so deep inside him in so many ways—such a part of his thoughts and his voice; his steady companion on the road from teenager to adult—how could he possibly think he could extract her from his soul and toss her away like a splinter or an unwanted piece of clothing? She was inextricably linked to everything he'd been and would ever become. Just seeing her had made him starved for her, not only now, but retro-actively, for the whole year and a half she'd been gone.

To hell with just convincing her to leave Vermont and come back to their professional partnership. He wanted her back in his life, in his bed. He wanted to stay up half the night talking, brainstorming, sharing their days, and the other half making love. He wanted her back—the real her—bursting with energy, glowing with excite-ment. Not this wan, wasting waif who barely seemed in-terested in the world around her, and who had developed an unnatural fondness for chickens.

"Okay. He doesn't kiss her." He got to his feet, still confused and disoriented. "Does he later?"

"Of course."

Why did she seem so calm and collected while he could barely remember what he'd just said? "When?"

She glanced at him as if he needed immediate psy-chiatric attention. "When he's changed enough so that their relationship will work. When he's chosen to accept her as she is. It becomes his reward for seeing the light about his own life."

"Okay." Again the blurry lines. Was she talking about the script? Or was this some kind of female coded message? "But she has to change, too. And accept him as he is."

"Of course. That's the moral of the story. First he changes, then she does."

They stared at each other. Gavin resisted the urge to scratch his head. "And then he can kiss her."

"Yes." She got to her feet and went back to her break-fast. He followed, struggling to return to Planet Sanity and organize his thoughts. Did *he* have to change? How? What did she mean? How did any of this—

Coffee. He glommed on to the double pot like a life raft in a hurricane-tossed sea. Coffee would help.

Two cups later he'd recovered his senses enough to take in what she was saying. The lines became clear and distinct again as they hashed through the rest of the treatment, and once again he was having the time of his life. Not just because of all the "yes!" moments as her unerring instinct zeroed mercilessly in on flaws he was too close to see, but because during the process she started to come to life.

When he was a kid, he'd loved the C.S. Lewis book *The Lion, the Witch and the Wardrobe*. In an unforgettable scene, Aslan the lion brought statues of unfortunate creatures turned to stone by the White Witch back to life. His breath caused them to revive, warm color replacing the white stone bit by bit until they were unquestionably and wholly living again, flesh and blood and heat and passion. Like Lindsay, doing again what she was meant to be doing. With him.

"Yes, yes, yes." He flipped over a page of his legal pad and scribbled furiously on the next sheet, trying to concentrate on the words, on the concepts, trying not to notice the bloom of color in Lindsay's cheeks or the new sparkle in her eye, the way she held her head higher, gestured more broadly, ate with more enthusiasm. In short, became herself again.

Then the last page was turned, the last comment was made, and she took a deep breath, let it out and met his eyes with her dark Audrey Hepburn ones.

The urge to kiss her was so intense he had to grip his

pen and force his body to stay in the plush velour seat. Too much too soon.

"Thank you, Lindsay. This is…perfect. It's just the focus the story needed. I knew you could help me."

"You're welcome." She took another breath, pushed her chair back a few inches from the table, looking slightly stunned. "My pleasure."

Damn right it had been. He needed to pound home how much. "So how is your novel going?"

The energy in her eyes started to fade. "Oh. Well. It's going fine."

It wasn't. He felt like cheering, selfish as that was. "Is this the one you wanted to write about the Shakespearean scholar who uncovers evidence Shakespeare was a powerful female wizard?"

She cringed. "No. This one is about a woman making a new life for herself."

"And…"

"And so…she does." She shrugged, didn't meet his eyes.

"In a small town in Vermont?"

"As a matter of fact, yes. Away from the smog and panic and appearance-driven shallowness of another certain city far, far away."

That was it? No alien invasions or international conspiracies or demons or werewolves? Oh my God. He really had to rescue her, before it was too late. "With chickens?"

She glared at him. "With. Chickens."

"How far along are you?"

"Oh…" She averted her eyes, started rubbing her hand along the arm of the chair. "Nearly done."

Liar. The book was tanking. Ha! Forget just getting her

to stay this week, he could practically feel her next to him in L.A. at the pitch meeting Friday. "Congratulations."

"Thanks." Her eyes stayed down, her posture sagged; her transition back into Pale Mournful Waif was nearly complete. And if he had any qualms about his selfishness wanting to kidnap her back into her old life and back into his, they were tempered radically by the certainty that Lindsay was miserable in Vermont.

So, his next move—slowly, deliberately—was to invite her out somewhere this week, somewhere big-city and exciting, to remind her how much she missed the fast lane without realizing it. Then, gradually, he'd entice her into coming with him to L.A. by convincing her he couldn't pitch the story effectively without her. Being back in L.A. would supply the rest of the missing hunger she needed.

He also wanted to find out if she was still as desperately in love with him as he was with her, so that when she did move back, it would be in the fullest sense, so they could live a fast-track thrilling life, conquering the film world together until death did them part.

THE RUSSET MAPLE LEAVES sang.

Lindsay frowned. No, not sang. Whispered. Leaves whispered.

Except every author had leaves whispering. She needed something more interesting than that.

She glanced up at the Central Park elm she sat near and frowned, listening, trying to think of what she could type that would be less clichéd.

The russet maple leaves overhead imparted their secrets to her eager ears. Ruby strained to listen, to learn from their wisdom, but once again, her thoughts drifted to Dirk, his dark deep eyes that saw—

Wait, Dirk's eyes were blue.

His deep blue eyes that wouldn't leave her alone.

Crap. All of it. But at least the words were there; they were coming slowly. Editing could come later.

She gave in to temptation and lay back on the warm grass, another sun-seeking body among way too many others. New Yorkers had rushed en masse outside to enjoy the summerlike Sunday. But at least it was blissfully peaceful away from the city panic. Tulips were blooming, trees were budding, spring was here—the fabulous time of rebirth. It would take a few more weeks before the season hit Vermont, but she could enjoy it there, too. Winter was not for sissies. She admitted there were days when she thought she'd lose her mind after so many years of California sunshine. But then the sky would clear, the snow would sparkle, she'd go out to feed Freia and Frieda, and listen to their morning greetings, which they'd repeat until she answered and they were satisfied their flock was complete.

Most days she felt her flock was complete, too. E-mail made it easy to stay in touch with friends and family. Her neighbors were gradually accepting her. The routines of her life had fallen easily into place. Long nights of sleep. Long naps. She didn't realize her body had such a capacity for sleep. She didn't seem to need it so much here. Maybe she had enough stored for a few days of deprivation. Maybe her stress adrenaline was keeping her running on empty.

Okay. She struggled back up to sitting. Leaves. Sharing secrets. Yada yada.

It had been days since she'd thought of Gavi—

Lindsay hit the backspace key frantically. The ex-husband's name was Dirk.

Days since she'd thought of Dirk. His hold on her was weakening, poisoned irrevocably by her proclamation of freedom from the marriage, by her survival instinct, which had finally surfaced after years of denial. Eventually the chains would drop off completely and rust to russet-nothing.

Wait, damn, she'd already used russet to describe the leaves.

Lindsay sighed and lay down again. The book was going nowhere. It was missing something, some spark, some mysterious element that would make it click. She closed her eyes, feeling the sun's warm weight on her face, and let her imagination roam back to Vermont to a house Ruby owned, which of course looked suspiciously like her own.

What did the book need? What did her character need to drive her forward?

Immediately a tall, dark, suspiciously like Gavin man entered the suspiciously like hers property, driving a TT Roadster, top down, past the huge maple on her front lawn, up the gravel drive. He got out, strode to the front door, lifted Ruby and—

No! For God's sake no. The entire point of the novel was that Ruby was going to make her own way, that men weren't the answer, that she had gotten over Dirk and taken charge of her life and she was content. Massively and totally and completely content.

Lindsay exited her fantasy and found herself stretched out rigidly, fists at her sides, face tightly scowling.

Oh dear.

Okay, so complete and total contentment could take time. At least she had done something important this weekend, which was to confront Gavin, spend alone time with him, show him how important quiet conversation could be. She smiled, remembering. He'd shown up for breakfast jittery, frantic, ready to race off to more overstimulation.

She wished she had a videotape of him gradually relaxing, focusing, more and more able to understand his script, to see where he'd gone wrong. She wished she could show him how the lines in his face had softened, how the tension around his mouth had released. How his movements and speech had slowed and flowed more gracefully, more naturally, more like himself, more like the man she knew.

No question but he was miserable in L.A. She couldn't help wanting to rescue him from the grind that would drive him to poor health, addiction or despair, as it had so many people before him. Somehow she had to lure him to Vermont, teach him a thing or two about real life, about real living, about the seasons and fresh air. And even a thing or two about chickens.

How could he help but be seduced to a better, healthier place?

Maybe Vermont was thinking too big right away; maybe she'd do better starting with time this week. A quiet afternoon right here in Central Park. On a weekday, when not so many of the office-imprisoned would be around. One step at a time, on the journey to recovering his sanity.

Except…what would that do for hers?

When he was about to kiss her... Oh my heaven. A year and a half apart and zap, right back to the way it was for those wonderful early years, when the universe was only big enough for the two of them, before he'd expanded it to include Marlie and Alex and now Kaytee, whoever she was, and everyone else who wanted a piece of him.

Where Lindsay got the strength to back away from that offered kiss she had no idea, except that being in Vermont had put her closer in touch with her feelings and instincts, and this instinct had served her well. Getting back together now would be like Katherine Hepburn and Cary Grant falling back in love again at the beginning of the movie. They'd simply repeat the same mistakes. Change had to happen, for them and for Lindsay and Gavin. Like Cary Grant's character, who'd kicked his drinking problem during their separation and was coming back to Kate Hepburn whole and sane at the movie's opening, Lindsay had reached a place of sanity. It remained for Gavin to reach that place, too. She didn't need to be dragged back into the hell it had taken so much strength to escape from.

Because—

"Gavin, look!"

Lindsay's eyes flew open, then closed instantly when she found herself staring into the sun. Ouch. She struggled up to her elbows, lifted her head to vertical and tried again. Gavin? Her Gavin? What were the odds?

No. Not her Gavin.

An elderly couple had stopped to admire a patch of tulips.

"Remind you of anything?" The woman turned blue eyes adoringly up to the man next to her, who was staring at the flowers with a troubled, vacant look.

"Flowers."

She smiled tenderly and adjusted his hat. "Tulips. You brought me a big bunch every day in high school until I'd agree to go to the dance with you, do you remember? Until Julie Wedford caught you pilfering out of her yard and told your mother."

His brow creased; his mouth worked ineffectually. "Flowers."

"That's right, dear." She took a handkerchief and wiped the corner of his mouth. "Tulips."

"Flowers."

She led him gently away, her tiny figure pressed close to his, supporting him, urging him on.

Tears rose in Lindsay's eyes. She grabbed up her laptop and wrote out everything she'd heard and seen. The couple could be her heroine Ruby's parents—her father with Alzheimer's, her mother caring for him. Or maybe he'd already died when the book opened, and the scene could be a memory; maybe Ruby's mother would come to live with her and the women would find strength in each other. Or maybe Ruby saw the couple and realized she and Dirk never could have made it to that stage, and the realization would set her free of divorce guilt later in the book.

Lindsay glanced at the two frail bodies moving slowly away, clinging to each other, the shade of the elm darkening the woman's blue coat and the man's gray jacket. She watched until they emerged into the sunlight on the other side, her heart full of bittersweet longing.

Or maybe her heroine would see them and realize that's what she still wanted. To grow old with the man she loved and to care for him, to live a simple, beautiful, gentle life, until death did them part.

"Ooh, that was so fun!" Kaytee burst into her hotel room ahead of Gavin, did a joyous if clumsy pirouette and fell onto the bed, sighing rapturously. "Wasn't that awesome?"

Gavin followed her, carrying roughly fifty thousand shopping bags, and dumped them on the floor beside her bed. "It was a nightmare."

"Aww, c'mon." She stroked the space next to her and smiled invitingly. "I promised you a reward...."

He only managed half a grin and sat at the foot of her bed, patted her ankle paternally. "I was thinking more along the lines of a banana split."

Her luscious lower lip extended in a pout and she rolled over onto her elbows. "It's her, isn't it."

He started, then didn't bother pretending not to know who she was talking about. "Yes."

Kaytee prowled over next to him and took his earlobe between her teeth, leaning so her impressive breasts swung freely in the dipping neckline of her dress.

His body managed mild interest, his brain not even that. He'd taken up with her soon after he heard through a mutual friend that Lindsay had bought a house in Vermont, though even after that thud of finality, it was many months before he stopped lunging for phones and doorbells. But a man had to do something besides wallow in misery, and Kaytee hadn't been shy about listing options.

The diversion had worked for the most part. She was a decent actress, full of life, funny, and made no demands except in the bedroom and for the occasional professional introduction. Having someone to go out with once in a while had brought him out of his stunned despair and made it worth going on. Eventually she became a comfortable, beautiful habit he was proud to have on his arm. In return he introduced her to people he knew—actors, agents, directors.

He hadn't even realized how much she bored him until he'd been with Lindsay again.

"I bet I can make you forge-e-et her." Her teeth recaptured his earlobe briefly.

"I don't think so, Kaytee." He smiled and kissed her forehead. "Not this time."

She drew back, scowling. "Don't tell me you're going back to her."

"I haven't been invited, no."

"But would you if she did?"

"I…" He twisted his mouth. "No, Kaytee, I—"

"Oh, come on."

"Okay." He gave her a sheepish look. "In a heartbeat."

"Thought so." She got off the bed and walked over to the window, twisting her hair rapidly into some knotty thing he could never figure out how she got to stay that way. "Bob Franklin offered me a trip to Cancun next week."

The sharp jab in Gavin's gut was more anger that Backstabbing Bob was trying to undercut him once again, than pain someone else would be with Kaytee. What was wrong with that picture? How many more signs did he need? "Do you want to go?"

She shrugged and turned, keeping her face tilted to one side—her best side, catching the light from the window.

Kaytee knew her camera angles.

"I'd rather be with you, Gavin. You're a lot of fun.

But he's a nice guy, well-connected, and if you're not into me anymore, I might as well."

He looked for pain and regret in her eyes and found them, but not in great quantity. Nor did he feel much of either himself. The situation struck him as incredibly surreal. They'd been sharing their bodies and an evening or two each week for over a year, and both were able to move on as if they were changing brands of deodorant? Since when had he settled for so little?

Since he'd known Lindsay. After he'd been with someone like her, what other option was there but to settle?

"It's not that I'm not into you, Kaytee. I'm just…"

"More into Lindsay."

He nodded, feeling like a complete male idiot. "I thought I was past it, but seeing her here again…"

"Gotcha." She blew out a sigh, walked to the door, opened it for him. "I had someone like that once. He was killed in a car crash about three years ago. You're lucky you can still get her back."

Her words shook him, both because he'd been jerk enough to attribute her somewhat passive attitude toward the relationship as lack of depth, and because it hit him that something could have happened to Lindsay in Cow Town, USA over the past year and a half and he'd be left with the same dull hopelessness Kaytee had perpetually in her eyes.

"God, Kaytee, I'm sorry."

"It's okay. A lot of people never find what we had. At least I did for a while."

Her voice broke, and Gavin reached out and hugged her tightly. She drew back, wound her arms around his neck and kissed him long and hard.

"Aw, Gavin." She sighed. "You were wonderful to—"

"Do we really need to hear how wonderful he was?" Lindsay's voice, dripping acid behind him, sent Gavin's heart into his stomach. Oh crap. Not just bad timing. The worst.

He pulled away from Kaytee, who gave him an uh-oh look of alarm.

"Lindsay, this isn't anything to get upset about, trust me."

"Who's upset?" She opened her eyes as wide as they'd go and shrugged so her shoulders practically bounced off her ears. She was right. She wasn't upset. She was livid.

Was he a complete idiot to be glad? Not that she was hurt, not ever that. But God knew if she'd ho-hummed past them without saying anything it would be a good sign his chances were nil.

Kaytee took a step back and gestured between them. "We were saying goodbye."

"Aww, about to be separated for twenty or thirty minutes, were we? How can you bear it?"

Gavin took another step back. "She means we're through."

"So early in the day? Did you remember to wash and zip?"

Out of his frustration and concern for her, crazy laughter threatened. Damn, he loved her. She was one of the sharpest, funniest, most fabulous women he'd ever known. And right now she was operating at full steam, at her most gloriously passionate best.

Er, okay, not her *most* gloriously passionate best. But that was too much to hope for this early in the week.

And after what she just thought she saw, maybe too early in the month. Or year, if he didn't clear it up soon.

"I'll disappear. Thanks for everything, Gavin." Kaytee gave him a sad sweet smile, kissed him on the cheek and went into her room, letting the door close behind her.

Gavin turned back to Lindsay and put his hands on his hips. "We need to talk about—"

"No, no, no." She backed down the hall, waving him away. "Don't let me bother you. I'm just going to the elevator. Please, go in and continue exchanging fluids."

He strode down the hall after her, breaking into a jog when she started running. He caught her right before she reached the bank of elevators, and hauled her up against the wall. "Afraid of something?"

"What do you mean?"

"You're running away. Again."

"I wanted to catch an elevator."

"You had one scheduled?"

She struggled halfheartedly. "Let go of me."

"Why?"

"You were kissing her."

"We were breaking up."

"Looked more like gluing together."

"A friendly breakup. You see, Lindsay, that's how most relationships should end. You come to a point where you no longer want to be together and you decide to end it. Which is very different from, oh, say, giving up and heading out of state."

"I told you I was leaving, you didn't listen. To that or anything else I was saying. You were too busy inviting anyone and everyone you met to come in between us."

He pushed his body suggestively close. "There's nobody between us now."

"Don't you dare." She struggled again, with a tiny quantity of the strength he knew she had, which gave him courage to hope she was enjoying the contact and sparring as much as he was.

"Don't dare what?"

"Flirt with me after you had your tongue down another woman's throat. Don't you dare even try to touch me in any way that resembles a romantic gesture or I'll…"

"What?" He suppressed a grin. Badly.

"I'll…" She darted a glance to the side, obviously frantically thinking of a suitable threat.

"You'll what?" He chuckled and leaned in for his prize.

"List all the men I've slept with since we broke up."

Ouch. He jumped back as if she'd burned him, only the pain wasn't on his fingers, but deep in his chest. The thought of her with anyone else… He wanted to smash things.

He was a fool. He'd expected her to take the sight of him and Kaytee calmly? While just the thought of her with someone else…

"Okay." The word barely made it past his lips, his voice was so hoarse and choked. "Touché."

He waited for her triumph, knowing he probably deserved it. How stupidly safe he'd felt imagining her in her lonely cabin at her computer. She was a sexual woman in her prime. What the hell made him think she'd stay faithful to a man she'd left?

No triumph. Instead she dropped her eyes to the turquoise-and-gold carpet. "Gavin."

"Yes." His voice still sounded as if it belonged to someone else.

"The list isn't very long."

"Lindsay, don't do this. I can't—"

"Gavin."

He closed his eyes. "What."

"There isn't even one name on it."

His eyes opened. The ache in his chest stopped expanding. Shame replaced it, and the irrational pain of having been the one who strayed, even if technically they hadn't been together when he and Kaytee hooked up. Shame, irrational pain, overwhelming tenderness—and okay, stupid macho relief. So shoot him, he was a man.

She raised her sad, shadowed eyes from staring at the carpet, and the power of what sprang to life between them was so huge, he wasn't sure he could bear it.

"Stay the week, Lindsay. Fly with me to L.A. Thursday night and come with me to pitch the story Friday at Universal."

She wouldn't. He'd asked much too early. He'd meant to do this slowly, spend time with her this week, have fun with her, seduce her with the memories of what they'd been, and the images of what they could still be. But the sight of her sweet, lost, pale face broke him, and he had to ask now. He had to know if there was any hope for a future together.

"I have my own life now, in—"

"Vermont. I know. I'm not asking you to give that up." Yet. At least he'd managed to hold that much back. "Just one meeting. The pitch is good."

"It's fabulous. You don't need me there to sell it."

"Maybe not to sell it." He reached across the hallway,

arm extended nearly straight, and touched her chin, feeling her soft hair brush the back of his hand. "But I need you there for me."

CLOSE SHAVE

lorem ipsum dolor sit amet, consectetur
adipiscing elit sed do eiusmod tempor
incididunt ut labore et dolore magna aliqua.

CHAPTER FOUR

A PICNIC IN CENTRAL PARK. Gavin lugged the laden
basket down Fifth Avenue toward the park entrance at
79th Street and the spread of green beyond, with a determined grin on his face. New York had some of the
finest restaurants in the world, he and Lindsay were
only here a short time, and she wanted deviled eggs,
ham sandwiches, bumpy ground and insects?

If he'd had any doubts about her sanity, they were
confirmed when she announced this little treat she had
in store for the two of them, after a day spent hard at
work revising the pitch. Worse, because the early
spring weather turned chilly at night and the sun set
by seven-thirty or so, she'd wanted to eat…early.
Before *six*.

He had to remind himself that she wasn't herself
right now, that she'd fallen under the spell of some
Vermont weirdness that had zapped the life right out of
her, made her turn to parks for picnics at a time of day
more suited to cocktails in elegant bars.

Poor Lindsay. If he survived this ordeal he'd do
whatever he could to save her. Starting right after the
picnic, when he took her dancing at Club Tigre.

"Here we go." She peered at a park map the concierge had given her. "Seventy-Ninth Street entrance. We're looking for Cedar Hill."

"Not Blueberry?"

She sent him her best prim glare. "No."

"Okeydokey." He forged on ahead, whistling the tune of "*I found my thrill...*" and was rewarded with soft laughter behind him.

They found Cedar Hill, a green expanse of sloping lawn, and trees trying hard to get their leaves going. He had to admit it was pretty. A few brave picnickers were already there, taking advantage of the warmer-than-usual week, though he saw a pretty hefty pile of coats near one family, waiting for when the sun started disappearing.

Hmm. Maybe Lindsay would need to be kept warm....

He liked that picture. Spooning on the hillside, maybe as darkness fell, getting themselves into some old-fashioned trouble, like that night on the beach in Santa Monica....

Though with Vermont in her blood and Southern California in his, more likely it would be him needing to be kept warm.

Lindsay found a spot fairly high on the slope with a view of trees and the Metropolitan Museum of Art jutting into the park, and spread the cloth the staff at The Hotel had given them along with the basket of food.

He sat, trying several positions before he found one he could tolerate. Even so, his back wasn't happy and his rear was negotiating a few rocks or clods of dirt that weren't going to be friends in an hour or so.

Nature boy he wasn't. What was wrong with a nice upholstered chair? Indoors? With waiters on call and a full bar?

"Mmm, pâté, crackers, chicken, some kind of sauce, salad, rolls. Strawberries! First ones of the season for me. And mmm, chocolate raspberry torte, looks totally decadent. Yum."

Gavin glanced over all the neat packages and ingeniously stored items as Lindsay unpacked. Hmm, well… Not a deviled egg or ham sandwich in sight. Maybe he could survive this, after all.

"Oh, and a bottle of sparkling grape juice. How fun."

Sparkling grape juice? Like grape soda? He shuddered. He could do without that. If alcohol wasn't allowed in Central Park, just let him drink water.

He fished around in the bag he'd brought and started setting up his portable CD player and speakers.

"What is that?" Lindsay halted her pâté spreading.

Gavin lifted his eyebrow. Uh-oh. Her displeased voice. "Music. I thought we could listen to some jazz."

"Why?"

He laughed, wanting to kiss the prissy expression right off her face. "Why not?"

"Because it's manmade, it's civilization, it's city, it's an intrusion into—"

"Lindsay, we're in the middle of one of the biggest cities in the world."

"I know." She got that troubled look on her face that always made him want to sweep her into his arms and make her world better. "But I want to pretend we're not."

"Okay." He put the CD player away. Not a problem. He'd follow her lead for now, then get her back when they went dancing later. "We'll pretend we're not. Where are we instead?"

She handed him a glass of sparkling grape juice—he couldn't bring himself to object—and clinked with him.

"We're on a forested hill in the middle of Canada." A helicopter roared overhead, nearly drowning her words, and she gestured to it with her glass. "Note the migration of the noble Canada goose."

"Ah, yes." He pointed to a band of way-hip teenagers passing by, flaunting as much attitude as they could. "And the abundant native wildlife."

"Exactly." She passed a paper plate with crackers spread with pâté. "Do you remember the last time the two of us had a picnic?"

He sipped his juice, surprised to find it tart and crisp and refreshing. No, he didn't remember their last one specifically. He remembered plenty early on in their relationship, and ones with the gang from UCLA before that, which invariably involved smuggled-in illegal refreshments. But if he started off pretending he remembered, maybe she'd jump in and rescue him. "I think so, yes. Sure. Weren't we in a…some kind of…"

A cut-the-crap glance was all it took for him to back down from the bull poop, feeling like a jerk. "No, I don't. I'm sorry."

"There were power outages that day, nothing was working. We packed peanut butter sandwiches and warm lemonade and drove to Charmlee Wilderness Park in—"

"Malibu."

"Yes. Do you remember how quiet it was?"

He did. It all came back to him, so clearly he couldn't believe he hadn't thought of it immediately. It had been quiet. Peaceful. Dusty hills and unexpected flowers. "It was great. We were so crabby at the blackout—"

"And then we ended up being glad because we had that perfect evening to relax. Without laptops, scripts, TV…"

"Yes." He bit into a cracker, spread the rich taste of the pâté over his tongue and felt his muscles letting go just at the memory.

"We lay there listening to the birds, watching the clouds roll by…."

"I think we did a few other things, too." He winked and watched the blush creep up her face. She was so beautiful. In this light especially, that rich time before sunset, when it seemed everything was set in particularly intense relief. Colors deepened; her soft dark hair and fresh-cream skin stood out vividly from the backdrop of dark green.

It was going to be physically impossible for the evening to end without him kissing her.

"Yes, we did a few other things, too." She turned away, beautiful pink still highlighting her cheeks, and prepared plates of food while he refilled their glasses and dug out napkins and silverware from the basket.

Frankly, he wouldn't mind if she'd send him one of those hot lustful glances that got him primed and ready in fewer than ten seconds, but it felt wonderful doing something even this simple together. They were partners, had always been. He and Kaytee generally ended up somewhere someone else was serving them.

He missed this.

They ate, talking of old times, catching each other up on basics of their time apart. She told him about her house, her land, and yes, her chickens, describing it all so vividly he could imagine her there, though in his mind she stood out like a whirlwind color character in a static black-and-white movie.

The sun went down; the air started to turn chilly. Time to move on. He wanted to take her dancing. Go somewhere to spark some excitement back into her fragile-seeming bones.

Mmm, but he was so comfortable lying here, listening to her beautiful voice conjure up memories of their long, wonderful past, feeling drowsy, full of good food and…content.

When was the last time he'd felt that?

He didn't want to think about it. In fact…he yawned, a big, wide-mouthed, satisfying yawn…he didn't want to think about anything….

LINDSAY FINISHED the last bite of her second piece of chocolate cake. She hadn't eaten this much in one sitting in months, but everything tasted so good she couldn't stop. And she couldn't stop staring at Gavin. He was so gorgeous, lying on the cloth, fast asleep. His face was relaxed, dark lashes resting on his cheeks, mouth soft and slightly open, breathing deep and regular. He looked as if he'd knocked five years off his age, looked as he had when they'd been working together awhile, before the stress got to him, before their success started seeming possible, before he caught the Hollywood bug and lost himself and then her.

She moved toward him, unable to resist, and it felt like the most natural thing in the world to lie down facing him, arm curled under her head, watching the man she loved sleep.

She did still love him. Any belief she'd retained in her proud and stubborn attempts to insist to herself she was over him had dissolved the second she saw him locking lips with Kaytee. Sure, okay, it was a breakup goodbye kiss. Gavin wouldn't lie to her; she had no problem believing him. But being faced that directly with the fact that he'd been with someone else, touched someone else, done…*that* with someone else… It only slammed home, extremely painfully, how deeply she still felt he belonged to her. And yes, she to him.

If she had to be honest with herself, she'd admit that she hadn't pursued any other relationship in the last year and a half for that reason. She'd told herself she'd chosen romantic isolation because she was rebounding, that she wasn't ready to date again. When the real reason was more likely that as long as Gavin was alive, she'd never be ready.

Yeah, it hurt that he'd run to someone else, but people coped with pain in different ways, and she had no doubt that he'd been hurting as much as she was, maybe more, since leaving had been her idea. And maybe…maybe if he broke up with Kaytee two days ago, after having seen Lindsay again…maybe he still felt they belonged together, too.

And while she was admitting all the ways she'd been fooling herself, she might as well add to the list that she didn't want to slow Gavin down and turn him on to Vermont only for his sake—to lead him to a healthier lifestyle. She was hoping they could find common ground that would enable them to get back together for good. Maybe even lead them to the altar this time, a place they'd always assumed they'd end up, but never got around to.

She'd won this round for sure. The second she got Gavin away from concrete, into nature, he'd relaxed and unwound. Right away his sleep-starved body had taken what it needed. Oh, she couldn't wait to tease him about this. A nap!

Her own lids fluttered down and she snuggled nearer for his warmth. Maybe it wasn't a good idea to fall asleep at twilight in Central Park. This wasn't Vermont. She should probably...stay awake....

Someone was touching her.

"Lindsay."

Gavin. She struggled up from sleep and lifted her head, wincing at the crick in her neck.

"What is it? You hurt?"

"Stiff neck." She yawned and winced again. "Time 's it?"

His watch glowed green as he lit the face to check. "Nine."

"Nine!" She sat up, rubbing her neck, twisting it side to side as far as it would go, which wasn't very.

"Why, you have somewhere to be?" His hands settled on her and started a slow, gentle massage. Given the distinct chill in the air, she had no idea how he kept his fingers so warm, but mmm, she was glad of it.

"No. Just glad we weren't dismembered. Were we?" She managed to turn her neck far enough to see his face, lit a funny pale shade by the lights lining the park paths.

"Not as far as I can tell." Then, just like that, he dropped a quick soft kiss on her lips, which sent thrills dancing over her skin, and started up a longing for a hell of a lot more than one quick one. "Let's go."

He got to his feet and started packing up their picnic.

"Go? Where?" Back to his room? Was that a good idea or not? Her body said yes; her mind wasn't sure.

She rotated her neck to find the crick was gone and she felt wide awake, thanks to his massage and his sneak-attack kiss.

"Dancing. A new club on Gansevoort Street, Club Tigre. Kaytee told me about it. Supposed to be the big new thing."

Not to his room. Out into the chaos and craziness of the New York party scene. *Oh Gavin.* Her stomach sank and she told herself to calm down. She couldn't expect to change him with one picnic. But after this blissful intimate time together, the last thing she wanted was to go somewhere and be stimulated out of her mind with noise and confusion.

"Okay." She heard herself say the word and cringed. Why didn't she just beg off and go to bed?

Because she wanted to be with him. Because the week was short, he had to be in L.A. by Friday, and she couldn't expect her neighbor Frank to feed Frieda and Freia forever. And because if there was any hope for her and Gavin to work out their differences and make a future together, it wasn't going to happen while he was out on the town and she was sleeping in a hotel room by herself.

"Fabulous." He finished folding the tablecloth and stood. "Ready?"

"Don't I need to be wearing something chic?"

He gestured toward the path and fell into step beside her. "Black is always chic."

She wasn't convinced, but then she hadn't brought anything chic, so guess what, she was doomed to feel even more out of place in this Club Whatever than she would anyway.

They got a cab on Fifth Avenue, took the basket back to The Hotel, where Lindsay insisted on freshening up over Gavin's insistence that she looked ravishing as is, and then proceeded in another taxi to Club Tigre.

Oh. Yippee. Lindsay got out of the car reluctantly, eyeing the more-chic-than-her crowd waiting to get in, which eyed her back. She walked with Gavin to the end of the line and waited, chatting uneasily here and there, eavesdropping on conversations about therapists and shopping trips and the baseball season starting. Music throbbed behind the entrance, louder as they approached, erupting into a blast whenever the door opened to consume those next in line.

Finally they were in, and immediately she wanted out again. Red lights, black corners, the feeling of someone's dank basement. Overwhelming. Gyrating bodies, music she could feel in her chest. Smoke and heat and the crush of too many people in a low-ceilinged space.

How had she ever stood this? She glanced ahead at Gavin, who was grinning, pushing his way through to the bar, clutching her hand, pulling her along. It was a metaphor for their entire life in L.A. Him leading the way, knowing what he wanted, where they were going. Her hanging on for dear life…

Somehow he got the bartender's attention, ordered and pushed a clear drink on the rocks into her hands.

"Soda water?" She had to shout to be heard. "Gin and tonic?"

He shook his head and shouted something back that sounded like "Ky-pee-reen-ya."

Whatever that was. She nodded, unwilling to shout further to clarify, and took a long sip.

Mmm.

Another sip.

Darn good. Limey and strong, but went down nice and easy.

They found a fairly uncrushy place to stand, and bellowed out an attempt at a conversation for a while until they gave up.

Or at least she did. She'd much rather stand here and sip her drink and watch people than have her vocal cords rupture.

As she neared the bottom of the glass, the noise didn't seem quite so bad—had the crowd thinned a bit? What's more, her body had started to move to the beat. First her foot, tap-tap-tapping, then her hips seemed to want to do a little pulsing motion. A permanent smile took charge of her lips, and she felt color surge to her face and a restless energy to her body.

Gavin pulled her over to bellow at someone he knew. Gavin knew everyone. Put him down in a pontoon plane in the middle of Alaska and someone he knew—or someone who knew someone he knew—would come along within twenty minutes. Forget six degrees of separation, Gavin only needed two.

She satisfied herself with nodding and smiling, catching phrases here and there, not really caring. A couple nearby danced suggestively and she watched the woman's face, fierce and sensual, the man's curled-lip response, their bodies undulating together, hands raised, then lowered, moving together then apart. It was beautiful. Fabulous. Lindsay loved everyone here tonight, in fact. Yes, even that guy standing alone, the one no one could possibly love, with too much gel in his hair and his insecurities written all over his desperate attempt to look nonchalant. She loved him, too. Everyone! All of New York.

And she wanted to dance till the cows came home. Wait, no cows here, those were in Vermont. That meant they'd never come home and she could dance forever!

Hot damn.

"Gavin." She yelled and he turned immediately. "Dance with me."

A slow triumphant grin lit his face, but she didn't care about what he might think he won. All she wanted was to get out there, get her body moving, be in the thick of humanity, be part of something big and exciting and energizing and fabulous.

He excused himself from what's-his-name and she grabbed his hand and yanked him onto the floor, threw up her hands and danced. And danced. And danced, lights flashing, music pounding in her chest. And the more she danced, the more the energy rose and flooded her. She felt light, transformed, euphoric; couldn't stop smiling, couldn't stop moving; the most incredible high of her life—except the night she and Gavin had fallen in love.

Hours later? Minutes later? Days later? The music slowed. Gavin clasped her to him; she was breathing hard, glowing, laughing, heated up and having the time of her life.

They started moving again, together, slowly this time. And without any words being spoken, she knew they were telling each other they were back. That they would always be together, no matter what.

She lifted her face, met his eyes, and the stupid cliché of the room falling away happened, as it always did when they were together, when they really looked and really saw each other. She smiled, a happy hey-there smile, but he didn't return it. Instead he leaned forward, a slow sway toward her that had her almost instantly dizzy with anticipation.

When their lips met, it was like the first time, on her couch in front of the TV as the credits rolled, that hot buzz of excitement and lust and the dawning of love. Only this time the love was reawakening to its full power.

She wrapped her arms around him, pushed her body close and kissed him until the need to do what came naturally was so strong she gasped with it. He broke away and ran with her to the exit—only figuratively, since there were too damn many people to get anywhere very quickly. But she felt like running and knew he did too.

Outside, they caught a cab, rode home in silence, holding hands. There seemed to be nothing to say, only to feel—this deep, rock-solid emotion she'd missed so desperately.

In his room they shed their smoky clothes, kissing frantically, trying to make up for a year and a half worth of missed kisses.

And on the bed they knew exactly what went where and when and for how long, because they knew each other inside out and nothing could ever change that or the magic that existed between them.

When she came, she cried out his name, as she had way too many times to count, alone in her bed in Vermont. But this time he was there with her, real and warm, accepting her gift, giving it back in a hoarse whisper as he rode the same ecstatic wave.

After, they lay together blissfully, legs tangled, arms around each other, neither interested in moving even an inch apart. And her feelings for him rose even further, until she knew they'd have to spill out or she'd burst.

"Gavin."

"Mmm."

"I have to tell you something."

"Mmm?"

"I...love you." Her voice broke on the last word; tears jumped into her eyes as if they'd been waiting for this all night long.

"Lindsay."

"Mmm?"

"Something to tell you, too."

"Yes?"

"I love you."

Happiness made the tears fall faster. She giggled and brushed them away. "No way."

"Seriously."

"That is *such* a coincidence."

He lifted his head off the pillow, grinning, relaxed, devastatingly alive and wonderful. "Isn't it?"

"I had a blast dancing."

"I noticed. Thank you for the picnic."

"You liked that?"

"Very much."

"You're welcome."

"I was thinking..." He laid his head back again, squeezing her close, gazing up at the ceiling.

"Ye-e-es?" Wasn't this the perfect scene and perfect time for him to say how he wished he lived someplace calm, where moments like this and the picnic were possible every day? Was she hoping too much?

"I was thinking of that night we got together. How

incredible it was that we were platonic friends, and then in that one instant we were so much more."

"Yes." Not what she'd hoped for but, oh, she'd take it. "Kind of like the instant flare-up while we were dancing?"

"Honey, I had an instant flare-up when we locked eyes in the theater on Saturday night."

"Really? Geez, not me."

He turned toward her, frowning. "No?"

"No." She shook her head gravely. "I felt nothing."

"Ha!" He caught on and laughed. "Liar."

"Moi?"

"I've got news for you. It happened one night—six years ago. Everything since then has been based on that."

"No going back?"

"No, this is it for us. Sorry."

She pouted. "You mean I never will get in Brad Pitt's pants?"

"Negative. You're stuck with me."

"Oh dear." She sighed, then traced a cautious circle on his chest with her fingertip. "So…what happens now?"

"We try again." His smile grew strained. "Come with me to L.A. on Thursday. See how it feels. Come to the pitch. Help me there. See how it feels to be back."

She took a deep breath. "Okay."

"Okay?" He raised himself up on his elbows. "Seriously? It was that simple?"

She smacked his shoulder. "Yes."

"Geez." He fell back on the pillow. "If I knew it was going to be that easy I never would have bothered with the picnic crap."

"Ha!" She smacked him again. "There is a condition."

He groaned. "I knew it."

"You come with me to Vermont after."

"Why?"

"Why?" She gaped at him. "So you can see how it feels."

"Are you kidding me? They make depressants. I don't need Vermont."

She rolled her eyes. "Gavin, it's only fair."

"Look." He took her face in his hands and kissed her, twice. "I'll visit there if you want. But the heart of everything I do is in L.A. The center of everything you are meant to do is there, too. Forget novel-writing, you're not cut out for it."

"What do you mean I—"

"Admit it."

She glared at him.

He nudged her. "C'mon."

"Okay, fine." Her throat thickened. It was the truth. She might as well face it. "I'm a crappy novelist and the book is duller than Mr. Bradford."

"Your neighbor?"

"High school chemistry teacher."

"Oh." Gavin squinted for a second, then his face cleared. "But you're a fabulous screenwriter. And L.A. *is* film. Everybody's there. The whole business is there. Hell, the whole world is there."

Not her world. Something sick and sad invaded her, a worm boring its way into her happiness. He didn't get it. Now she understood his triumphant smile at Club Tigre. The same triumphant smile she must have been wearing when he fell asleep in Central Park. Both of them thought they'd gotten their way, thought they'd convinced the other their lifestyle choice was the right one.

Maybe neither of them really got it. Maybe they underestimated the depth of the gulf between them.

She sighed and got out of bed.

"Where are you going?"

"Shower. I feel sticky and tobacco-gross."

"Want company?"

She smiled at him. She did want company. Now and for the rest of her life. And she wanted that company to be him.

So she'd go to L.A. Try it on. See how it felt. Maybe she could handle it again. For his sake and theirs. She certainly owed it to their history and the depth of her love for him, to try.

"Yes." She laughed uncertainly. "Yes, I do want company."

"Mine?" He blinked teasingly at her from the bed, his body strong and graceful and so dear to her it almost hurt to look at him. How could she live without him?

But how could she go back to living with only the small part he had left over to give her in L.A.?

"Oh yes." She laughed again, hollowly. "Only yours."

At least for as long as it lasted.

CHAPTER FIVE

"YOU NERVOUS?"

Lindsay suppressed a chuckle at Gavin's question. Was *who* nervous? He hadn't sat in one position on the black chair in producer John Saxman's reception area at Universal Pictures for more than ten seconds, and when he was seated, his leg jiggled the entire time.

This wasn't her world anymore; she had no stake in this. If she was nervous it was only because she so desperately wanted Gavin to get what he wanted and what his talent deserved.

"A little nervous." Okay, more than a little. Maybe she did have a tiny stake in this. The project had belonged to both of them at one time.

"Don't worry, Linds, we're going to be fabulous."

She laughed openly this time. "*You* are going to be fabulous, Gavin. This is what you were born to do."

He shook his head. "Both of us. Together."

She smiled tenderly, knowing he was talking about what he wanted to be true more than what could be.

Granted, some things about being back in L.A. had felt like coming home. Sleeping in Gavin's bed last night—er, tossing and turning while listening to him toss and turn—in the familiar tiny house had been delicious. Even being back in L.A. was fun. The shops, the restaurants, the sunny glow and energy of the place…

Hell, she'd spent nearly a decade here, so that wasn't so surprising. But a big part of her was still back in Vermont. She worried about Frieda and Freia, worried about foxes and hawks frightening them or getting past the coop's defenses. She worried about her plants, which her neighbor Frank's housekeeper had promised to water for her. And she missed the green, just starting to work its way into the season. She missed the seasons themselves. Vermont fit her. It felt like home, like security and safety, in a way L.A. never had.

John Saxman's secretary poked her elegant head out of the inner office. "He's ready. Come on in."

Lindsay turned to give Gavin a comforting smile. But he was up already, head held high, shoulders back, chest out, spine straight, nary a jiggle or twitch, every inch the cool confident operator.

She followed him into the office, her comforting smile fading and drooping into an uncomfortable frown. He lived here. Literally, yes, but figuratively as well. She could take him to picnics in the park until she shredded her fingers carrying baskets, but he'd always live here in his heart.

Tears popped up for a quick hello, but before they could settle in, she was saved from humiliation by the appearance of John Saxman.

"Gavin, Lindsay, hey, how are you two, glad to see you."

He was her perfect image of a studio executive. In his fifties, medium height, with brown hair whose color she was pretty sure came from a box, and with a hearty manner that would probably come from a box, too, if that were possible. His greeting was cordial enough, but under it, assessment, as he tried to figure out if she and Gavin would be his ticket to immortality or a giant pain in the afternoon.

"So, the dynamic duo are back together again, eh? Sit down, sit down." He indicated white swively chairs that appeared to be suspended midair, hanging off shiny metal poles. How chic. And uncomfortable. But then Mr. John Saxman, Producer, probably did it on purpose to keep his meetings short. "How was New York? Congratulations on the award, Gavin."

"Thank you." Gavin somehow managed to look at ease on the chair. "I was thrilled. New York was fabulous as always, but it's good to be home in L.A. Right, Lindsay?"

She gave a fake smile. "As ever."

John seated himself at his minimalist black desk, folded his hands on its spotless surface and zeroed in on Lindsay. "You're back for good?"

"Just for a visit this time."

His eyes narrowed, and she didn't even need to look at Gavin to see that his had, too. "Tough to make a career here long-distance."

Who said I wanted a career here? She added teeth to her fake smile. No way would she hurt Gavin's chances by telling the truth. "I'm in the process of moving back."

Might be a sixty-year process, but he didn't need to know that.

"Glad to hear it." He pushed away from the table, crossed his legs, his posture and face challenging. *So what have you got for me to hate today?*

"Let me tell you what we've got here, John. A remake of *The Philadelphia Story*. We're seeing Nicole Kidman leading, with George Clooney as her ex, and John Cusack as the Jimmy Stewart character."

"Hmm." Their hopes and dreams rested his elbows on the arms of his chair and tented his fingers in a classic go-on-I'm-listening pose.

"The film opens with a prologue. We see George Clooney, workaholic ad man, being tossed out of the house by his wife, Nicole, while he's still talking on his cell. She grabs it from him and throws it into their koi pond. He advances on her, picks her up, looks like he's going to kiss her, then throws *her* in the koi pond.

"Fast-forward two years and Nicole's decorating business, what George always called her 'little hobby,' has taken off. She is now as much a workaholic as he was when she threw him out. She's about to marry one of her clients—we're seeing Greg Kinnear in this role—a self-made billionaire who doesn't work and wants her to quit to travel the world with him."

Gavin went on, gesturing broadly, turning the floor over to Lindsay from time to time as they'd planned, when the point of view belonged to the Nicole Kidman character, and Lindsay could outline her gradual realization that she'd become just as driven and career-relentless as her ex was when she threw him out.

Lindsay was nervous at first, stuttered a few times, lost her place and barely caught it in time. Then Gavin looked over at her and smiled as if she was the only person in the room, and from then on, she was fine.

And, bit by bit, more than fine. The excitement started building in her, the desire to paint the script as carefully and faithfully as possible, to sex it up, fire it up, make it as commercially viable as she could.

Her own gestures broadened; she felt herself straightening, ad libbing a few times, adding extra details, extra emotional depth. Damn, it was a good story. She and Gavin should be able to tell it so the world could see it again, so that new generations could fall in love with the characters, the fabulous plot, the dialogue and sheer brainy complexity of movies the way they should be made.

They stood together, trading lines, shooting sparks off each other, outlining the fun and powerful scenes between Clooney and Kidman and the ultimate change in Kidman's character—her growing humility and self-understanding and finally, grand finale, her acceptance that she and her ex were birds of a feather meant to be together.

And there it was. Over. Done. Gone like gangbusters. If Universal didn't buy their work, it wouldn't be because of this performance.

She stood opposite Gavin, smiling into his eyes, her breath coming fast, adrenaline rushing. A happy ending on the silver screen. Now they wanted one in this office.

John Saxman, Producer, still sat with his fingers tented under his nose.

Did he love it? Hate it? Had he been deeply moved or had he suddenly suffered a paralyzing heart attack?

Finally he took his hands down. "Is the script written?"

"Say the word and it will be."

"Both of you?" He gestured between them.

"Yes." They answered in unison.

"I love it."

Lindsay held her breath. Yes. *Yes*. This was it. Gavin

glanced at her; she hardly dared look back for fear of erupting into squeals of excitement.

"I really love it." He started nodding, then a big grin spread over his face. "I've got people who would be interested in this for sure."

"That's fabulous, John." Gavin didn't let out an ounce of the emotion she knew he was feeling. Ever the consummate professional. "Thank you."

She added her thanks, barely getting the syllables past the squeeze of emotion in her throat.

They'd done it. *They'd done it.*

How the hell were they supposed to get out of here with their dignity intact? She wanted to throw up her arms and howl, act like a linebacker in the end zone after catching the winning Superbowl touchdown. They'd done it. Okay, no sale yet, but hell, this was as good as they could get out of the meeting today.

They shook hands calmly with a beaming John and walked into the outer office, calmly saying goodbye to his secretary. They even made it out of the building and into the studio parking lot and the glorious sunshine of Los Angeles, California.

"Yes!" Lindsay shouted the word and jumped into Gavin's arms. He whooped and spun her in a jubilant circle.

"We did it." His face was glowing; he put her down, and kissed her. "This is it, Lindsay. We're on our way."

She laughed, unable to contain her joy, needing some kind of outlet, any kind. On their way. The script of their heart. As good as sold. No need to think about everything that could and often did go wrong in this business. Right now they could enjoy their dream still untarnished by directors, actors, studio policies, box office uncertainties. Forget all of them. Right now it was Gavin and Lindsay, the Dynamic Duo, ready to take off for the stars together.

"Gavin, to celebrate, we should go to that little place near UCLA we went to all the time when—"

His cell rang; he checked the number and punched the phone on. "It's Barry. Hey, Barry, guess what?"

She took a step away from him while he filled his agent in on how the pitch had gone. The sun was hot, and she was suddenly incredibly thirsty. She tugged on his sleeve; he smiled and nodded at her, but kept talking.

"Okay, Barry. Right. Bye. Damn. He's excited." Gavin laughed and squeezed her close.

"Of course he is. It's money in his pocket, too. Now I'm dying of thirst. Let's go   "

"Oh, crap, I forgot. I have to call Tom and Sharlee. And then Mom and Dad. I promised I would the second we got done. Okay? Only be a sec, I promise. Then we'll go wherever you want."

She must have had an I'll-get-you-for-this look on her face because he kissed her while he was waiting for the first call to connect. "They've lived with me through a lot of this, they deserve to know. And if I don't call now, one or both of them will call me, and if we're somewhere having fun and get interrupted, that will be worse."

"You're right." Yeah, he was right. It was just too typical.

Fifteen minutes later, Tom and Sharlee and David and Joyce had apparently heard enough details to satisfy them, and Lindsay was hot and cranky and wishing

Universal had a koi pond around here for Gavin's cell to have a nice cool swim.

"Okay, bye." He punched off the phone and rushed her, swung her around, growling. "Now, my one true love, I am all yours."

She giggled. Okay, she was a sap; she couldn't help it. "It's about time. Let's go to that little Thai place where we used to—"

"Gavin, hey, buddy."

Her giggle died a swift and terrible death. Oh yippee. Backstabbing Bob Franklin. With Hanger-On Marlie, the Gavin-attachment he'd never bothered to shake off even for Lindsay's sake. And Alex, who'd taken such pains to snark at Lindsay and her dress the night of the awards in New York. And two other people she didn't recognize, but who looked suited up and important.

"Let's go." She waved at the approaching throng and tugged Gavin's sleeve. "Now."

"Okay. Just let me get rid of them." He greeted the quintet. "How's it going?"

"Good meeting?"

He nodded smugly, though Lindsay knew he'd rather put his thumbs in his ears, waggle his fingers and say, "Neener-neener."

"Great. Gavin, I'd like you to meet George Conklin and Bruce Russell."

Lindsay wilted. George and Bruce, big-time decision makers for Universal, exactly the kind of people Gavin most wanted to butt-kiss. She could see disaster coming a mile away. A big train, single light glowing in the dark, and she and Gavin tied to the tracks.

After polite introductions all around, the inevitable came.

"We were on our way to Marica's Cantina to have a few drinks. Join us." This command came from George Conklin, causing Bob's face to turn an unattractive shade of I-hate-you.

"Oh, well…" Gavin turned to her. He wouldn't accept unless she said yes. He wasn't that bad. But the plea was there in his eyes, and if she said no, he'd fidget the entire evening, imagining all the fabulous opportunities for networking he might have blown by not accepting the invitation.

She sighed. "We'd love to, thank you."

He smiled gratefully, bent close and kissed her, using the move to whisper, "Just a quick one, then we can go to dinner."

"Sure." She smiled at him, hoping the sadness didn't show in her eyes, and walked with him to his car. They wouldn't make it to dinner. These were studio execs on an expense account and it was five o'clock on a Friday. Drinks would make everyone jolly and chatty and ravenous, and food would start appearing… And Gavin wouldn't feel he could leave even if he wanted to, or risk insulting his hosts. She'd lived it so many times.

"Hey, you." He opened the passenger door for her. "Thank you for understanding.

"You're welcome."

She did understand. She understood very well. Much better than he thought she did. She understood that for him it would always be about L.A. It would always be about filmmaking.

And it would never be enough about them.

WERE THEY EVER GOING to stop talking?

Gavin let out yet another hearty ha-ha-ha at a story he didn't find funny. He'd been looking for an opportunity to leave for the last half hour, ever since he'd noticed Lindsay had gone stone-cold quiet beside him and then excused herself. Damn it. He'd said a quick drink. But the talk had flowed, entrées had been ordered, important business was being discussed. These people could make his and Lindsay's career. He couldn't stand up and walk out unless his exit would seem completely natural.

He turned impatiently to see if Lindsay had come back from the restroom yet. He hoped she wasn't in there sick or upset. He'd seen her talking to the bartender at one point, but then he'd lost track of where she went.

"Right, Gavin?"

He forced his attention back to the conversation, smile back in place. Damn it, where was she? She'd only had one drink, a margarita she'd nursed for nearly an hour, and hadn't eaten much, maybe some chips and salsa. He knew she had her heart set on the Thai place they used to go to near UCLA when they were students there. They could still go. Sort of. Maybe for dessert.

Okay, so he was a jerk. He'd let her down. But this was—

He sighed. Why was he sitting here arguing with himself? It was Lindsay he needed to apologize to, or else take a stand and insist being here was important and they could always go out another night.

So where was she?

He excused himself from the table and stood by the ladies' room until a woman came out.

"Hi, sorry. Would you mind—was there a brunette in there, petite, Audrey Hepburn type, about this high?" He put his hand up by his collarbone.

"Sorry, no. I was alone in there."

Crap.

He lunged for the bar, waved frantically until the Matt Dillon look-alike bartender came over. "Yeah?"

"Do you remember the brunette who was over here talking to you before?"

"Who, Lindsay?"

"Yes, Lindsay." It galled Gavin unreasonably that this guy knew her name. "Where is she, do you know?"

He shrugged. "Asked me to call her a cab. Said she was going to Venice."

To his house. Okay. He needed to do some minorly serious groveling to George and Bruce, then go home and do some seriously serious groveling to Lindsay.

He returned to the table, feeling uneasy.

"Hey, where's your better half?" Backstabbing Bob had a grin on that said he smelled a lover's spat and wasn't above trying to rub Gavin's nose in it. "She go running off to Vermont again?"

He couldn't quell the stab of panic. "Not this time."

"You better be nicer to her...."

Gavin dropped all pretense at friendliness. "Or what? You'll invite her to Cancun behind my back?"

Bob look startled, then shrugged. "You'll lose her again."

"Not going to happen." Gavin forced a smug smile on his face, which dropped as soon as he said his goodbyes and thanks and swung around to leave. Using every last bit of self-control, he kept himself from running out of the restaurant and into his car.

Traffic was hell. Traffic was always hell in Los Angeles, so that made today's traffic superhell. The ninth circle, the ultimate torture, Satan's special misery supreme.

Just to make sure Gavin suffered as much as possible.

Nonsense. He told himself he was being ridiculous. That Lindsay had learned she couldn't live without him, without L.A. During the meeting he'd seen her catch fire, the way she'd caught fire on the dance floor in New York. But this time it was all about the work, all about the story and the passion she had for telling a good one.

She wouldn't make the same mistake twice. Even if she did need to go back to Vermont for chicken maintenance, at least she wouldn't run out on him. She'd talk to him, they'd discuss things, come to some solution that would work for both of them. Like she'd give up this depressing isolated farmhouse obsession, admit she came alive here in L.A., deeply involved in the work she was born to do, and they'd settle back into their life together, older and wiser.

Sounded reasonable to him.

Unfortunately, it would take seeing her, talking to her, and holding her tonight in his house to rid himself of the uneasiness Bob had planted.

If the Fates were kind, next week in Mexico Kaytee would give The Backstabber a coronary in bed.

Finally, an hour after Gavin left the restaurant, he pulled into the driveway of his tiny Venice bungalow, scrambled out of his Mazda and barreled up to the front door. Locked. That meant nothing. She would lock the door behind her, of course. Safety reasons.

He went inside, scoured the living room, kitchen, guest bedroom.

"Lindsay?"

Nothing. He peered into the backyard—using the term loosely for a postage stamp patio of concrete and a strip of what was supposed to be a garden—and hurtled to the rear of the house and his bedroom. "Lindsay?"

What he least wanted to see—her things were gone. And there was a note on the bed.

Gavin. I've gone back to Vermont. I need to regroup. Too much has happened in too short a time and I need peace and room to think it all through. I'd love to work on the script with you, but I can't do it here. L.A. has too much of you for there to be room for me.

All my love,

Lindsay

He crushed the note in his fist, stiffening every muscle until it hurt, and let out a bellow of frustration.

How could she do this to him again?

He slumped down on the bed, the one he'd be in alone tonight, with the memory of her in his arms so fresh. He'd have to go through that pain *again*.

He'd been on his way home to apologize. To make everything right. And she gave him no chance to do it. No chance at all.

When had things gone wrong? When had she

changed her mind? She'd been so full of fire and excitement after the deal....

And then Bob and company had shown up.

Gavin groaned and flung himself backward on the bed, gazing up at the ceiling, wanting it to fall on him and crush this horrible emotional pain out of him with a new simpler physical one.

She'd been trying to get him to go somewhere with her. With no L.A. No film people. No crowds, no dancing. The two of them, alone, as they were in Central Park, where he'd felt more contentment than he had in years.

And he'd given her no chance to do it.

No chance at all.

CHAPTER SIX

AHHH. Lindsay switched off the motor of her yellow Volkswagen Beetle, leaped out and took in huge lungfuls of crisp clean pine-scented Vermont air.

God, it was good to be home. Away from the crowds, away from the smog and the heat and the asphalt and steel everywhere. Back to her three-story white Victorian farmhouse, welcoming and regal, all the more so for being nobly weathered.

She wouldn't think about how it felt being away from Gavin. Not yet. Not just yet. She'd come here to regroup, and she would take time to do that first.

She grabbed her bag out of the back seat and sprinted behind the house to the chicken pen. "Frieda, Freia, I'm home!"

Both of her sweeties had already rushed to the wire of their pen to greet her, cackling their special greeting, "Wuuhhhh? Wuuuuhhh?"

"It's all right, babies, it's me." She half sang her standard response, knowing if she didn't, they'd keep calling louder until she answered.

She opened the pen and let them out, kneeling on the grass to say hello properly, heart brimming with happiness. Frieda hopped up onto her lap, crooning with joy, and Freia flapped up to perch on her shoulder, making sounds of contentment.

"Hey, pretty birds," she sang in the voice they knew as praise, stroking their beautiful silver-and-black feathers. "I'm sorry I was gone so long."

She stayed out in the yard until she felt she'd atoned for her sin of absence, that she'd reassured them she hadn't fallen to a predator, and that their flock was still intact. Then she went into the house, delighting in every beautiful peaceful familiar corner of it, ignoring the tug of pain in her heart. This was home. She needed to be back here to be whole again.

She unpacked her bags, changed out of the black pants she was sick to death of wearing and into soft pale blue jeans, hung the formal gown up to air until she could get it to the dry cleaner—God knew how long it would be before she'd wear it again. Certainly not around here.

There. All unpacked. Back home. All settled.

So.

She yawned—of course she was tired from her flight—and went back downstairs to call her neighbor.

"Hey, Frank, I'm home. Thank you so much for taking such good care of Frieda and Freia. They're looking great, healthy and full of spirit, and—"

"No trouble. Good trip?"

"Oh, yes, tiring, but it was fun. I first went to New York, then an unexpected detour to Los Angeles. I—"

"All right. We'll be seeing you."

"Right." She chuckled. She'd forgotten herself and turned back into Chatty Cathy. "Bye. Oh, and thanks again, for—"

"Ayup."

Click.

Well. Obviously she needed to relearn Vermontese.

Lindsay let out a great sigh of happiness, which didn't feel quite happy enough, and stood in her quiet, cozy, neat kitchen. Did she mention quiet?

So. What had she been going to do? Something…

Maybe…a nap?

Sure, why not. She felt awfully sleepy. Stress of the last few days and so on.

She went back upstairs and lay on her bed, forcing thoughts of Gavin out of her mind.

It must have worked, because when she opened her eyes it was two hours later. She lay there dreamily, letting her body adjust to the concept of being awake.

Unfortunately, her mind was too sleepy to keep up the blockade, so all the thoughts about Gavin she didn't want to be having burst over her.

She shouldn't have left like this. She'd panicked, and it was wrong and childish. When he'd ignored her and spent the evening with those idiots, it had broken her heart, and she'd thought only of running as far and fast as she could from even the threat of that pain again. Bad move. Same mistake twice. She should have sat down calmly and talked it over with him. Even if it hadn't done any good, she owed him more than a disappearing act.

But that was the problem with L.A. Here she saw everything more clearly. Here she was a rational, sane…she yawned…sleepy human being. There she was a mass of nerves and anxieties and stresses, and she didn't behave like herself.

She dragged herself out of bed and went down to the

sunny, plant-filled, closed-in porch she used as an office, and flipped open her laptop. Checked e-mail from friends, family and spammers, then pulled up a new one and addressed it to Gavin.

Hi. I'm home safely. I panicked and I'm sorry, truly. I didn't mean to put you through this again, but then I can't go through the whole L.A. routine again, either. If we're going to make this work, we need to do things differently. I love you,
Lindsay

She hit Send, deleted the spam, responded to family and friends. Made herself a cup of tea. Drank it. Made another, decaf this time. Drank that.

So.

She yawned in spite of the tea, and played about eight games of Spider Solitaire while her incoming mail notifier remained stubbornly silent. Apparently Gavin wasn't anywhere he could get e-mail.

Well.

She could take the rest of the day off and not worry about her novel, which she thought she might try to rewrite as a romance, since she couldn't get that image of the tall dark stranger in the TT Roadster out of her mind. Or the image of the old couple, hanging tough, spreading tenderness in good times and bad, sickness and health.

Why hadn't she and Gavin ever talked marriage other than in an abstract way? They'd had this unspoken agreement—she thought—that when their careers took off, that would be the time.

Now she thought maybe the postponement had been

an excuse. Maybe they both realized they were too different for things to work out, and they'd kept postponing facing the issues until they exploded.

Maybe she needed to let go this time. They'd had their second chance. They could have a third, a fourth, a fifth, and really, nothing would change unless everything about them did.

Tears slipped out from under her lids and she got up, grabbed a tissue and indulged in a good honking blow, staring out at the wandering hills, adorned with maples, birch, pines, farmland. It all looked so beautiful…so, so beautiful. And quiet. And real.

And so, so lonely.

ARRRGH! Lindsay drove her Beetle up the driveway, switched it off in front of her house and rested her head on the steering wheel.

Terrific.

She was just back from the second visit to the doctor in three days, after spending two weeks either asleep for ten hours a night, napping or wishing she could nap. The scale had showed her weight dropping. Finally she'd been scared enough to get a medical evaluation.

Diagnosis? Not anemia. Not cancer. Not thyroid.

Depression.

Recommendation? A therapist, a regime of antidepressants, or…a major life change.

Great. Spectacular. Sweet as hell. Her wonderful contentment here, her communion with nature, her reaching for and finally touching the reality of existence, finally grasping what truly mattered to her…was a form of mental illness.

When wonderful Dr. Bolton, who reminded her of her own black-eyebrowed, white-haired grandfather, had made his pronouncement, after the shock and denial, Lindsay had slowly started to remember. Remember how she'd come alive that night she and Gavin went out dancing. Hell, how she'd come alive just setting eyes on him that first night at the Reel New York awards. And the next day, in her hotel room, when he'd shown up to talk over the script. And the day after that when they'd been working on the pitch.

She wasn't happy here. She was miserable, especially without him. She couldn't write; she could barely function. And somehow she'd managed to call this nirvana?

Nirvana was being with him, having him drive her crazy, and driving him crazy back. Nirvana was being in his arms, peaceful and cuddling or writhing and sweaty.

Nirvana was not Vermont if Vermont was without him. And she was pretty sure he hadn't found much nirvana in L.A. without her, either.

He'd e-mailed a short reply to her note of two weeks ago, sounding busy and pressured, setting up a time this week when they could discuss moving forward on the script. Today at two o'clock. And all she'd wanted to say was, No, I can't, that's my nap time.

Hello? Shouldn't that have been a dead giveaway?

Yeah. Hindsight didn't require vision adjustment.

She yanked open the door to her car, marched up the front walk, into her house, up to her bedroom, and packed her two biggest suitcases. She was going back to L.A. and then she'd sell her house and move there permanently, assuming they could find a place zoned for backyard chickens. She didn't love L.A., but it didn't matter. She and Gavin needed to be together, and he'd made it obvious that he wasn't leaving. Maybe he was so miserable right now without her that he was promising himself he'd change....

Unless he'd just shrugged and moved on to Kaytee2.

Lindsay's lip curled in a snarl. *Just let him try.*

She'd need to get Frank to take care of Frieda and Freia again. Oh, gosh, she hated leaving them so soon. Frank had said it was days until they stopped calling for her.

She glanced at her watch, adrenaline pumping, and realized that she'd been in her bedroom over an hour and hadn't once wanted to fall asleep.

Things were looking up.

She ran downstairs and into the kitchen. She'd have time to eat lunch before Gavin called at two. Then the trick would be talking to him without giving away the surprise.

Ha! She couldn't wait to see his face when he saw she'd come back to stay this time. She'd just have to live with the part of her that dreaded being in the city again.

She wolfed down her usual half sandwich, was still hungry, made another half and wolfed that, too. Followed it with an apple, then got inspired and rushed to make a batch of brownies, which she shoved into the oven. Excellent. She was halfway cured already.

A glance at the clock and she went upstairs to use the bathroom and brush her teeth, not that Gavin could possibly smell her lunch two thousand miles away, but women held that kind of illogic dear. She even fussed with her hair and put on a little makeup.

There. Two o'clock. On the dot. He'd call any second; he was extremely punctual.

She sat smugly by the phone in her office and waited.

And waited.

Two-o-five.

Two-ten...

Two-fifteen, and time to take out the brownies.

Maybe she should call him?

Frieda and Freia set up a ruckus in the backyard and she put the brownies on a rack to cool and went to peek out the window. What was bothering her sweeties?

Her jaw dropped.

She pushed open the back door and stood stupidly on the step, watching Gavin bend over, peering at her frantic chickens.

She grabbed a handful of hen scratch and walked forward, nearly laughing when she heard what he was saying.

"Heeere, chicky chicky chicky."

"They think you're a predator, since you're not part of the flock." Her voice came out rusty and she had to clear her throat.

"Yeah?" He straightened and turned, and the gentle Vermont sun hit his face and made his eyes vivid and intense, erased the shadows and softened his too-harsh cheekbones. "Are you part of it?"

"Yes." She wanted to say it but it sounded absurd. *Join us! Be one of our flock forever!*

"What do you suggest I do to be part of the gang?"

"This will help. Watch." She pitched her voice slightly higher. "Treat! Treat!"

At the sound of their favorite word, her chickens came rushing back to the gate.

"Now give it to them."

He accepted the feed, stared at the excited birds, then glanced at her again. "They understand words?"

"Quite a few." She sent him a wry grin. "They probably communicate more clearly than we do."

"Undoubtedly." He fed the chickens corn and seed treats until they were gone, and the birds went back to scratching, calmed by Lindsay's presence. "So I'm an honorary chicken now?"

"On your way if you want to be, yes."

"I want to be."

Her heart threatened to stop from happiness. "Then you're more than welcome."

"Thanks." He smiled and did a three-sixty of her fabulous view. "You were right, Linds. This is beautiful country. I feel more relaxed than I have since…"

"I left?"

He frowned slightly, tilted his head, not unlike one of her feathered babies. "I guess maybe, yeah."

"Uh huh. I have a theory about that. Come inside. I made your favorite brownies."

"You knew I was coming?"

"Subconsciously I must have." She couldn't stop smiling, couldn't stop her heart from pounding like crazy any more than she could stop it hoping. He'd come here. Maybe things could change enough so they'd both be happy.

He eyed her critically, holding open the screen door for her to pass through ahead of him. "You don't look like you've been eating many of them."

"That's about to change."

She had three. Gavin had four. They washed them down with big glasses of milk from Vermont cows and talked business. The deal on *The Philadelphia Story* would go through. But Saxman was bringing in other writers. Bob Franklin for one.

Lindsay's heart sank. Damn it. What a crappy business. Hadn't they heard the too-many-cooks saying? If Bob was in on it, the purity and sophistication of Gavin's planned script would be compromised. Bob would put in transvestites for cheap disrespectful laughs, and stuff the screenplay with overblown physical sight gags that weren't funny. "They'll ruin it."

"I know." Gavin got up from the table. "I'll bring my bags in."

"Are you okay?"

He turned back, looking perplexed. "Strangely, yes. I seem to have decided there are one or two things more important than scripts. One in particular."

"Oh." She couldn't say more, just sat there, glowing like a lighthouse. "Need help with your bags?"

He shook his head, smiled at her in a strangely calm way and went out to the car.

Lindsay sank down at the table, since her legs weren't planning on holding her for much longer. Something was up. Something big. She didn't know what, but her instincts were telling her she was going to like it.

Gavin came back in, carrying two enormous suitcases. Lindsay sat bolt upright. "Planning a long stay?"

"Planning a move."

"A *move?*"

"Yeah." He grinned, as if he'd just bought her the moon. "What, you don't want me here?"

"*No.*"

His grin froze in horror before she realized what she'd said.

"No, I mean, you don't belong here. Even I don't belong here. Look." She grabbed his hand and pulled him up the stairs into her room, where her two enormous suitcases still lay on her bed. "I'm planning a move, too."

"Lindsay, you hate L.A."

"Yes, but I love you." She slid her arms around his neck and gazed at him adoringly. "And not to sound like a screenwriter who found the perfect line, but darling, wherever you are is where I want to be."

She went up on tiptoes, asking for a kiss, and oh my goodness did she get one, strong and warm and containing every ounce of passion that they shared. Which was considerable. And therefore it was a full minute before she could make her brain function again and realize he was speaking.

"You'd move to Tinseltown for me and I was ready to join a chicken flock for you."

"Can you believe it? To heck with film awards, we should be sainted."

"Um." He moved suggestively against her. "I'm not feeling very spiritual at the moment."

"No?"

"More…earthly."

She smiled sweetly. "Rocklike, you mean?"

"Yesss."

"Gavin."

"Mmm?"

"Let's do something we've never done."

"I like it already. Tell me."

"Compromise."

"Compromise?" He pretended shock. "But no one *wins* that way."

She wrinkled her nose. "I know, doesn't it stink? But I hear it's the way to go in relationships."

"Well, you know me, I'm always about what's hot." He started walking her backward, a slow, sexy meander toward her bed. "Which is why I'm always about you, Ms. Kenyon."

"Oh, good line, Mr. Garvey."

"Thank you. So what's your plan?"

"Six months here, six months in L.A.?" She tilted her head, watching him.

He frowned for twenty endless seconds, then nodded firmly. "I could live with that. July through December here, January through June there?"

"Oh perfect, Christmas in Vermont, but February in sunny California." The backs of her knees encountered the side of her bed and she knew she was about to be loved more thoroughly than any woman had ever been before. "You got yourself a deal."

"I've got myself the perfect woman."

"Ooh, another good line." She slid her hands down until she encountered the waistband of his jeans, and pulled his shirt out of them. "You should be a screenwriter."

"Interesting thought." His hands were similarly occupied and her shirt lifted up and over her head. "I'll keep it in mind."

"Write a script with me." She stopped undressing him, hit by a bolt of pure joyous inspiration. "About a headstrong woman who runs away from something instead of dealing with it, and a man who leads her to what truly makes her happy."

"I like it." He bent and kissed her bare shoulder, following the line to the base of her neck, sending shivers all over her skin. "As long as there's a happy ending."

"There definitely is going to be a happy ending, Gavin."

His head stilled next to hers; his breath stopped warming her shoulder. "With marriage?"

Lindsay inhaled sharply. "Do you think they should?"

"Yes. We should." He lifted his head, looking at her slightly anxiously. "That is if you—"

"Yes." She beamed at him, picturing the two of them, old and content here in this house, spry and still kicking in L.A. "I do."

He chuckled and kissed her until she was breathless again, his fingers trailing up and down her bare sides. "So what will you call this blockbuster of ours?"

"It Happened One Night."

"It did, didn't it." He lifted her suitcases off onto the floor to make room for the two of them on the bed that would be theirs to share, in her half of their life together. "And sweetheart, it's about to happen again."

Everything you love about romance...
and more!

Please turn the page for Signature Select™
Bonus Features.

And the envelope, Please...

BONUS FEATURES INSIDE

12 Secrets to Great Photos
by Julie Monahan Wyatt

You may not have a red carpet or paparazzi in your future, but that doesn't mean some time soon you won't find yourself being asked to smile for the camera when you need new business cards, at your best friend's wedding, your goddaughter's christening or at your own surprise birthday party. Knowing how to put your best face forward at a moment's notice is a skill we can all use.

Short of signing up for a package deal with a cosmetic surgeon, there isn't much we can do to alter our DNA, but when it comes to facing the unblinking eye of the camera, it helps to have a few tricks up your sleeve.

Let's hear what the experts have to say.

1. Author Barbara Bretton admits she has made more than a few mistakes. "If you know you'll be faced with photographers on a given date, don't experiment with new makeup techniques or hair colors the night—or even the week—

4

before. Stay away from the scissors! Try a test run a few weeks before the big day so you have time to get it right. If you're feeling self-conscious about the way you look, you're doomed."

2. Top Harlequin Presents author Sandra Marton gets right to the point. "Wet your lips and widen your eyes before each shot and make sure you use a lighter shade of eye shadow."

3. Yasmine Galenorn, author of the popular Chintz 'n' China mystery series, offers this reminder: "The key is to try all sorts of variations and be prepared to go through a number of shots. After a while, amidst the serious poses and the gaffes and the inadvertent goofs, something usually creeps in that captures the 'you' that you feel is really you."

4. Take a close look at red-carpet photos of celebrities and you'll notice that none of those photo-savvy ladies ever faces the lens head-on. Susan Lacy owned and managed a chain of modeling/talent agencies in Georgia and Florida. Susan advises, "Stand so you're perpendicular to the camera. Your hips are at the three o'clock position. Twist your shoulders to the twelve o'clock position so they are square in the lens. This makes hips look tiny and shoulders wide—the fabulous V! It might be uncomfortable, but you'll look so great you

won't care. Place one hand on your hip, one stretched down your leg. Try this in the privacy of your own home and you'll see exactly what I mean."

5. Mary Kennedy, author of the young-adult novel *Confessions of an Almost Movie Star*, advises: "Try looking down, as the photographer fiddles with the lights, and just look up at the last moment when she says, 'Ready.' If you stare steadily at the camera for too long, it gives you that deer-in-the-headlights look, along with a frozen smile. If you want a look that is fresh and spontaneous, look up and smile as she snaps the picture."

6. Christine Rimmer, author of *The Bravo Family Way*, offers this: "I use my vivid author's imagination. I pretend the photographer is passionately in love with me and thinks I'm the most gorgeous woman on earth. This helps me loosen up."

7. Publicist and author Binnie Syril Braunstein recommends the following: "Role play. Put a chair in front of a full-length mirror and do some poses. Talk to someone (that person in the mirror) while you're doing it. Don't talk about the depressing process of having a photo taken. Every once in a while, see how the pose is going."

8. Alesia Holliday, author of *Nice Girls Finish First*, takes a playful approach. "Drink a glass of wine just before you go. Take a good friend or somebody who can make you laugh. The photographer's little "tricks"—no matter how good he or she is—just make me tense up more. But a friend can help you poke fun at yourself and relax."

9. Bertrice Small, the beloved *New York Times* bestselling author of *Lara*, speaks from experience. "Get a facial, manicure, pedicure and massage so you are totally relaxed and feeling really good about yourself. Pick an outfit you love and feel incredible in, and get your makeup and hair done. When the picture is being taken, just keep thinking how fabulous you are, and what a wonderful picture it's going to be."

10. Author Melanie Jackson uses props. "Wear a large hat or glasses, hide behind a fan or a book or a pet (Pets are especially good. People seem to love animals)."

11. Bestselling reader-favorite Dallas Schulze enjoys being in front of the camera. "I never minded being photographed and am very comfortable in front of the camera. The only specific tip I remember on posing for photographs is to relax your mouth. Even if the photo doesn't show any teeth, pressing

your lips together tightens your whole expression. Once the photographer told me that, the whole thing seemed to go better."

12. Nancy Herkness, the award-winning romance author of *Shower of Stars*, has come up with her own formula for success. "I found a photographer who was willing to come to my house so I was in a familiar, natural setting and I wore clothes that I love and feel comfortable in."

Practice, prepare and before you know it, you too will be able to relax and have fun in front of the camera. The results will surprise you!

Hollywood Tales Magazine
The DQT Column—
Dish with Queen Tinsel

It's not often this fabulous celebrity interviewer is called on to interview screenwriters. It's even less often this interviewer actually looks forward to it. But writing team Gavin Harvey and Lindsay Kenyon are not your average pair of old-movie lovers. Start with Gavin, who looks like a combo Cary Grant/Gregory Peck. Throw in Lindsay, who could be Audrey Hepburn's daughter, and it's like being in the presence of royalty...only fun.

Coming soon to a theater near you, their latest collaboration, a first for them from Universal Pictures, *Take Me Back*, a remake of the 1940 classic *The Philadelphia Story*.

I spoke to Hollywood's Dynamic Duo over lunch at The Ivy.

Q: Why The Philadelphia Story?

Gavin: It's a classic second-chance-at-love story, but with lots of twists and turns along the way. Who will our leading lady marry? The dull fiancé...?

Lindsay: Oh, God forbid

Gavin: The handsome reporter...?

Lindsay: Mmm, that might be nice.

Gavin: (sends her a killer glare) Or the wildly sexy ex?

Lindsay: (beams back) Yeah, how about him.

Q: At one point I heard Universal was bringing in other writers, true?

Gavin: Uh, yes, Bob Franklin was going to work on it with us.

¹⁰ **Q: What happened?**

Lindsay has a sudden coughing fit that makes this interviewer raise her beautifully shaped eyebrows.

Gavin: Bob had an accident during a trip to Mexico.

Lindsay: An unfortunate accident. In the bedroom. At night.

Gavin: Very unfortunate.

Lindsay: Very painful.

At this point your lovely and talented interviewer decides to let the topic drop. Must keep my G rating. But obviously Bob was out of commission for a while after being overly...

enthusiastic. Note to self: Stay out of Bob's way at night in bedrooms.

Q: So they let you write the script on your own?

Gavin: No, they brought in Bill Angleterre. We'd worked with him before.

Lindsay: Very happily.

Gavin: And did so again. In fact, we're really pleased with the way everyone involved with the film agreed with our original vision.

Q: Well, I can't wait to see the movie. What's next for you two?

Lindsay: Universal is producing our next script.

Gavin: Another rewrite—*It Happened One Night.*

Q: I love that movie!

Lindsay: (does the beaming-in-love thing again) Same here.

Q: My "spidey" signals are tingling. I sense there's a story there.

Lindsay: We were watching that movie the night we fell in love.

Q: You fell in love in one night?

Gavin: We'd been friends for a while.

Q: Did they bring anyone else in on this script?

Lindsay: No, they let us write this one on our own, which was great.

Q: So what about the rumors that you two are finally going to tie the knot?

Lindsay: (laughs) They're true. We've been through a lot together, and it's the right thing to do.

Q: When is the big day?

Gavin: (puts his arm around Lindsay) After the premiere of *It Happened One Night*.

Q: When is that going to be?

Lindsay: Not soon enough.

Q: So you guys live half the year in L.A. and half in Vermont. How does that work?

Lindsay: Pretty well, actually. I think we both need the quiet—

Gavin: And after the quiet we need the craziness—

Lindsay: Then we definitely need quiet again. It's turned out to be ideal. Lots of compromises at first, but—

Gavin: I've learned to love chickens.

Lindsay: And I've learned to party till I drop.

Q: How perfect. Any bambinos planned?

Gavin: Twelve.

Lindsay: Two.

Q: (laughs, she can't help it, even though she risks lines) I can see more compromises ahead.

Lindsay: That's what makes it work.

Gavin: That and good nooky.

Lindsay: Gavin! This is going in print.

Gavin: (shrugs) It's true. Let the world read.

Lindsay: (rolls eyes and smiles) Fine. Let 'em. Good nooky definitely helps.

Q: And with those immortal words, Lindsay, Gavin, it's been a pleasure talking with you.

Lindsay: For us, too.

Gavin: Thanks very much.

They get up, smiling at each other in a way that makes this jaded interviewer smile, too, and oh, we hate to smile.

Celebrity divorces have become more common than boob jobs. Will these kids make it?

This gorgeous but oh-so-cynical chick is betting yes.

Biltmore House
by Emilie Rose

If we could linger with Jenna and Conrad for a few
more pages I imagine they'd be married quietly
on the extensive grounds of the Biltmore Estate
in Asheville, North Carolina, Jenna's hometown.

Biltmore House is the largest privately owned
home in the United States. In the late 1880s
George Vanderbilt, youngest grandson of
American shipping and railroad tycoon Cornelius
Vanderbilt, bought 125,000 acres of land in
Asheville, an upper-class health retreat.

He commissioned architect Richard Morris
Hunt, designer of famous structures such as
the pedestal of the Statue of Liberty and the
entrances to Central Park in New York City, to
build him a home worthy of the Chateau de Blois,
a grand chateau in the Loire Valley of France. The
undertaking was so immense that a separate
railroad spur had to be constructed to carry the
materials and equipment to the site, and a private
brick factory was required.

The massive limestone structure formally opened on Christmas Eve in 1895. Biltmore House boasts 175,000 square feet (four acres of floor space), 250 rooms, 34 bedrooms, 43 bathrooms and 3 kitchens. The mansion has central heating, hot and cold running water to the bathrooms, electricity, a fire alarm and a mechanical refrigeration system. And just in case Mr. Vanderbilt didn't want to trudge up and down the 102-step stone staircase for a midnight snack, he had an elevator and an electric intercom system installed. Oh, yes, and he had one of those newfangled things...a telephone. Many basements are dark and dingy. Not this one. Vanderbilt's had an indoor pool with underwater lighting, a bowling alley and a gymnasium installed in his basement. For a home completed in 1895, Biltmore was amazingly state of the art.

You can't plop a Hope diamond of a house like that down in the dirt and throw out a handful of grass seed and be done with it. Vanderbilt contracted Frederick Law Olmsted, designer of Central Park, the U.S. Capitol grounds and the campuses of Yale and Stanford to design his grounds.

The grounds of Biltmore Estate are a combination of formal and natural areas. Considering the rough material of overworked farmland that Olmsted began with, he worked nothing short of a miracle, filling the acreage with both native and non-native plants. Today there are more than 250 acres of landscaped gardens, 2,300 roses, 1,000 azaleas, 50,000 Dutch tulips and 3 reflecting pools. It's an impressive place and a fairy-tale setting for a movie star's wedding at any time of the year. Speaking of movies, a number of them have been filmed in the Biltmore mansion or on its grounds.

Back to our newlyweds. If Jenna and Conrad ever make it out of their 1200-square-foot suite in the Biltmore Inn, I expect they'll take time to admire the collection of old masters artwork adorning the walls of the mansion. They'd probably take time to view the chess set that once belonged to Napoleon, the beautiful antique furniture, the Ming dynasty bowls and sixteenth-century Flemish tapestries. No doubt they'd tour the former dairy barn, which has been converted into Biltmore Estate Winery. Or perhaps they'd lunch in the café located in an old stable.

If Conrad needs a testosterone rush while Jenna is enjoying the flora and fauna, he can take the Land Rover off-road driving course. It offers participants two hours of instruction and a chance to ride off the beaten path. Or he can join Jenna in a mountain bike or horseback ride.

After George Vanderbilt's death his widow donated 87,000 acres of land to the federal government. That parcel became the Pisgah Forest.

The Biltmore Estate, while still privately owned, holds both the riches of a European museum and a study in world history. Sadly, no one has lived in this palatial home since the 1950s. I can't image a more perfect setting for a couple's married life to begin. Can you?

For more information visit www.Biltmore.com.

Here's a sneak peek...

18

Sugar and Spikes
by
Heather MacAllister

Enjoy this excerpt from one of next month's exciting releases, "Sugar and Spikes" by Heather MacAllister, part of BOOTCAMP, the March 2006 Signature Select Collection.

CHAPTER 1

REBECCA IRONWOOD didn't handle humiliation at all well. It made her do things like fire her personal assistant and plunk down ten thousand dollars to attend the Warfield Retreat north of Houston, Texas, in hopes of making herself more attractive to people in general and men in particular. Actually, one man in particular. Cy Benedict.

Yes, Cy Benedict's rejection had driven Rebecca to the Warfield Retreat. "Leveling the playing field by teaching the Womanly Art of Romance" Warfield Retreat. The pink brochure with purple ink Warfield Retreat.

Rebecca sat in her car in the pine-needle-covered parking lot and stared at the rustic building with the, oh, God, yes, pink door.

What had she been thinking? Rebecca thunked her head on the steering wheel of her BMW SUV, and then quickly checked the parking lot to see if any other women were in their cars banging their heads on their steering wheels. Or if anyone had seen her, period. This was so embarrassing.

The lot was filled with BMWs, Mercedes, Cadillac Escalades and pretty much any luxury car imaginable, but they were unoccupied, their drivers presumably already behind the pink door.

It should have made Rebecca feel better that other clearly successful women were here, but it didn't.

Focus. Rebecca picked up the glossy-paper newsletter and read the headline once again: Lonely At The Top—Houston Female Business Owner Of The Year Goes Solo To Awards Banquet.

Well so what? was Rebecca's first thought when she saw the headline. She'd been interviewed by a couple of college interns for this article in the *Future Businesswoman's Journal*. She'd been encouraging, witty, charming and generous in her advice—in other words, fabulous as usual.

But had these two little chippies quoted any of her generous advice? No, they'd quoted her assistant Adrienne's whining. Make that *former* assistant's whining.

Rebecca had hired that whiner right out of college four years ago, mentored her, given her a job where she could learn firsthand from the best—that would be Rebecca—and how had Adrienne repaid her? By smearing Rebecca's carefully established reputation.

There in print for everyone—friend, foe or male—to read were the details of Adrienne's unsuccessful attempt to find Rebecca an escort for the awards banquet.

Frankly, Rebecca vaguely remembered suggesting names and having Adrienne make the phone calls, but she hadn't kept track of just how many names...and Adrienne clearly had.

"Eight," the article quoted her as saying. Rebecca imagined her whiny little voice. "And those were only the men she suggested. I came up with a couple on my own. They all turned me down. Some weren't even nice about it. I wasn't surprised. If there's one thing I've learned working from Ms. Ironwood, it's that you can be successful or you can have a man in your life— but not both."

That was just wrong on so many levels.

Rebecca gripped the steering wheel and stared at the pink door. The problem was that if a man was intimidated by her, she didn't want him and if he wasn't, she didn't like him. That left a very shallow pool of candidates, so no, she currently didn't have a man in her life. She had a broken marriage in her past, so it wasn't as

BONUS FEATURE

though she'd never had a man, but printing something like the garbage equating success with loneliness for the next generation to read was hideous. What were these girls—women—future business leaders going to think?

And the worst of it was that not having an escort at the banquet actually bothered Rebecca. As she gave her acceptance speech and soaked up the applause, the entire time Rebecca had been aware of a radiant Patricia Eggelston, sitting at the first group of tables just below the dais, cooing into the ear of her new husband.

It was sickening. Last year, Patricia had owned the top-ranked female-owned company and she'd sold it—which was why Rebecca was number one this year and don't think that didn't rankle.

Patricia kept telling everyone how blissfully happy she was. Adrienne had helpfully pointed that out in the article, too.

But bad as it was, that wasn't what had ultimately cost Adrienne her job or sent Rebecca heading to the Warfield Retreat. No, the disloyal Adrienne apparently told the interns that Cy Benedict, the personnel consultant Rebecca had hired, would only be her escort if he would be paid his hourly rate.

Rebecca hadn't known until she read the article.

"'The only way I'd spend one minute more than I have to with the Iron Lady is if you paid me.'"

That's what Adrienne had told Rebecca when confronted, but in her mind, Rebecca could hear Cy saying it. Saying it in that honey-wrapped-in-smoke voice that he had. The voice that she had a crush on.

Rebecca rolled down the windows of her SUV as her face heated. She'd called him several times asking for clarification on his reports just so she could hear that voice.

She'd seen him from a distance, but had never spoken to him face-to-face. He was a tall man with brown hair shot with silver and looked as though he spent a lot of time outdoors. He looked vibrant and alive and very much like someone she would like to get to know.

Rebecca had thought asking him to accompany her to a business-oriented event was the perfect way to approach him. If they clicked, then great, and if they didn't, well, it was just business after all.

His brutal rejection stung. This stupid article stung. The fact that she wouldn't have been number one unless Patricia had sold her business stung.

And life just stung in general.

She was successful, wealthy, had social stature and was strikingly attractive—that was a quote. From a woman, but still a quote.

But she was forty-three and manless and apparently that was what counted in the world.

So, okay. She'd deal with it. Rebecca got out of her car, slammed the door and locked it, then strode toward the pink door of the Warfield Retreat before she could change her mind.

She pushed open said pink door, ripped off her sunglasses and approached the receptionist, relieved to find a woman of about her own age exuding calm.

"Welcome to the Warfield Retreat," said the woman. Her pink-and-purple plastic name tag read "Maxine." "May I have your name?"

Had she given her real name when she made the reservation? Had she truly been that stupid? Rebecca couldn't remember, but she must have done so. What if word of this got out? If anyone knew she was here, especially after that article...

Rebecca wanted to leave. Yes, she, Rebecca Ironwood, who had founded Ironwood Executive Staffing with an annual gross of over fifty million dollars, wanted to back down from a challenge.

The receptionist noted her hesitation. "Our discretion is assured. And there is nothing to be ashamed of in seeking help."

"It shouldn't matter!" Rebecca burst out. "I am a successful, contributing member of society and it shouldn't matter whether or not there is a man in my personal life. I shouldn't be willing to change myself back to the female equivalent of the dark ages just to get a man, let alone pay an exorbitant amount to do so!"

"But you are and you did," replied the implacable Maxine. "Fill out this form and I'll show you to your cabin."

Yes, she was and she had. There was the form to prove it. Rebecca dutifully filled it out and followed Maxine, meekly rolling her suitcase over the rough Italian tile in the hallway and out a side door.

Meekly. Yes, Rebecca Ironwood was doing meek and the world still spun. Did the woman even notice Rebecca's meekness? For pity's sake, she was making an effort here. She was also lugging a carryall, her makeup case, a computer satchel and another satchel bulging with papers and files. And Cy Benedict's report, a report in which he'd stated that she appeared remote and unapproachable to her employees, but she wasn't thinking about that now.

Now she was thinking about a bellman, only there appeared to be no bellmen. Had she complained? No. Not yet, anyway.

"You're in cabin number thirteen."

It figured.

"You and your roommates have been deliberately matched to form an optimum support group after you leave here."

As if Rebecca would ever blab her problems to strangers. Except this once—for which she was paying a lot of money and expected THEM to provide the support. But, she was being meek so she said nothing, even though everything within her wanted to rebel. She'd spent years—decades—counseling young women not to be meek.

"As part of the Warfield method, we expect you to practice the strategies you'll learn in our workshops to get along with your roommates. Remember—breathe...consider...act."

Rebecca found herself breathing right along with Maxine as she swiped a card in the security lockbox for cabin thirteen and stepped inside.

Well, now, this was okay. Very okay. Cabin, bungalow or whatever, this was not the primitive Girl Scout camp she'd been tortured with in her youth. This was rustic chic. Lush carpets, classic neutral colors and separate bedrooms. It was the kind of place where the roof didn't leak. Things were looking up.

Still meek, and feeling like a pack mule, Rebecca wheeled her suitcase into the only unoccupied bedroom. Queen-sized bed and good lighting. Excellent.

"You have only a few minutes to get settled," Maxine said. "The morning session will begin shortly."

Rebecca let the bags fall from her shoulders onto the bed. "I thought it wasn't going to start until ten o'clock."

"It IS nearly ten." Maxine glanced first at the clock radio beside on the nightstand and then at her watch.

Five minutes until ten. Rebecca must have spent more time banging her head on the steering wheel than she'd thought. "You're right." She added a smile. Smiles were good, weren't they? This woman wasn't giving her a whole lot of positive reinforcement. So why was she bothering?

Out of touch. Unapproachable. Cold. Iron lady.

And it cost ten thousand dollars.

So the last one had the most influence. Sue her.

"The conference center is a five-minute walk from this cabin." Maxine handed her a pamphlet that unfolded into a map of the Warfield Retreat. "Head along this path and follow the signs. I'm going that way now."

Be more approachable. "Could I walk with you?" Rebecca abandoned the thought of unpacking now. She could have her clothes pressed later.

Maxine hesitated as though she actually considered giving up the chance for five minutes alone with Houston's Female Business Owner of the Year. Was she nuts? Did she not know that Rebecca was a valuable contact? Rebecca's agency staffed dozens of companies and this woman was what? A receptionist? Didn't she want a better job?

Rebecca knew for a fact that Adrienne—the whiner—had been bribed to set up just such chance encounters. It had amused Rebecca until she discovered that Adrienne had actually accepted one of the bribes. But since the bribe in question was a Hermès Fleur de Lis bag, Rebecca could hardly blame her. Especially when Adrienne, caught red-handed—or bagged—had insisted that the Fleur de Lis had been meant as a present for Rebecca.

Rebecca had been on the waiting list for that very bag—though in navy and not red—but she accepted Adrienne's gesture, met with the client and allowed Adrienne to escape unscathed. See? She could be nice. Wasn't that being nice?

Maxine set a brisk pace along a springy mulched path through the pine trees. The grounds were manicured and still managed to preserve the "we're roughing it" tone of the retreat, Rebecca noted with approval. This showed an attention to detail she appreciated. So many people let details slide these days.

"Since you were running late, I didn't get an opportunity to show you the cabin."

Rebecca heard the rebuke in Maxine's voice and let it pass. She had *not* been running late. She'd been distracted.

Maxine continued. "In addition to the three bedrooms, there is a living area and full kitchen, as well as a common business center with a printer and fax. And wireless Internet, of course. Land-lines are available in each room for secure calls."

"I'm relieved that there will be time to check in with my company," Rebecca said. "I wasn't sure of the schedule of activities here." She figured it was understood that check in meant spend several hours working.

"We're not unrealistic. We're aware that our clients find it difficult to spend two weeks away from their work and social responsibilities."

But apparently, this realistic attitude didn't extend to living arrangements as Rebecca then learned that she and her roommates would be responsible for their own meals, cleaning and laundry. Clearly, the "rustic" part of rustic chic.

They reached the central lodge housing the conference center before Rebecca could formulate a diplomatic way of telling Maxine that she was crazy.

What kind of a chintzy place was this? And was it too late to back out? What about a refund?

Cy Benedict's report sounded in her head. *Out of touch. Cold. Unrealistic expectations.*

Oh, shut up.

Maxine pulled open yet another pink door and Rebecca heard the murmur of female voices. She was instantly soothed because this was the murmur of professionals networking, not the chirpy babble of a women's coffee club.

"I'll find your roommates and introduce you to them," Maxine said.

"Thank you," Rebecca said demurely. *Demurely.* She nearly gagged. How long could she keep this up?

She signed in at a table and slapped on a name tag, thinking this was like the countless other seminars and business conferences she'd attended. Maxine beckoned her across the room where two women stood with her. One was flawlessly made up in a way that told Rebecca she was in a business where appearances counted. The other, near her own average height, had the expensive shoulder-length, straight hair and sophisticated clothes of the very rich. "This is Cassandra Devane and Barbara Powers. You three will be roommates for the next two weeks."

In a show of the Warfield spirit, Rebecca suggested that they sit together, Barbara pointed out the spaces she'd already commandeered, and Cassandra handed her a bottle of chilled water.

Rebecca smiled her first genuine smile in days. Strategic planning. These were her kind of people.

Maxine strode, unmeekly, to the lectern in the front of the room. "Please take a seat and we'll get started."

"'They call her Mad Max,'" Barbara whispered.

Maxine pasted a professionally pleasant smile on her face, one every woman in the room knew, and waited, undemurely, as everyone quickly took a seat in the sudden silence. Nobody wanted to waste time here.

"Hello, I'm Maxine Warfield. Welcome to the Warfield Retreat."

Maxine Warfield. Rebecca cringed. Just a receptionist. Right. At least she'd behaved herself.

"Let's get one thing straight right now—you are all successful women and have the privileges, trappings and responsibilities that come with that success. You deserve them. You've worked hard and are the target of envy and resentment from those who have no idea what it takes to get where you are and stay there. If you were men, you'd be admired and respected, but you're women. And you want to be liked and you're hurt that you aren't. You're called cold, aggressive, ball breakers—

Rebecca wanted to know why no one was standing up yelling, "Right on, sister!" Maybe she would.

"—and it's not fair. Let's all agree on that up front. It's not fair." Maxine paused, clearly expecting something from the group.

There was polite murmured agreement as Rebecca still considered leaping to her feet with 32 a rallying cry.

"You're here because you're women and you need the social connection. There are virtually no programs for men quite like this one. For them, being disliked or feared in business and social situations is a badge of honor. But we're wired differently, so we're going to accept that and then let it go and move on with our life's journey. Got it?"

Not fair. Oh, so right. Move on. Good advice. Rebecca exhaled, feeling inexplicably lighter and heard her sigh echoed by others. They were right and the world was wrong. Validation was good.

"During the next two weeks, you will relearn the basics of interacting with others. And when

I say basics, I mean housework, grocery shopping, driving in traffic—the chores of daily life. You can call it connecting with ordinary people—but you didn't hear me say that."

Polite laughter rippled through the crowd as Rebecca thought about Cy Benedict and how he wasn't ordinary.

Maxine delivered her next comment as though she'd read Rebecca's mind. "If this group is like past groups, you're all single. By single, I'm including women friends as well as male lovers."

Rebecca flipped through her mental close friends file and, even stretching the definition, came away with few names. Okay, two. And one, she hadn't seen for seven years. As for male lovers, the file was empty.

"You need people in your life." Music began playing. "And when you have those people, you'll find you are much more effective in your life."

It took Rebecca a few moments to realize she was listening to a recording of Barbra Streisand singing "People." Oh, how hokey. She suppressed a giggle, but someone started laughing and they were all lost.

It was the perfect tension breaker and when the laughter eventually quieted, Rebecca gazed at Maxine Warfield with new respect.

And, she dared to admit, hope.

...NOT THE END...

Look for the continuation of this story in BOOTCAMP, *available from Signature Select in March 2006.*

**From the author of the bestselling
COLBY AGENCY miniseries**

DEBRA
WEBB

VOWS *of* SILENCE

A gripping new novel of romantic suspense.

A secret pact made long ago between best
friends Lacy, Melinda, Cassidy and Kira resurfaces
when a ten-year-old murder is uncovered. Chief
Rick Summers knows they're hiding something, but
isn't sure he can be objective…especially if his
old flame Lacy is guilty of murder.

**"Debra Webb's fast-paced thriller will
make you shiver in passion and fear."**
—*Romantic Times*

Vows of Silence…coming in March 2006.

THE FORTUNES OF TEXAS: Reunion

Coming in March...
a brand-new Fortunes story
by *USA TODAY* bestselling author

Marie Ferrarella...

MILITARY MAN

A dangerous predator escapes from prison
near Red Rock, Texas—and Collin Jamison,
CIA Special Operations, is the only person who
can get inside the murderer's mind. Med student
Lucy Gatling thinks she has a lead. The police
aren't biting, but Collin is—even if it is only
to get closer to Lucy!

The Fortunes of Texas: Reunion
The price of privilege. The power of family.

Where love comes alive™

Signature Select™

All's fair in love and war…
So why not do both?

BOOTCAMP

Three brand-new stories in one Collection

National bestselling authors

Leslie Kelly

Heather MacAllister

Cindi Myers

Strong-willed females Cassandra, Rebecca and
Barbara enroll in the two-week Warfield crash
course to figure out how to get what they
want in life and romance!

Experience *Bootcamp* in March 2006.

COMING NEXT MONTH

Signature Select Collection
BOOTCAMP by Leslie Kelly, Heather MacAllister, Cindi Myers
Strong-willed females Cassandra, Rebecca and Barbara enroll in the
two-week Warfield crash course to figure out how to get what they
want in life and romance!

Signature Select Saga
QUIET AS THE GRAVE by Kathleen O'Brien
Mike Frome's ex-wife is found suspiciously dead—making him the
prime murder suspect. Believing in his innocence, Mike's ex-flame
Suzie Strickland offers her support. But sudden murder evidence
against Mike is discovered, testing their newfound trust and love....

Signature Select Miniseries
COFFEE IN THE MORNING by Roz Denny Fox
A heartwarming volume of two classic stories with the miniseries
characters you love! A wagon-train journey along the Santa Fe Trail
is a catalyst for romance as Emily Benton and Sherry Campbell
each find love.

Signature Select Spotlight
VOWS OF SILENCE by Debra Webb
A secret pact made long ago between best friends—Lacy, Melinda,
Cassidy and Kira—resurfaces when a ten-year-old murder is
uncovered. Chief Rick Summers knows they're hiding something,
but isn't sure he can be objective...especially if his old flame Lacy is
guilty of murder.

Signature Select Showcase
LADY'S CHOICE by Jayne Ann Krentz
Juliana Grant knows she's found "the one" in high-octane real-
estate developer Travis Sawyer—even if *he* doesn't realize it yet.
But Travis has arrived back in Jewel Harbour for retribution, not
for romance. And it doesn't help that the target of his revenge is
her family!

Signature Select™

BARBARA BRETTON

sold her first book on Monday, February 2, 1982, when Vivian Stephens uttered the magic words, "We want to buy your manuscript," and changed her life forever. Writing had been Barbara's dream since childhood and the Harlequin American Romance line was about to make that dream come true. Her first book, *Love Changes,* became a launch title and she went on to write almost two dozen books for the line. Today, Barbara Bretton is a *USA TODAY* bestselling, award-winning author of more than forty novels. In addition to writing for the Harlequin American Romance line, Barbara has written for Harlequin Historical, Harlequin Intrigue, MIRA Books, Pocket Books, Crown Books and Berkley Books.

Barbara, a New Jersey resident, loves to spend as much time as possible in Maine with her husband, walking the rocky beaches and dreaming up plots for upcoming books. If she could walk and knit and read at the same time, her life would be just about perfect.

ISABEL SHARPE

started reading romance in high school, back when it should have been called, "Men who plunder honeyed depths and the women who let them." After she quit work ten years ago to be with her firstborn son, and nearly went out of her mind with boredom, she started writing. Yes, she was the clichéd bored housewife writing romance, but it was either that cliché or seduce the mailman, and her mailman was unattractive. Twenty-two sales later, to Duets, Temptation and Blaze as well as Signature and eHarlequin, the mailman is still ugly and Isabel can safely say she made the better choice.

EMILIE ROSE

lives in North Carolina with her college sweetheart husband and four sons. This bestselling author's love for romance novels developed when she was twelve years old and her mother hid them under sofa cushions each time Emilie entered the room. Emilie grew up riding and showing horses. She's a devoted baseball mom during the season and can usually be found in the bleachers watching one of her sons play. Her hobbies include quilting, cooking (especially cheesecake) and anything cowboy. Her favorite TV shows include Discovery Channel's medical programs, *ER, CSI* and *Boston Public.* Emilie's a country music fan because there's an entire book in nearly every song.

Emilie loves to hear from her readers and can be reached at P.O. Box 20145, Raleigh, NC 27619 or at www. EmilieRose.com.